TO
SERVE
AND
PROTECT

MAGICAL SEDUCTION
by Cathryn Fox, Mandy M. Roth, & Anya Bast

GOOD GIRL SEEKS BAD RIDER
by Vonna Harper, Lena Matthews, & Ruth D. Kerce

ROAD TRIP TO PASSION
by Sahara Kelly, Lani Aames, & Vonna Harper

OVERTIME, UNDER HIM
by N. J. Walters, Susie Charles, & Jan Springer

GETTING WHAT SHE WANTS
by Diana Hunter, S. L. Carpenter, & Chris Tanglen

INSATIABLE
by Sherri L. King, Elizabeth Jewell, & S. L. Carpenter

HIS FANTASIES, HER DREAMS
by Sherri L. King, S.L. Carpenter, & Trista Ann Michaels

MASTER OF SECRET DESIRES
by S. L. Carpenter, Elizabeth Jewell, & Tawny Taylor

BEDTIME, PLAYTIME
by Jaid Black, Sherri L. King, & Ruth D. Kerce

HURTS SO GOOD
by Gail Faulkner, Lisa Renee Jones, & Sahara Kelly

LOVER FROM ANOTHER WORLD
by Rachel Carrington, Elizabeth Jewell, & Shiloh Walker

FEVER-HOT DREAMS
by Sherri L. King, Jaci Burton, & Samantha Winston

TAMING
by Kimberly Dean, Summer Devon, & Michelle M. Pillow

ALL SHE WANTS
by Jaid Black, Dominique Adair, & Shiloh Walker

TO
SERVE
AND
PROTECT

ARIANNA HART
KIT TUNSTALL
TRISTA ANN MICHAELS
DELILAH DEVLIN

POCKET BOOKS
New York   London   Toronto   Sydney

Pocket Books
A Division of Simon & Schuster, Inc.
1230 Avenue of the Americas
New York, NY 10020

First Pocket Books trade paperback edition November 2009

POCKET and colophon are registered trademarks of Simon & Schuster, Inc.

For information about special discounts for bulk purchases, please contact Simon & Schuster Special Sales at 1-800-506-1949 or business@simonandschuster.com

The Simon & Schuster Speakers Bureau can bring authors to your live event. For more information or to book an event contact the Simon & Schuster Speakers Bureau at 1-866-248-3049 or visit our website at www.simonspeakers.com.

Designed by Renata Di Biase

Manufactured in the United States of America

10 9 8 7 6 5 4 3 2 1

ISBN 978-1-4391-3154-1

These stories have previously appeared in Ellora's Cave anthologies published by Pocket Books. "Convince Me" appeared in *Bad Girls Have More Fun*. "Ablaze" appeared in *Asking for It*. "Fantasy Bar" appeared in *His Fantasies, Her Dreams*. "Ride a Cowboy" appeared in *A Hot Man Is the Best Revenge*.

CONTENTS

CONVINCE ME

Arianna Hart

1

ABLAZE

Kit Tunstall

69

FANTASY BAR

Trista Ann Michaels

129

RIDE A COWBOY

Delilah Devlin

215

CONVINCE ME

ARIANNA HART

DEDICATION

This book is dedicated to my husband, who had to convince me to go on that first date with him. I'm so glad we decided to be more than "just friends."

I'd also like to thank all the people who work and volunteer to help abused women in shelters across the country. Leaving an abusive relationship is a near-impossible thing to do. Thank you all so much for providing places for women and their children to go to when they find the strength to make that decision.

Although the shelter in this story is fictitious, if you are interested in finding out more about battered women's shelters in your area, look in the yellow pages of your phone book under Domestic Violence or contact your local police department.

1

SAREENA'S EYES PRACTICALLY glazed over as the mayor droned on and on. She loved raising money for the battered women's shelter, but these charity dinners were beyond boring. The only thing that kept this one from being a total yawn fest was her seat assignment.

Eye candy at twelve o'clock sharp.

Officer Brogan Donahue had a polite smile on his face but it didn't reach those gorgeous blue eyes of his. They'd been working together on fund-raisers for months now and she hadn't wrangled so much as an invitation for a cup of coffee. He was unfailingly pleasant but distant.

That had to change.

They'd worked side by side remodeling the shelter and she'd flirted outrageously with him. A few times—usually when she was covered in paint or drywall dust—he'd let down his guard and flirted back. She'd thought she'd finally made some progress with him, only to have him slam those damn walls up as soon as they went their separate ways.

Every time she saw him she had to start from scratch, breaking down the barriers he placed between them. Boy, was he stubborn. But then again, so was she. If it was the last thing she did, she'd get him to take her out on a date.

A shiver of sexual hunger raced through her as she thought about how she'd like that date to end if she ever got the chance.

Better get those thoughts out of your head right now, girlie. Sareena glanced down to make sure her nipples weren't poking out under her emerald green silk sheath. She had to speak next and didn't need to put on a show for half of New York City's wealthiest citizens. With her luck there'd be a close-up of her "high beams" in the society section tomorrow morning. Or worse, a picture of her with a wet spot because she decided to forgo underwear tonight to avoid panty lines in the tight dress.

Being an heiress had its drawbacks.

"And now, it gives me great pleasure to introduce the woman of the hour, Ms. Sareena Wilton."

Sareena approached the podium as the polite applause died. After the mayor's never-ending speech the audience was probably more than ready to listen to someone who didn't say "as you well know" every other sentence.

"Thank you, Mr. Mayor. Good evening everyone. I hope you enjoyed your dinner and the entertainment provided by the Williams Jazz Ensemble. I promise I won't keep you much longer." It was already eleven-thirty and she really didn't want to be hanging around with the socialites come midnight. Then again, having a huge black cat stroll through the lobby of a five-star hotel would liven things up a little.

Now *that* would make the papers for sure.

"Domestic violence is one of the most vile of all societal ills. It doesn't discriminate by race, color or economics. Many women are at risk from murder by the very men who vowed to love and protect them. The city's shelters are in desperate need of provisions to help these women and their children find better, safer lives. Your contributions this evening will help make that possible. Mr. Stevenson, I'm thrilled to be able to present this check for twenty-five thousand dollars to the Phelps House of Brooklyn."

She paused and waited for the director of the Phelps House to make his way to the raised platform.

"Fucking bitch!"

Sareena's ultra-sensitive hearing picked up a disturbance in the lobby, even over the enthusiastic applause. The double doors in the back of the ballroom crashed open.

"I want my wife back!"

A burly man pushed his way through the crowd and charged toward the podium. "It's my God-given right to show her who's boss!"

No one moved to stop the raging lunatic as he knocked over anything in his path. Murder was in his eyes and it was directed at her. Fear sent adrenaline shooting through her bloodstream. Her hackles rose at the threat and her muscles bunched in preparation to change.

Not now!

She fought the pull of the moon and her survival instincts and managed to stay calm and upright at the podium. Barely.

The enraged man had made it halfway through the room before security caught up to him. Sareena relaxed slightly as they grabbed his arms and fought him to the floor. A flash of copper-bright hair snagged her attention and she realized Brogan had jumped into the fray as well. Her heart leapt into her throat as she watched him dodge a kick before he tackled the bull of a man.

"I don't care how much money you have! I'm gonna kill you! You have no right to keep a man from his wife. No right!"

The man continued to scream threats even as security dragged him out of the ballroom. Cameras flashed in her face and Sareena remembered she was still at the podium.

"Well, that wasn't part of tonight's festivities." A nervous twitter ran through the crowd. "As you can see, your continued support is desperately needed to prevent men such as him from continuing their abuse. Thank you all for your participation. Should you have any questions or wish to help further, Mr. Stevenson will be on hand to take additional donations. Thank you and good night."

Sareena's muscles trembled with the effort to hold back the change as she smiled brightly for the still snapping cameras. It was all she could do to walk calmly to the manager's office and not snarl at the microphones being shoved into her face.

"My secretary will have a statement for you all tomorrow. Right now I need to talk to the police. I'm sure you understand," she said as she walked through the mob of reporters surrounding her.

The media was a necessary evil. She needed them on her side to win additional support for the shelters, but right now she wanted them out of her face.

BROGAN WATCHED WITH a combination of lust and awe as Sareena Wilton crossed the lobby toward him. Not a sable hair was out of place and her long stride didn't show even the slightest of hitches.

Un-fucking-believable.

Some wife-beating motherfucker just threatened to kill her and she waltzed across the hotel in shoes that cost more than a car like nothing happened. Did nothing faze her? He'd seen her deal with snot-nosed kids, hysterical women and now an enraged man. Nothing disturbed the calm façade she presented to the world. He wondered what it would take for Sareena to lose her cool—for him to make her lose her cool.

Don't go there, Donahue. She ain't for you.

But damn, sometimes it was hard to remember that. He'd been attracted to her the first time he saw her playing peek-a-boo with a toddler at the shelter. She didn't look anything like the Wilton heiress with her hair in a ponytail and dressed in faded jeans and a denim work shirt.

Thank God he'd figured out who she was before he'd asked her out on a date. Wouldn't that have been a fucking joke? She'd have laughed her ass off at the idea of a cop asking her to the movies. Christ, didn't her family own a production company or something?

Not that he'd researched her or anything.

Her sultry fragrance reached him a second before she did and his cock twitched in his rented tux. Just because his head knew he didn't belong in the same room as her didn't mean his body agreed.

"Thank you, Brogan, for your timely intervention. I'd hate to think of what that man would have done if you hadn't stepped in."

"The hotel's security had him pretty much under control by the time I got there. I just made sure he wouldn't get up."

"Well, it was a lot more than any other man in there did, and don't think I didn't notice."

"I'm a cop, it's what I'm trained for." *And those other idiots wouldn't know how to stop a cab, forget a pissed-off bastard like that.*

A commotion in the foyer snapped the spell ensnaring Brogan's senses.

"I'll get you, bitch! You can't escape me!"

Security struggled to control the attacker and keep him away from Sareena. The man's eyes blazed with either extreme fury or insanity. It took two security guards and another cop to wrestle him out the door and away from Sareena.

"Ms. Wilton, do you want to press charges?" A beat cop stood off to the side as they finally hauled the handcuffed attacker out.

Brogan looked at Sareena to see if she was upset by the situation but she only glanced at her watch nervously.

"Is it something I can do tomorrow? I'm still a little shaken up now."

"Of course. Stop by the precinct house in the morning and we'll take care of it."

Brogan didn't think she looked shaken up at all. In fact, she looked more irritated than scared. His instinct said something was up, but he couldn't put a finger on what it was. Shouldn't she be a little more upset by all this? At least nervous for Christ's sake? She had amazing control over her emotions and once again he couldn't help but wonder what it would take to break that control.

Any other thoughts were sucked out of his brain along with the blood supply when Sareena pressed against him. That tempting perfume infused his senses as her silk-covered chest brushed his arm. Images of peeling that scrap of fabric off her inch by inch flashed in his brain as she reached up to give him a quick peck on the cheek.

"Thanks again, my hero. I'll have to come up with a suitable reward for your bravery."

Her smile reminded him of a cat with a bowl full of cream— hungry and looking forward to every taste.

He could think of several ways she could reward him but somehow he didn't think she'd go for them. Despite her flirting, he knew she didn't have any intention of following up on the promise her eyes made.

"Just doing my job."

"I think tonight you went above and beyond the call of duty."

She shot him another sultry glance from those mysterious cat eyes before she walked out of the hotel and into her waiting limo.

He shoved his hands in his pockets to hide his growing erection. Sareena Wilton might not be the typical trust fund party girl, but she was still way out of his league. The only thing they had in common was the volunteer work they did for the shelter. He was blue-collar all the way and she was diamonds and limos.

She'd flirted with him every time they'd worked together but he didn't take it seriously. With any other socialite he'd think they'd want to try slumming or use him as a boy toy or something. Sareena was different. She worked damn hard for the shelter, not only raising money with gigs like this but also cleaning and hauling supplies to the building.

Hell, she'd even helped paint and drywall. No, she definitely wasn't a pampered princess. She put her heart and soul into the shelter, not just her money. He respected that, even if he didn't really understand it.

There had to be a story there somewhere but she'd never mentioned it and he was too polite to ask. Hell, polite had nothing to do with it. He didn't want her asking him why he worked so hard for the shelter, so he'd kept his mouth shut.

A disturbance on the sidewalk caught his attention and Brogan ran for the door. He hit the cement reaching for his gun, which wasn't holstered in his tux.

"Stop him!"

The squeal of brakes and a crunch of metal meeting metal echoed against the building. Two taxis were smashed together and several other cars were haphazardly scattered along the street.

"What the fuck happened?" Brogan asked the uniformed officer who dabbed at a cut on his mouth.

"Just as I was loading him into the back of the cruiser the bastard slammed his head into my face and took off."

"Didn't you have him cuffed?"

"Hell yeah, whatdaya think, I'm a rookie or something? His

hands were cuffed behind his back. Shit, they still are. He took off across the street, scrambled over the cab and disappeared with the cuffs on tight."

"Why didn't you chase after him?"

"I was still picking myself up off the ground when he caused the two-car accident out there. Murphy was helping me get the bastard in the car. He almost got flattened by the cab when he ran after him."

"Well, call it in."

"No shit, Columbo."

Horns blared from all directions as the congestion spread up the block. Brogan didn't mind helping out but he was not directing traffic in a rented tux all night long. Good thing Sareena's limo pulled out before that bastard escaped.

Oh shit, Sareena!

This guy was after her in the first place. Brogan would bet his last dollar the jerk was heading uptown to finish what he started. Fuck. He cursed the tell-all book by a fading pop star that dished many of the city's celebrities' addresses. Including Sareena's. The guy shouldn't be able to get into her place but he shouldn't have been able to get away from two cops while handcuffed either.

He yanked his phone out and called dispatch to send a unit to cruise by her Central Park condo. But with this traffic snarl, if there wasn't a car in the neighborhood they'd never get there in time. His conscience prodded him. Did he take the chance that a patrol car would get there before the sick bastard that was after her? Not when he could walk there in five minutes.

His feet were moving before he even finished the thought. If he remembered correctly, she lived on Fifty-Seventh Street along Fifth and Sixth Avenue. He didn't know exactly which building was hers, but he could scope it out and keep his eyes peeled for an asshole wearing handcuffs.

Damn, he wished he had his gun with him. Central Park was freaking creepy at night. It always took him by surprise that there were so many trees in the middle of the city. When he was a kid he'd hide in there and pretend he was a jungle explorer. Right now he could almost believe there was a jungle hidden in the darkness out there.

The dress shoes pinched his toes something fierce. They weren't meant for walking five city blocks. Brogan leaned against a bench and considered taking the shoes off and going the rest of the way in his socks.

Probably not a good idea. If he had to take the assailant down he'd rather have a little protection, no matter how uncomfortable. He straightened as a limo ghosted by his spot on the bench. That couldn't be Sareena's limo, could it? She had to have made better time than that. He took a quick glance at his watch. It was midnight already.

Sure enough, Sareena stepped out of the back of the long black car with the help of the uniformed chauffer. He walked her to the front of the building where a doorman waited for her, then drove off.

Good, she'd be safe once she was in her building. These places were guarded better than Fort Knox.

He felt a little stupid for walking all the way here with some half-assed idea of protecting her. She had all the protection money could buy. Now he'd have to schlep all the way back to midtown just to get a cab. The chances of finding one on this street were slim to none.

With one last look at Sareena's sexy bod, Brogan prepared to head home.

A flash of movement caught his eye as he turned. Something rustled behind the decorative shrubbery. Before he could call out a warning, a man jumped out and attacked the doorman, knocking him to the ground with a sickening thud.

The wife beater had found Sareena!

Somehow he'd freed one hand from the cuffs and found a knife—a knife he now held to Sareena's throat.

Brogan sprinted forward, cursing the slippery shoes that slowed him down. He was still a hundred yards away when a roar rent the night air.

He couldn't believe his eyes. A huge black cat stood where

Sareena had been seconds before. The attacker couldn't believe it either but he wasn't as stunned. He took off across the street for Central Park. The cat—a jaguar or something—leapt after him with a growl. Where the hell had it come from? He swore a blue streak as he raced for the fence, intent on following the cat and the attacker, but a cry of distress stopped him.

"Sareena?" Brogan changed direction and ran back toward the building.

"Help me, please." The doorman lay on the sidewalk, blood dripping down his face from a gash on his temple.

Brogan growled in frustration. He wanted to go after the jaguar and the wife beater to make sure Sareena was safe, but he couldn't leave the doorman in this condition. He bit back another swear before yanking his cell phone out of his pocket yet again.

"Just hold on a little longer. Help is on the way." He searched the sidewalk for something he could use as a bandage to apply pressure to the wound but didn't see anything.

Except for a pile of glimmering green silk lying on the sidewalk next to a pair of skyscraper heels.

2

*Y*ES! POWER SURGED through her muscles as she jumped over the fence into Central Park. The Conservatory was *her* territory. It was about time the wife-beating bastard felt what it was like to run for his life.

Sareena lifted her nose and sifted through the scents coloring the air. Her ears perked up to listen for the smallest movement from her prey.

What was that? Over to the left, off the path. There. The foolish man had stripped off his shirt and hung it in a tree to try to distract her. Maybe if she was a regular jaguar that might work, but she retained her human thought processes and knew a decoy when she saw one.

She slunk into the trees, the soft loam cushioning her steps. The glow from the streetlights didn't reach this deep into the woods and she knew her black coat made her invisible to the human's weak eyesight.

He'd never know what hit him.

The part of her that was pure jungle cat let out a roar of triumph when she found her target. The chase was on. The man took off through the trees in a blind panic. His ragged breathing was as loud as thunder to her sensitive hearing and she could smell his sweat and his fear.

Good. Let him fear. He liked to pick on those weaker than him, now he was the weakling. And she'd make him pay dearly.

Her muscles bunched and stretched as she raced through the forest after her prey. It felt good to be free, to run through the night, to hunt. The knife wound on her neck stung a little but she ignored it. It was infinitely more satisfying to feel the wind on her coat and the dirt under her claws.

The wife beater had managed to trap himself against the fence on the far side of the Conservatory. He cried in fear as she slunk toward him. He wasn't issuing threats now.

"N-nice kitty."

Fat chance, asshole.

She prowled closer, her belly low to the ground, prepared to pounce on him if he jumped to the side. The feline part of her urged her to let him go just so she could chase him down again but she forced it back. She needed to deal with him quickly, not play with him all night. No matter how sweet his fear smelled or how much fun it would be to toy with him, it was time to be done with this.

He held the knife in front of him. Ha! As if that puny blade could stop her.

Inching closer, she allowed her fangs to show as a growl rumbled low in her chest.

"Fuck!"

He darted to the side and she was on him in a second. Her roar echoed through the trees as she knocked him down and rolled with him. Sharp claws dug into his soft belly and she clamped her powerful jaws over his head.

Some last bit of sanity stopped her from instinctively crushing his skull like a wayward doe. Since she wasn't about to eat this piece of filth she couldn't kill him without bringing undue notice from the authorities. The police already wanted him. If they found him dead from a jaguar attack near her condo there'd be too many questions she couldn't answer.

It was almost painful to release him. Every cat instinct she possessed cried out for her to finish the kill. With a growl of frustration she sheathed her claws and released her prey. Her tail lashed with fury but she backed off.

Blood dripped down the man's torso but his entrails were still inside his abdomen, so she hadn't fatally wounded him. Too bad. The bastard didn't deserve to live.

He didn't look so damn dangerous now, cowering in fear and curled up into the fetal position. Maybe he'd remember what this felt like, to be afraid for his life, the next time he wanted to strike a woman.

Anger churned in her gut and she sprang away from him before she did something she'd regret.

No, she wouldn't regret killing him but it would cause problems for her she didn't need. She'd expend the fire in her blood on something else tonight.

B ROGAN CALLED AN ambulance to take care of the doorman and alerted dispatch *again* about the maniac on the loose. It pissed him off to no end that he couldn't go after the guy but he couldn't let the doorman bleed to death either.

While he waited for the rig and squad car to arrive, he picked up the green dress lying on the ground. Sareena's perfume wafted up from the delicate silk, leaving no doubt that it was indeed hers.

If this was her dress, where was Sareena? And what was she wearing?

A black fur pelt?

No fucking way. There was no way she had turned into a cat right in front of his eyes. Shit like that didn't happen in real life. And it especially didn't happen to millionaire heiresses whose lives were examined in the newspapers daily.

Sure, he'd heard the urban myths of alligators in the sewer system and escaped lions and shit like that, but that was just crap made up on the Internet. If someone actually turned into a big freaking cat, that would be all over the news. Or at least in the tabloids. Especially if it was about someone as famous as Sareena.

There had to be some sort of logical explanation for how she escaped from the wife beater and why her dress was left behind.

And he was going to camp out on her front doorstep until he got it.

The wail of sirens bounced off the buildings, alerting him to either the ambulance's or the police car's imminent arrival. Brogan suddenly remembered he still held Sareena's dress. He scooped up her shoes and wrapped them in the length of silk and stuck the bundle under a nearby bush. If she complained about the condition of her dress she could send him the cleaning bill.

The ambulance beat the police unit by a minute. Brogan stayed out of the way as the EMTs packed up their patient and got his information from the building supervisor. He gave the beat cop as much information about the suspect as he could. How hard would it be to identify a guy wearing half a handcuff anyway? Then again, this was New York.

He watched the cop go in pursuit and moved off to the side. Brogan's brain spun and he needed to pull his thoughts together. This whole night was unreal. First the attack at the banquet, then seeing a big black jungle cat appear before his eyes on Fifth Avenue. The only thing that could make it more surreal would be seeing . . .

Sareena emerging buck naked from the shadow of the building.

Brogan blinked his eyes to make sure it was really her creeping around the corner of the building.

Probably looking for a side entrance.

She moved damn silently. If he hadn't been standing off to the side he'd have never noticed her. With as much stealth as he could muster in dress shoes, Brogan retrieved her clothes and followed her.

When she reached an unmarked door on the side of the building, he stepped behind her and slammed his hand against the door before she could open it.

"Looking for these?"

"Brogan! I didn't know you were there."

"Obviously. Aren't you a little underdressed?"

She stood straight and proud and made no attempt to hide her nakedness. Even barefoot and windblown, she still had the carriage and demeanor of a queen. Brogan couldn't stop himself from visually exploring every creamy hill and valley. His cock tightened painfully and his blood caught fire.

Her skin was smooth and golden, every flawless inch of it was mouthwateringly perfect. He wanted to run his fingers over her body and see if it felt as silky as she looked. The tight curls between her luscious thighs begged for his touch and her dusky nipples pebbled in the cool night air. He could stare at her for hours, finding something new to admire with every glance, but she spoke and brought him back to reality.

"I'm perfectly dressed . . . for some activities." Her eyes glowed with heat, sparking a new blaze in his veins. "But I thank you for returning my dress. It's one of my favorites." She held out her hand imperiously.

"I don't think so. You have some explaining to do."

"Oh really?" She arched a brow. "I don't believe I owe you any explanations for my actions. Unless you're going to arrest me for indecent exposure."

"If you're not going to give me the answers I'm looking for, maybe I'll do some digging. And if that digging takes me to the newspapers and tabloids, oh well."

"You're blackmailing me?"

"I prefer to call it bargaining. You tell me what the hell is going on, and what happened to that bastard who attacked you, and maybe I'll keep my mouth shut."

Sareena tapped her foot while she eyed him up speculatively "Fine. But it'll take a while to fill you in on everything. Let me find the secret key I leave out here and we can continue this discussion in the comfort of my condo."

Brogan held back a groan as she bent over and searched the ground. Her sweet ass gleamed in the light of the full moon. It was all he could do to keep his hands to himself and not caress those luscious globes. He'd be lucky if he could find a working brain cell by the time she got around to explaining herself.

"Here it is." She held up a rusty key triumphantly and unlocked the door. "Unfortunately, I don't keep the key to my private elevator here so we'll have to take the stairs."

"I think I can handle it." His apartment was on the third floor and there were no elevators in the building. He was used to stairs.

As he followed her through the dimly lit stairway, he admired the curves of her backside. She was more muscular than he'd thought. Although, he'd never had much of a chance to examine her legs and ass this closely before. She'd always seemed trim and fit to him but now he realized she was all tightly coiled muscles and sinews.

Except for the most important areas. Those were nicely plump and soft.

Get your head out of your pants and pay attention. Brogan needed to focus on what she said, not on her body. He couldn't let his dick distract him from finding out what the hell happened tonight.

The memory of that bastard holding a knife to Sareena's throat deflated his erection. He pulled his eyes from her shapely legs and examined her throat for any sign of injury. It was hard to see anything in the murky light of the stairwell but he thought he detected a glimmer of blood marring her smooth skin.

"Hey, are you okay? Did he hurt you?"

"Nothing a shower won't cure."

When they reached the fifth floor she entered a code on the door and yanked it open. Brogan stepped in front of her before she could walk through.

"Hold on a second. Let me check to make sure the coast is clear. Don't think you want your neighbors seeing you like this."

"Aren't you sweet? But don't worry. I own the entire floor."

She brushed by him and all he could do was follow. The door opened into a mudroom type area with a washer and dryer against one wall and coat hooks against the other. Brogan imagined this was probably the servants' entrance.

"You can leave my dress over there. Lana will take care of it on Monday."

"Sure. Who's Lana?"

"My housekeeper. She was my nanny when I was a child and I couldn't stand to let her go once I grew up. She refused to retire so I hired her as my housekeeper."

"And does she know about your penchant for running around naked?"

"Of course. If you'll excuse me, I'd like to take a shower before we get down to business discussions. Make yourself at home. I won't be long."

She strode through the little mudroom into a gleaming kitchen filled with stainless-steel appliances and shining chrome. Brogan trailed in her wake until he came to the enormous living room. He gasped and almost stumbled as he took the two steps into the sunken room.

"If you're hungry there should be something in the fridge. Help yourself to anything behind the bar," she called over her shoulder as she disappeared down a long hallway.

Brogan barely heard her, he was still trying to take in his surroundings. This one room was easily twice the size of his apartment. The freaking place had a cathedral ceiling complete with crystal chandelier. Enormous bay windows looked out over Central Park and a floor-to-ceiling entertainment center took up one whole wall.

So this was how the other half lived?

He kicked off his shoes so he wouldn't trail any dirt onto the thick white rug and crossed to the oak bar next to the entertainment center. A U-shaped leather couch that could seat his entire softball team took up a good section of the room. The image of Sareena's black hair spread over her naked body on the white cushions flashed into his brain.

Damn, he needed a beer. She probably didn't carry anything as pedestrian as that but he really needed something to cool the fire raging in his blood. If ever he thought the two of them could get together, seeing how she lived trashed that notion in a hurry.

She might flirt with him when she saw him but he knew now it meant less than nothing. What could she see in him? Christ, his mother was a cleaning lady and his father . . . best not to even think about what his father was.

Miracle of miracles, she had beer. It was even domestic. Hallelujah. He twisted off the top and downed half of it in one gulp. This was some place. The track lighting was dimmed but the full moon shone in through the huge windows and made the room glow.

The soft leather couch looked inviting but Brogan was afraid to sit on it. He probably had something on his pants from the wrestling match in the banquet room and would end up staining the white cushions.

"You don't have to sit here in the dark," Sareena said as she walked into the room.

Her hair was still damp and gleamed darkly against her white silk robe. She flicked on the overhead lights then crossed the room. Brogan smelled her perfume as she passed him and got a bottled water from the bar's refrigerator.

The shiny fabric of her robe clung to her curves and showed a hint of leg with every step she took. All the moisture in his mouth dried up as he watched her breasts shift freely under the scanty covering.

"Please sit. You might as well get comfortable while you interrogate me." She curled up in the corner of the couch and tucked her legs beneath her.

"You seem pretty relaxed after everything that's happened tonight." He joined her on the couch, sitting gingerly on the edge. This thing probably cost as much as his truck.

"I'm not prone to excess displays of emotion."

No shit. "So why is this asshole after you?"

"I don't even know who he is but I can hazard a guess. When he grabbed me by my front door he said, 'Tell me where my wife is or you'll take her place.' I can only believe he blames me for hiding his wife in one of the shelters."

"I figured that much out. But why blame you?"

"Maybe because I'm the most visual target?"

That made sense. The people who worked at battered women's shelters tended to keep a low profile to protect their clients.

"I'll buy that. Now tell me how you got away from him and why you were naked?"

"I don't suppose you'll believe I know an ancient form of martial arts?"

"I was there. I saw him with a knife to your throat one second and then you were gone the next." He didn't mention the part about seeing the big cat there. That was just too freaky.

"What else did you see?"

"Who's asking the questions here? Tell me what's going on, Sareena."

"How come the first time you don't call me Ms. Wilton has to be when you're angry?"

"Just answer the question."

"Why don't I show you instead? You won't believe me otherwise."

She uncurled from the sofa and let the robe slip from her shoulders. Brogan's cock stirred to life yet again.

"Not that I don't appreciate the show but this isn't telling me anything other than you have a beautiful body."

She smiled slyly and closed her eyes. Her muscles shifted and writhed beneath her skin and he swore he saw her bones move. Seconds later, a gigantic black jaguar stood where Sareena had just been.

"What the fuck?" Brogan jumped to his feet, knocking his half-empty beer bottle over. "Sareena?"

The jungle cat gave a sinuous stretch then padded lazily across to him. It nudged its head against his leg as if waiting to be petted.

"Is that really you in there?"

Emerald green eyes flashed at him as the cat let out a deep purr.

"Holy Mother of God! That is you." Brogan collapsed on the couch, stunned.

He'd seen the cat before but didn't believe his eyes. Now there was no denying it. Sareena Wilton had turned into a jaguar right in front of him.

"Shit. What are you, some sort of werewolf—err, werecat?"

Sareena rubbed against his knee before hopping onto the couch. Ropey muscles rippled under the glossy coat and moments later Sareena—the woman—sat next to him.

"I'm a *jaguatium,* a shapeshifter."

"Are there more of you?" His hands shook as he straightened his fallen beer. It was almost impossible to keep his eyes on her face and not on her naked body but he tried damn hard.

"Lots. There are clans scattered all over the world. My family is in the United States mostly, and all of us can shift. Some better than others."

"I didn't realize there were degrees to this sort of thing." Was he really having this conversation?

"Oh yes. Some shifters can only change when the moon is full and once changed can't turn back until daybreak. Others can shift at any time but the effort is extraordinary. Some can barely change at all. Everyone is different."

"And you?"

"I can shift at any time and can go back and forth at will. Although it's easier on nights like tonight when the moon is full. If I change too often it takes a lot out of me though."

"So you can control when you turn?"

"Pretty much."

"Pretty much? You mean sometimes you *can't* control it?" Brogan's muscles tensed in nervous reaction.

Sareena sighed and moved off the couch. She picked up her robe and slipped it back on. "During the full moon it's more difficult for me to keep my cat in check, which is why I usually avoid staying out past midnight during that time."

"I can't believe this. If I didn't just see it, I *wouldn't* believe it. You're a millionaire fucking heiress and you turn into a cat."

"Believe it." She got another beer from behind the bar and handed it to him.

Brogan drank half of it without even realizing it. A few strands of short black hair lay on the white carpet and he couldn't seem to take his eyes off them.

"So are you going to keep my secret? Or are you going to go to the tabloids?"

Anger shook him out of his daze. "What do I look like to you? Some sleazeoid gold digger?"

"It doesn't matter what I *think*. I need to know you won't betray me. If it were made public that I'm a *jaguatium* scientists would want to study me. They'd capture my people and lock us in cages. Or worse yet, put us on display like some freak show."

"How many of you are there?"

"I don't have an exact number. My clan is spread out between the States and Europe. We're not like werewolves who run in packs.

We mostly go our own ways except for the occasional family gathering or business meeting. There are more *jaguatium* in Asia and I'm sure there are some other shifters here that I don't know about. We don't exactly broadcast our presence."

"Are they all wealthy like you?"

Sareena gathered some paper towels and blotted up the spilt beer. "Lana's going to have a fit if this stains. It's bad enough I had to change in here and there'll be cat hair over everything. If she smells beer on the rug she'll kill me."

"Isn't she your housekeeper?"

"Only in the sense that I pay her. She's more like my mother than an employee. But to answer your previous question, no, we're not all wealthy. Although it helps. Money buys silence and loyalty. Very few not of the blood know about us."

"Who else knows you're a shapeshifter?"

"Only Lana, her husband Sanders and now you."

"Don't forget the guy who attacked you."

Guarding a secret this big was an enormous responsibility. It implied a level of trust that he wasn't sure they had yet. What if he screwed up?

"Isn't it dangerous for you to be in the public eye so much? I mean, whenever you go out there's cameras following you. Aren't you afraid someone will catch you in the act?"

"There's always that worry but I take precautions. Tonight, for instance, I had another limo waiting for me on a side street. The car I got into at the hotel went off to a club in the Village while my real ride circled around before coming here."

"Pretty slick." So that was why he beat her back here.

"I'm very careful when it's a matter of life and death."

"Then why do the work for the shelters? That puts you in the public eye even more. I mean, every time you do a function like tonight, during a full moon, isn't that a risk?"

"Some risks are worth taking. Protecting abused women is important to me and I'm willing to chance my safety in order to help them." Her eyes glittered with emotion.

Oh yeah, there was a story here.

"What happened to the bastard who attacked you? Did you kill him?"

"Unfortunately, no. I thought it might look a tad suspicious if the police found him with a crushed skull and his intestines hanging out."

"So he could come back to attack you. Or worse, he could go to the tabloids and tell them how you turned into a jaguar."

"Perhaps, but would anyone believe him? It would be one thing if a respected officer of the law came forward and said that Sareena Wilton was a shapeshifter. It's a totally different story if the man who attacked me in full view of several reporters claimed I became a cat."

"So why do you believe I won't say anything?"

Her fingers toyed with the edge of her robe where it made a V between her breasts. The blood roared in his ears in its rush to reach his cock as her long legs stretched out along the cushions just inches from him. Sweat dripped down his back and the collar of his fancy shirt felt way too tight.

"I guess I'll just have to convince you it's in your best interests to keep quiet."

3

SAREENA'S NIPPLES TIGHTENED as Brogan's eyes zeroed in on her drifting hands. She'd wanted him in her bed for a long time but he'd been too aware of their different income brackets. Maybe now that he had some leverage over her he'd be willing to overlook the disparity in their bank accounts.

The thought of him having leverage over her in bed made cream flood her pussy and her body heat. Shifting always made her hot and needy but smelling Brogan's arousal pushed her further than usual. How wonderful would it be to actually make love to someone and not have to worry about revealing her secret?

No, how wonderful would it be to finally make love with Brogan? His honest face and boy-next-door good looks had captured her attention from the start but it was that hint of danger about him that hooked her but good. He might look like Opie but a serious bad boy lurked behind those beautiful blue eyes.

It was that hint of bad boy that she was hoping to bring out now. Granted, she wanted to make sure he wouldn't tell the world about her, but she knew she didn't have to ply him with sex to ensure his silence.

But oh how she wanted to.

Brogan polished off the rest of his beer and toyed with the empty bottle. He looked flushed and slightly nervous and couldn't keep his eyes off her chest.

Good.

"I can't thank you enough for taking care of that man during the banquet. If he had managed to attack me I don't know if I could have kept myself from changing. The survival instinct is strong, especially during the full moon."

"I didn't do much, security already had him by the time I got there." He loosened his bow tie and unbuttoned his collar.

"I still think you deserve the reward I promised you earlier." She slid across the couch to him and unfastened his shirt the rest of the way.

His chest had only a sprinkling of light hair across his muscular pecs. Her pussy lips swelled as she scented his increased arousal. A glance down showed his cock pushing at the fabric of his pants. Her heart beat faster and her breathing hitched.

A shiver of anticipation raced down her spine as his masculine scent drifted through her sensitive nostrils. Finally, she could explore his body like she'd wanted to for months. Every time he'd helped out at the shelter she'd wanted to see what he hid under his jeans and tight T-shirt. She'd seen his muscles ripple as he'd swung a hammer and wanted to feel them bunch and move against her. Now she could.

Her fingers trembled with lust as she trailed her fingers down his torso.

"You don't need to do this to keep me quiet," he said as she reached for the snap of his pants.

"I know. But I want to."

Oh God how she wanted to.

Sareena knelt between his legs and worked his zipper down. When his cock sprung out of his boxers she let out a purr of anticipation. He was thick and hard, waiting for her touch.

"I've wanted to do this since the first day I saw you."

Her hand shook as she grasped his cock. It felt like silk over steel. The texture was soft and smooth but his shaft was oh so very hard. He was so hot and full it made her mouth water. Licking her lips, she blew a stream of warm air over his pulsing tip. His groan was music to her ears but she was far from done with him. She wrapped her lips around the head of his cock and drew the tip into her mouth. He tasted salty and wonderful.

"Holy shit," he gasped as she drew him the rest of the way in.

His hands clawed at the couch as she cupped his balls and slid her tongue along his length. She loved the taste as she pulled him deeper into her mouth.

Fire raced through her as she continued to make love to his cock. Her breasts grew heavy with need and the feel of the silk sliding over them made her nipples tingle. His tortured breathing grew more labored and she knew he fought to hold back his orgasm.

Not for long. She'd wanted to touch him like this forever. She'd dreamed for months of sucking his cock and stroking him.

The reality was so much better than her fantasies.

She hummed in pleasure as she felt his balls tighten in preparation.

"I'm going to come." He threaded his fingers in her hair and tugged, as if to pull her off before he exploded in her mouth.

No way. Sareena sucked harder, wanting to taste his essence.

A harsh shout tore through him as he arched off the couch in pleasure. She lapped up every drop of fluid, loving the weak quivers each touch set off. Her heart beat faster as she watched him collapse against the cushions. His shirt was undone but still on and his cock lay slightly erect.

"That was . . . indescribable." He looked at her lazily through half-closed eyes.

"My pleasure." She stood and crossed to the fridge, feeling his eyes on her every step of the way. "Do you want another beer?"

"No thanks. I'll take a water if you're getting one."

Sareena grabbed two bottles of water and headed back to the couch. He'd made no move to cover himself and she shivered with desire at his rumpled appearance. Her pulse raced at the thought of exploring his muscles and feeling them over her. She took a big gulp of water to cool down. He didn't need to be attacked ten seconds after he'd come.

Screw it.

Slipping off the robe, she tossed it to the side before straddling his lap. "I know you need some recovery time but I've waited so long to get you here, I just can't keep my hands off you." She pushed his shirt and jacket off and ran her nails down his bare chest.

"I know that feeling."

He cupped her breasts and tweaked her nipples with his thumbs. Searing heat spread from his fingers to her core.

"What took you so long? I made it pretty clear I was interested in you."

"I didn't know if you were serious or playing games. We don't exactly travel in the same circles."

He placed nibbling kisses along the column of her throat. Shivers of lust made her tremble.

"I don't mind playing games but my attraction to you has always been a hundred percent serious." She could feel his cock stirring under her pussy and need raced through her. Her hips rocked against him in mute supplication.

"How far is it to your bedroom?" His hands drifted over her ribs and across her torso.

When his fingers reached her ass and squeezed, she thought she'd die if she had to wait any longer. "Too far."

She rolled off his lap and pulled him on top of her. The couch was as wide as a twin bed and twice as long. She thanked the stars she'd gone against Lana's advice and bought it.

Brogan pushed his pants off and slid between her thighs. "Do you have any protection?" he asked as he nuzzled her breast.

"Somewhere. I don't have many occasions to use it so it's not handy." She gasped as he drew her nipple between his lips and sucked hard.

"Good thing I have a spare in my wallet."

"I always knew you were a Boy Scout."

"Honey, nothing could prepare me for tonight."

A brief flash of worry tried to fight its way through the fog of her desire. Would he regret this in the morning?

Brogan took a sip of water then drew her nipple into his mouth. The coolness flooded her burning tip and sent bolts of need straight to her pussy. She rocked her hips against him to ease the ache but the contact only made it worse. Sunbursts of desire grew in her core, scorching every cell in her body.

Morning was a long way off. She'd worry about regrets later.

As he swallowed, he tugged her nipple harder and she whimpered in need. Brogan trailed his fingers lightly across her heaving chest and down her stomach. Fire trailed in his wake as he slowly drew closer to where she wanted him. Too slowly. She was going to die if he didn't reach her clit soon.

Sweat dripped down her face as she bit her tongue to keep from begging. At last he slipped his hand through her curls and caressed her slick lips with one finger. It felt good but not good enough. She shifted her hips to get him where she wanted but he only laughed. It took eons before he drifted lower. He teased her swollen nub, shooting hot sparks across her body.

"You have the softest skin. It's like satin under me." His tongue speared her belly button and swirled around a bit before he moved on. "I can't wait to feel your softest spots surrounding me, squeezing me."

Sareena's inner muscles clenched as he slipped a finger into her. He slowly drew the digit in and out, teasing her with a preview of what was to come. Tingles rushed through her bloodstream like champagne, fizzing faster and faster as she felt his face brush against her thigh.

Please God, let him hurry. She couldn't hold on much longer.

Her legs trembled as he nuzzled the crease of her pelvis. She felt his hot breath against her pussy and whimpered when he moved away from it to fondle the back of her bent knee. Sareena's head whipped side to side against the leather cushions. Her body burned with need yet Brogan took his time nipping and licking every inch of her skin. Every inch—except for the ones she really wanted.

"Do you know how often I dreamed of feeling these long, gorgeous legs around me?"

"Do you know how often I wanted them around you? You've proved to be a most elusive prey."

"All good things are worth waiting for." Blazing blue eyes stared up at her before he lowered his head.

His lips captured her desperate clit and sucked it into the warm cavern of his mouth. Sareena practically shot off the couch as his tongue stroked her over-sensitized nubbin. A scream tore from her as the wave of her orgasm crested.

Spasms rocked her body but Brogan didn't stop the exquisite torture. He stroked her G-spot slowly while licking her clit.

"Stop. I can't take it anymore." Sareena's hips bucked as another delicious quiver shook her to the core.

"But I don't want to stop. I want to bring you over again and again. I want to take you in so many different ways you'll come just thinking about it. If I have my way, you'll be spasming into next week."

His sexy tenor rumbled through her. Sareena felt another orgasm build just from the vibrations of his voice next to her pussy.

She wanted to come back with a snappy retort but her brain had ceased functioning. Her entire focus was on Brogan's lips and tongue on her pussy, his finger inside her channel and his body between her legs. The force of her pleasure grew until she couldn't take it anymore and shuddered to completion.

Vaguely she realized he'd grabbed the condom but she was still too busy shooting to the stars to pay attention to his actions. At least until he knelt between her spread legs and pulled her hips snug to his. She could feel the blunt tip of his cock probing her moist entrance and licked her lips in anticipation.

"Look at me, Sareena. I want to see those beautiful cat eyes of yours when I make you mine."

It was a Herculean effort to raise her eyelids but she managed it. Brogan's blue eyes stared at her with an intensity that stunned her. His muscled chest gleamed with sweat and his pulse throbbed visibly in his neck.

Slowly, he pushed his way into her creamy pussy. His steely hardness stretched and filled her. Sareena raised her hips higher to get more of him in.

With a groan he slid in to the hilt. Brogan lay still for a moment, letting her get used to his size. Sareena felt him along every cell of her channel. Her inner muscles wrapped around his cock and pulled him even deeper.

There was something so very right about having Brogan in her home and in her body. She wanted to keep him there forever and almost sobbed when he began to pull out.

"Easy, sweetheart. I'm not going far." He drew back slightly then slammed in again. Every glide of his cock spiraled her higher.

Sareena, so used to being in control, could only lay back and revel in the sensations rolling over her. The sheer pleasure of Brogan's skin touching hers had reduced her brain to mush.

"Look at us," he ordered when her eyes closed again.

Sareena glanced down to where their bodies joined. Brogan's light skin rubbed against her darker tones as his cock disappeared and withdrew from her pussy. The scent of their lovemaking drifted through her nostrils, musky and hot.

She was drowning in sensations. The taste of him remained on her lips, his scent filled her mind, his touch drove her to madness and the sounds of their bodies straining to attain the highest pleasure was too much for her to resist. Sareena pulled him on top of her and dug her nails into his back as yet another tidal wave of pleasure swamped her.

Brogan's heart raced and his cock quivered with aftershocks. He'd felt that orgasm down to his toes and back up again. It was like every atom of his body had come and was now basking in the afterglow. Sareena lay soft and still beneath him. Too still. If he couldn't feel her pulse pounding as hard as his own he'd think she was dead.

He lifted his upper body off her to keep from crushing her. "You okay, sweetheart?" Her cheeks were flushed and sweat had made the hair along her face curl.

"I'm not sure. When I can feel my extremities again I'll let you know."

"Then I won't bother to ask if it was good for you."

"If it got any better I wouldn't be able to walk."

Brogan slid out of her warm body with a shudder of pleasure. As quickly and unobtrusively as he could, he disposed of the condom in a tissue then returned to the couch. Sareena's beautiful hair and golden-toned complexion were a stark contrast to the white cushions. She didn't appear the least bit embarrassed to be naked while he stared at her.

He couldn't keep his eyes off her. She'd cast a spell over him and he wanted to do nothing more than touch, taste and look at her for hours. Her breasts were rosy from his kisses and her hips and thighs were lush and ripe. The subtle, sexy perfume that was such a part of her mingled with the scent of their lovemaking and did nothing to help slow down his pulse.

It was well after midnight and he had to be to work early in the morning but he couldn't care less. He'd gladly spend every waking moment worshiping the very pores of her skin.

Bending over, he scooped her off the couch and cradled her in his arms. "I hear walking is overrated anyway. Where's your bedroom?"

Sareena let out a purr of contentment and nuzzled his neck. "I like how you think, Officer Donahue. Now I'm even more upset it took me so long to get you in my clutches." She curled her fingers into claws and raked his chest lightly.

"I'm making up for lost time. The bedroom?"

"Down the hall, last door on the left."

With every step he took over the plush carpet her body rubbed against his, reminding him of what it felt like to have her under him. The hallway seemed to stretch for miles as he hurried to get to the bedroom.

"How big is this freaking place anyway? If your bedroom's much farther I'm not going to make it."

"Umm." She licked the hollow over his collarbone. "I think it's nine thousand square feet, give or take. But most of that is the gym and pool. My bedroom isn't much farther."

Nine thousand square feet? His entire neighborhood wasn't nine thousand freaking square feet. "You have a gym and a pool in your apartment?"

"Pretentious, isn't it?"

"I wouldn't think a cat would have much need for an indoor pool."

"Actually, jaguars love water. If you think you can handle it, I'll take you for a swim sometime."

"Later. Much later." Brogan captured her lips with a kiss to tide him over until he could find her damn bedroom.

The differences in their lifestyles were as wide as the Grand Canyon. At least when he was touching her, the disparities didn't seem so bad.

At last, he made it to the bedroom. Light from the full moon shone down through the skylights onto an acre-wide bed. A black satin comforter covered the mammoth piece of furniture and red, black and white pillows lay piled against the headboard.

He was too preoccupied with picturing Sareena spread out on there to pay attention to the rest of the room but he vaguely noticed a bathroom off to the left and a door that must lead to a closet on the right.

Brogan laid her down amongst the pillows and admired the picture she made in all her naked glory. "I'm going to dream about this for years to come."

Sareena knelt on the bed and pulled him down to her. "I'll give you something much better to dream about."

With a strength that surprised him she flipped him on his back so he now lay across the silky pillows.

"Stay here, I'll be right back."

"Honey, I'm not going anywhere."

A jolt of heat slammed him in the gut when she tossed a sultry smile over her shoulder. She scampered across the bed to what looked like a built-in closet on the other side of the room. It was actually a refrigerator, and the light from it caressed the curves of her breasts and ass.

When she bent over to fumble around for something, Brogan felt his cock twitch with desire. Unreal. He'd come twice and already he was gearing up to pounce on her again. What the hell had gotten into him? Had someone slipped an aphrodisiac into his dinner?

Sareena closed the refrigerator door with her hip and walked toward the bed. Even with her arms full of containers she moved with power and grace. His heart flipped over in his chest as he watched her approach him, her slanted eyes gleaming with satisfaction.

"Lana must know something I don't, because she stocked my private stash before she left tonight."

"Oh really? And what did the ever-resourceful Lana pack for you?"

"If I tell you, it'll ruin the surprise. Just lie back and enjoy."

"It'll be tough but I think I'm up to the challenge."

She placed the items on the nightstand and pulled a few more things out of a drawer before crawling on the bed.

"So, Officer Donahue, how do you feel about handcuffs?"

Her smile sent a thrill straight to his groin. A pair of red, fuzzy handcuffs dangled from her elegant fingers. Anticipation and excitement snaked down his spine.

"Only if I get to return the favor."

"But you get to handcuff people all the time," she pouted but her eyes gleamed. "I've never had a chance to use these before."

Wasn't that interesting? She had a kinky side but hadn't done anything about it. Considering how tightly controlled she was that wasn't a big surprise. What shocked him was that she trusted him enough to explore her sexual fantasies with him. Could he convince her to trust him further?

"I'll make it worth your while."

She appeared to think for a minute before smiling at him. "Okay, but I get to cuff you first."

"Go right ahead." He held out his wrists.

As she leaned over to secure his hands above his head, Brogan couldn't help but swipe his tongue along her pointed nipple. A shudder shook her body and he hid a smile. She might think that by cuffing him she was in control but he could do a hell of a lot without using his hands.

"You're a naughty boy," she said but didn't move away.

He drew her luscious tip into his mouth and bit it gently before laving it to take away the sting. Sareena trembled and finally pulled back. Her breathing had increased and her eyelids lowered partway.

"You look like the innocent boy next door but you sure hide an evil streak behind that guileless face." She grabbed a few more things and put them in easy reach before moving between his legs.

"I have multiple layers." He watched as she clicked a remote and soft bluesy music drifted through unseen speakers.

"And I plan on uncovering several of them tonight."

Brogan's pulse raced as she knelt between his thighs and shook her hair back over her shoulders. The moonlight kissed her full breasts and made her look like a goddess come down to Earth.

"I hope you like strawberries," she said in a throaty whisper.

She took one of the juicy berries from a bowl next to her and bit it in half. Staring him right in the eye, as if daring him to look away, she trailed the sweet fruit down her sternum and under the curve of her breast.

Searing heat filled him as he watched the circular path she made over her luscious mound and then around her nipple. When she finished one creamy globe, she took another bite of the strawberry and traced her other breast.

"I think they've become my favorite fruit."

Sareena said nothing but a sly smile crossed her beautiful face. Her skin glistened with sticky juice and he couldn't wait to lick it off her. His mouth watered for a taste of her sweet skin.

The smoky music surrounded them and Sareena swayed to its beat. She picked up another strawberry and took a bite of it. Her white teeth and full lips sucked at the berry, making him envious of the tiny fruit.

With no regard for what the sticky juice would do to her comforter, Sareena slid down between his legs and ran the berry up his thigh. Brogan jumped from the coolness of it against his overheated skin. Her warm breath against his thigh sent licks of flame straight to his cock.

When she traced his balls and his length with the crushed fruit he thought he'd shoot off the bed.

"You know, they say you should get at least five servings of fruit a day," she said as she wrapped her berry-stained lips around the head of his cock.

Brogan could do nothing but groan in pleasure as she licked and sucked him into a pleasure coma. He strained at the cuffs preventing him from clutching her hair but didn't break free. Sweat trickled along his forehead as he fought to hold back his release for the third time that night.

"I just love fresh produce, don't you?"

"I'll never look at a fruit salad the same way again."

Heat rolled off him in waves as he watched her take yet another berry and crush it between her fingers before popping it in her mouth. She ran her sticky hands over her breasts and squeezed them like he was dying to do. He licked his lips, anticipating what she'd do next.

Sareena threw her head back as her fingers parted her sable curls and teased her clit. Little cries of pleasure blended with the music and she traced her pussy lips and circled her nubbin.

Every single muscle in his body tensed as he fought for control. His eyes flew from her enraptured face, over her glistening breasts to where she played with herself and back up again. He couldn't decide which was hotter—her fingers toying with her pussy or her reaction to it.

She gave a low moan as her hips bucked with her pleasure. Brogan had to bite down on his cheek to keep from following her over.

"Holy Mother of God." He closed his eyes for a minute to recover his senses.

Unfortunately, his lack of vision only made his other senses sharper. He could smell the sweetness of the berries mingled with the musk of Sareena's womanly cream. The feel of the cool satin next to his heated body competed with the hot silk of Sareena's fingers across his chest. And when she leaned down and brushed her lips against his mouth, his taste buds exploded with the varied flavors that were uniquely hers.

"Would you like a strawberry of your own?" she asked, holding a plump berry to his lips.

He ate it, relishing the burst of wetness over his desert-dry mouth.

"Good, huh?"

"Not bad. But it isn't the berry I really want."

"Oh? And what berry might that be?"

"The one between your legs."

Sareena gasped and her rapid breath fluttered over his lips. He couldn't use his hands to move her into position but he didn't need to worry. With a lithe twist she scooted on top of him, her dewy pussy just inches from his waiting mouth.

Her clit was red and plump like the berry he'd named it and when he sucked it into his mouth, it far surpassed the fruit's sweetness. He wanted to drink her juices for hours, to gorge on her flavor and drown in her essence. Her taste and texture had him so enraptured he didn't realize what she was doing until her hot mouth captured his cock and sucked him deep.

No longer could he keep his hands still. With a flick of his wrist he unsnapped the toy cuffs and freed himself of his restraints. He pressed a finger into her slick channel and searched for the slightly different texture of her G-spot. A sudden flood of cream told him he'd found it and he pressed harder.

He used his free hand to caress her delicious ass. He couldn't stop from giving her behind a tiny nip—it was too rosy and inviting to pass up. Her derrière was nicely rounded and slightly muscled. Gathering moisture from her dripping pussy, Brogan pressed his finger against her tight, pink rosebud. He stroked the sensitive nerves at her rear entrance and smiled against her pussy lips as she shouted in pleasure around his cock.

When she stroked the soft spot beneath his balls and pressed his nerve-rich perineum it was his turn to gasp in pleasure.

"I want to be in you." He blew a hot stream of air over her swollen clit. "I want to fuck your brains out. I want to drive into you until all you can think about is the next thrust."

Sareena whimpered and rolled off him only to turn around and straddle his hips. She didn't try to tease him or prolong the agony but sank her warm sheath over his throbbing cock until he was in deep.

"Sonofabitch that feels incredible," he swore softly, reaching around to gently pinch her ass.

"Uh huh." Sareena's eyes were closed and her head thrown back as she rocked her hips over him.

With every lift and fall of her hips she tightened her inner muscles and squeezed his cock in a fist of hot velvet. Brogan leaned forward and captured a berry-covered nipple in his mouth. He rolled the bud over his tongue and sucked it hard. When she didn't protest the slight pain, he bit down then laved away the sting.

"I can't hold back," she panted, her head whipping side to side. "Don't."

Brogan sucked her other nipple and flicked her clit at the same time. The combination pushed Sareena over and she spasmed around him before collapsing across his chest.

Thank God.

He didn't think he could last another second. Clenching her hips, Brogan thrust up into her still quivering warmth. It barely took three strokes before he too found a welcome oblivion.

It was only when Sareena finally rolled to his side that he realized they hadn't used any protection.

4

"FUCK!"

"Again? I need a few minutes," Sareena murmured sleepily.

"That's not what I meant. Not that I'd mind, but that isn't what I was saying."

Sareena forced her eyes open and peered at Brogan. He appeared flustered and upset. "What's the problem?"

"I didn't exactly come dressed for the party. We didn't use protection."

"Oh that. It's not an issue. One of the benefits of being a shapeshifter is immunity to diseases. It counterbalances our low birthrate. I'm clean as a whistle. The only reason I didn't mention it the first time was because I didn't want to freak you out and have you stop."

"Like that was gonna happen. But what about pregnancy? You can still get pregnant. That could be a problem."

A tiny pang of sadness rang in her heart. It was too easy to imagine carrying Brogan's baby. The fact that it was not only a long shot but also not something he'd want hurt a little bit.

"Don't worry. It's the wrong time of the month. And even if it was the perfect time, the chances of me getting pregnant are slim to none."

She pushed away from him and grabbed one of the bottles of water she'd taken from the fridge earlier.

"I didn't mean to insult you. It's just . . ."

"It's just you hadn't planned on sleeping with Sareena the heiress, never mind Sareena the shapeshifter, and the thought of an unwanted pregnancy scares the freckles off your face. I understand.

I'm not insulted." *Much*. She slid off the bed and headed toward the bathroom to wash.

"Now just wait a damn minute!" He followed her to the bathroom and cornered her against the vanity. "Don't put words in my mouth. Just because I hadn't *planned* on having sex with you didn't mean I didn't *want* to."

Sareena sighed and forced her irrational irritation away. Brogan had handled the strangeness of the night admirably. It was ridiculous for her to feel hurt because he wasn't doing handsprings of joy at the thought of getting her pregnant. *Grow up, Reena.*

"I'm sorry. You've explained about your discomfort with my bank account. That's not going to go away just because we had good sex. And you've handled the whole shapeshifter thing a lot better than I could have ever hoped for. I didn't mean to act like a spoiled brat."

"Come here." Brogan pulled her into his arms and she nuzzled the valley between his muscular pecs.

His musky, manly fragrance rolled over her and she cuddled closer, trying to absorb his scent. Unconsciously, she rubbed her cheek against his slightly sweaty chest. Her inner cat purred at the marking of so strong a mate.

Hold on there a minute!

Brogan wasn't her mate. Sure, she'd worked with him for months but this was the first night they'd ever spent together. It was way too soon to start thinking about anything permanent.

"So tell me, which bothers you more? My money or the fact I turn into a jaguar?"

He chuckled and she felt it vibrate through his torso. "Apparently it's your money because seeing you turn fuzzy didn't stop me from making love to you the first chance I got."

"Oh good. I could give my money away but there's not much I can do about being a shifter."

As soon as the words were out of her mouth she wanted to yank them back. When Brogan stiffened against her she could have kicked herself. She racked her brain for something to break the tension oozing from him.

"Not that *that* will ever happen." She slid to the side and smiled up at him. "But, since you're here now, would you like to go for a swim in my hot tub?" She pointed to the black marble bathtub that took up half the room.

"Swim is right. Do you realize I've been in pools smaller than your damn tub?"

"Ah, but I bet they didn't have jets. If you're really nice to me I'll even put in some of my sandalwood bath salts so you won't smell like a girl when you leave."

She bent over and turned on the faucets, not waiting for him to answer. His low groan made her smile to herself. He might not be sure about everything that had happened tonight but he still wanted her. It wasn't perfect but it was a start.

"That would go over big at the precinct. I'd never hear the end of it. The guys busted my balls already for wearing a tux."

"But you looked so good in it."

"It was a rental. I don't go around wearing monkey suits on a regular basis."

"That's a shame." She flicked the water from her fingers in his direction.

"We can't all attend black-tie events every night, princess."

She narrowed her eyes at him. "Don't call me princess. It makes me sound like either a spoiled poodle or a pampered rich girl. I don't know which is worse."

"Are you trying to tell me you're not rich?"

"Yes, I have money, but I don't spend all my time jet-setting from one hedonistic playground to another. I know having great wealth also means having great responsibility."

He grabbed her hand and pulled her close again. "I was kidding. I know how hard you work. I've seen you covered in paint from when we did the renovations on the shelter. A lot of folks would have just been happy giving the money to make the construction possible. Not many of them would have pitched in to help do the grunt work."

"I didn't think I'd ever get that awful ceiling paint out of my hair."

"You made a pretty good painter, for an heiress."

"I did a great job with the paint. It was the drywall that beat me. Every time I go in the recreation room I see that damn seam in the wall. It mocks me."

"I'll buy a picture to put up in front of it so you'll never have to see it again."

Sareena's shoulders relaxed as the tension evaporated. She might only have this one night with Brogan, she didn't want to waste it arguing. Leaning over again, she checked the temperature of the water. It was nice and hot so she added the bath salts and turned on the jets.

"Can I ask you a personal question?" Brogan asked as he settled into one of the carved-out seats in the tub.

"Sure. It's not like I have much more to hide."

"Why the battered women's shelter? There are a lot of charities out there, how come you picked domestic violence?"

"You couldn't ask me something easy, could you?"

"You don't have to answer it if you don't want to. I was just curious."

"How much do you know about animal behavior?"

"I know dogs poop a lot, especially on the damn sidewalk outside the precinct."

Sareena laughed and let her legs float over to mingle with Brogan's. "Jaguars aren't pack animals, but there's still a pecking order. In my clan, my father and mother are the Alphas, which is why I can't live too near them."

"I think I get it. It's like the old saying, you can't have two women in one kitchen, or something like that."

"Exactly. I love my parents but if you think two women in the same house is rough, two Alpha women in the same house is a nightmare. Cats need to have their own territories. Which is why I'm here in New York City and my folks are in London. Having an ocean between us helps keep family harmony."

"I bet."

"Someday I'll be the Alpha of my own clan. Someday far, far away if I have any say about it." Just the thought of juggling all the responsibilities she already had with those of a clan leader was enough to give her hives.

"So if there are Alphas that means there has to be . . . Betas?"

"Bingo. It's not as bad as with some of the wolf packs but there's still a pecking order. Anyway, one of my good friends was a sub—a Beta. The thought of being in charge of anything was enough to send her into a panic attack. She liked being told what to do and liked to be dominated."

A shudder of revulsion snaked down Sareena's spine. She had to force herself to relax and not let the anger control her. She'd already changed twice tonight—if she let herself turn furry again she'd be too exhausted to move.

"Theresa, my friend, seemed to attract the worst men for her. She could be in a room of a thousand nice guys and manage to find the one wife beater there."

"I know the type. It's like they have a bastard magnet on their foreheads."

"Exactly. I can't tell you the number of times I picked her up at the hospital with broken bones, concussions and internal injuries. No sooner would she heal then she'd find a new guy to beat her up. It got to the point where I set aside a special fund for her to access in case she needed to run away and I wasn't around."

"Did she use it?"

Pain slammed her in the gut and tears burned her throat. "Not soon enough. I was in India, acting as an ambassador in my mother's place. The cell phone coverage in the mountains is spotty to say the least. Theresa called for help but I didn't get the call until days later. By then it was too late. Her boyfriend had beaten her to death in front of a bus station full of people."

"Why didn't she turn into a jaguar to save herself? I mean, that's what you did tonight, right?"

"She wasn't a full-blooded *jaguatium* so she could only shift when the moon was full and with a great deal of effort."

Brogan swore a blue streak as Sareena tried to fight back the lump in her throat.

"What happened to the guy who killed her?"

"He got seven years in prison for manslaughter and was out with good behavior after five."

"Fucking figures. Is that why you set up the legal fund for the shelter?"

"Yes. It's important that women trying to get away from their abusers have a safe place to go. But it's also imperative that they legally protect themselves and their children."

"You got that right."

Silence stretched between them as they were both lost in their thoughts. The rushing of the water through the jets was the only sound.

"So," Sareena cleared her throat to get rid of the huskiness. "Why do you volunteer at the shelter? I know you work close to sixty hours a week for the department. Why use your precious free time to fix holes in the walls and leaky plumbing?"

Brogan's gut clenched at Sareena's question. He owed her an answer, a real answer, not the usual bullshit he told everyone else. But how could he explain it to her? She'd either be repulsed or, worse, pity him.

He looked around at the opulent bathroom, gleaming with chrome and black marble. How could she ever look at him again with anything but loathing if she knew the truth?

"You don't have to tell me if it's something personal," she said, obviously sensing his apprehension.

Oh Christ. Now he felt like an ass. Here she'd laid out all her deep dark secrets, trusting him with her very life, and he couldn't even utter a peep about his shitty father. What a fucking hypocrite.

He sunk lower in the bubbles, feeling vulnerable and massively uncomfortable with what he was about to say.

"I volunteer at the shelter because I used to live there. My father beat the shit out of my mother on a regular basis. When I was seven he hit me so hard he broke my arm. That was the last straw for Mom. She could handle him hitting her but when he went after me she ran."

Tears swam in Sareena's eyes and he could see her struggling with what to say.

"Look, it could have been a lot worse. At least my mom got out in time. She was one of the lucky ones—she never went back. It wasn't easy for her either. She had to raise me on her own working minimum-wage jobs and accepting food stamps. Her pride took a beating over that but she never went back to him."

"I'm so sorry."

"Don't be. I got over it and so did my mom. Neither one of us want your pity." He pushed himself up and prepared to get out of the tub but Sareena flew at him and he splashed back down.

"I don't pity you. I admire you and your mother for escaping that vicious cycle. I know how often it doesn't happen."

"You and me both." He released a pent-up breath. "I worry that someday I'll turn into him. That I'll become an abuser too. I don't just work at the shelter because I owe them, I'm there so I don't ever forget what it's like to be a little kid watching your mom get smacked around."

"You could never do that. Just because your father was a batterer doesn't mean you'll turn into one."

"How can you say that? You barely know me."

"Bullshit. I've been working with you for almost a year now. I've seen how you play with the kids to give their mothers a break. And I've seen how you interact with the women there. You treat them with respect, you never look down on them. You're the only man they'll let in there, did you know that?"

"Yeah, I know that. But part of the reason is Janice was the director when I was there too. She's known me most of my life."

"Do you think she'd let a potential batterer into her domain? She's more protective of her clients than a mother bear."

Brogan relaxed slightly and considered Sareena's words. A tiny knot of fear he carried around inside of him loosened slightly. It was still there but not as strong as before.

"You know, you're pretty damn smart."

"I know. It's just one of my many qualities," she laughed.

"You're already rich and beautiful, how many more qualities do you need?"

"A lot, apparently, since it's taken me this long to get you into my bed."

"I wanted to be in your bed the first time I looked at you, it was only when I found out who you were that I eighty-sixed that idea."

"You know, I've always had to worry about men coming on to me because of my money. You're the first guy I've met who *wouldn't* come on to me because of it."

"Nope, I just want you for your mind." He wiggled his eyebrows suggestively.

"Right, and I bet you read girlie magazines for the articles too."

Her wet breast slipped over his chest and her legs tangled with his. Any remaining anger or sorrow was pushed aside by the feel of her skin against him and her hands on his body.

"You can never do too much research. In fact, I think I'll do some right now." He ended the conversation by capturing her mouth with a kiss.

Sareena sighed into the kiss and relaxed against him. Her nipples pressed into his chest and he felt his cock stir yet again. She might not be the only one unable to walk by the end of the night.

Brogan's cock thickened against her thigh and Sareena's pussy tingled in anticipation. His large hands, strong but so gentle, stroked her back and she arched into the delicious pressure.

"Does my little cat want to be petted?" he teased.

"Depends on where you're talking about touching." She slipped her hand between their bodies and grasped his rock-hard cock. "And with what."

"You're insatiable. I like that in a woman."

Sareena laughed and faked a punch at him. The movement sent her sliding and she splashed him with bubble-laden water. "I'm not the only insatiable one here. You're the one with a tent pole sticking up between your legs. For the fourth time tonight, I might add."

"It's your fault. I've never recovered so fast or so often in my life."

"That really could be my fault. During a full moon *jaguatium* emit pheromones for mating. That could be influencing you and getting you more worked up than normal."

"Honey, being in the same room with you works me up. If the pheromones are helping me recover faster, I say bring 'em on, this is a new record for me."

"Well, you know what they say about records. They were made to be broken." She crawled across the tub to him and jumped when one of the jets sprayed water over her clit. "Oh my." She closed her eyes and enjoyed the feel of the hot water teasing her nub.

"Do you want a moment alone?" Brogan asked, watching her with hungry eyes.

"I'd rather have you but this feels damn good. I may have to start using this thing more often."

"Cripes. After only one night I'm being replaced by plumbing." He reached out and fondled her breasts.

Her position made them hang down, ripe for his touch. She closed her eyes and enjoyed the double assault on her senses.

"Guess I'll have to find some way to make myself more memorable."

Brogan wrapped a steely arm around her stomach and moved her to the other side of the tub. "Put your hands up here and don't move them. I don't have the handcuffs to make sure you hold still so I'm going to have to trust you."

"Like the cuffs held you for long."

"Are you complaining?" He gave her a swat on her wet bottom.

The stinging slap took her by surprise but didn't really hurt. In fact the burn quickly turned quite pleasurable.

"I wouldn't dream of arguing with an officer of the law."

Another slap, this one on the other cheek, increased the fire heading straight for her pussy.

"Don't you forget it."

The echo of Brogan's spanks reverberated through the marble-filled bathroom—and through every atom of her being. Juice ran freely down her legs and her pussy lips were swollen and achy.

Another jet of hot water pulsed against her nipples like many tiny tongues licking her. Sareena whimpered in frustration but didn't want the sweet torture to end.

When her butt was as hot as her pussy, Brogan stopped spanking her and began kissing every inch he'd abused so pleasurably. The feel of his soft lips over her super-sensitive ass made her groan out loud. She was the closest to begging that she'd ever been in her entire life.

"Please," she gasped.

"Please what?" he murmured against the soft flesh where her thighs met her ass.

"Lick me, fill me, fuck me!"

Tears leaked down her face but she didn't move her hands to wipe them away. Her grip on the edge of the tub was the only thing keeping her anchored. She was afraid if she let go she'd fly into a million pieces.

"All in good time."

His finger probed at her entrance and she thrust her hips back to give him better access. He stroked her slowly, never building her high enough to come. Her breath came in heaving gasps as she strained for the orgasm he held just out of reach.

She was sure she'd explode as soon as his hot mouth lapped at her clit but he backed off before she could go over.

"Brogan!" Her chest heaved with her labored breathing.

"Do you want me, Sareena?" Another fleeting lap of his tongue on her nub.

"Yes!"

He drove into her forcefully but Sareena didn't care. Her pussy welcomed his cock like a hand in a glove and she lifted her hips to let him in as deeply as possible. Water sloshed over the sides of the tub as he thrust into her from behind. His balls slapped her super-sensitive skin and added another caress to her overloaded body.

Brogan held her hips still, preventing her from rushing the pace. She cried out with frustration. She wanted him hard and fast and *now*! He was killing her. There was no way she'd survive another minute without an orgasm.

"Hurry!"

"Not yet, sweetheart." He leaned over, pressing his entire body over hers.

Almost every inch of their skin touched. She could feel his legs brushing along her inner thighs and his pelvis against her stinging behind. His hand crept down from her hip to part the curls of her pussy. One finger swirled around her clit as he slowly pulled his cock out of her and then pressed back in.

Sareena could feel the pressure ready to explode inside her. If he'd only move a little faster she'd fly over the edge in a second. She tried to move back against him when he withdrew but he bit down on the cord of her neck and stopped her.

The feel of his teeth against such a vulnerable spot sent an eruption of lust through her. Whether knowingly or not, Brogan had laid claim to her in an age-old feline manner and the cat inside her responded with a ferocity that shook her to the core.

The orgasm that tore through her ripped the very fabric of her being. It felt like her soul burst through the thin shell that was her body and scattered to the stars. Brogan's hips pistoned against her, making the orgasm go on and on. If it weren't for his arm around her middle, she was sure she'd have slipped under the water and drowned.

God knows she didn't have the energy to move.

"Shit. I think I might have bit a little too hard when I came." He kissed her gently.

"'S okay," she murmured in a daze. The slight sting on her neck barely registered. Her body was still humming from the most incredible orgasm of her life. He could have bit straight down to the bone and she probably wouldn't have noticed.

"No really, you're bleeding."

Brogan pulled out of her and Sareena shuddered from another wave of pleasure. Her legs shook as he pulled her to her feet. She felt loose and boneless and sublimely happy.

"Can you stand on your own?"

"Maybe."

A satisfied chuckle rumbled from him as he grabbed a hand

towel off the rack. Her body fairly sang when he held her close to dab at the tiny bite mark he'd left on the back of her neck.

"I guess it's not too bad. I don't know what got into me. I just *had* to bite that sweet spot and then you convulsed around me and I couldn't hold back any longer."

"Your bite was what made me come so hard. It's a cat thing."

"I'll have to remember that for future reference."

He took another towel off the heated rack and rubbed it over his hair. All too quickly he wrapped the bath sheet around his waist, hiding his delicious ass from her view.

"Will there be a future between the two of us?" The warm towel she patted herself with did nothing to warm the chill of nervousness in her blood.

Brogan ran a hand through his hair. "I want there to be."

"But?"

"But it isn't going to be easy."

"Most relationships aren't. At least not the ones that mean anything." She pushed out of the misty bathroom and plunked down on the couch in her bedroom.

"Yeah but most relationships don't occur between the son of a batterer and a fucking heiress."

Sareena looked up in shock. "I turned into a jaguar in front of you tonight. Twice! And the biggest issue you have is with my money? What is wrong with you? There are a million reasons why things might not work. My family, my race, your schedule and any number of other things but the fact I'm rich should be the least of the problems."

"I know. Damn it, I know I shouldn't care but all I think of is every time we're out together people are going to think I'm with you for your money. Or that you're using me as some sort of boy toy. The flack I caught for going to the benefit dinner will be nothing compared to what I'll have to deal with if you pick me up at work in that goddamn limo."

"Do you want to pretend we're just business acquaintances?" Anger and frustration boiled in her chest. She was trying her hardest to understand his point of view but he made it seem like he'd be embarrassed to be seen with her.

"No. I'm not going to sneak around and see you on the sly. That isn't fair to you."

A lump formed in her throat and she pushed it down before it strangled her. "It's not too late to back out. Even if you don't want to . . . be with me, I know you'd never betray me."

"Damn it, I do want to be with you!" he shouted and kicked a throw pillow across the room. "I just don't know how. I can barely remember what fork to use at those fancy-schmancy dinners. I'll end up doing something to embarrass you."

"Oh, Brogan, you could never embarrass me. I really don't give a damn what others think. You're a kind, caring, intelligent man. Let people believe what they want. I know that you're not with me for my money. Shouldn't that be what matters?"

"No offense but that's easy for you to say. It's not you who'll be branded as a gold digger in the supermarket tabloids. I may not have much but I do have my pride. No man wants to be seen as a sponge."

"Oh please. I can't see you quitting your job to be my boy toy."

"Hell, if the paparazzi hound me as badly as they do you I won't have a job. I can't see my captain being too pleased with me if I screw up a bust because a mob of reporters is on my back."

"I-I never thought of that." Damn. How would they ever work this out?

"Trust me, I have. Otherwise I would have knocked on your door the minute you gave me a second glance. I've wanted you for a long time. I just couldn't figure out how we could make it work. I still don't."

She took a deep breath and prayed for patience. "Listen, we don't have to figure this all out tonight . . . err, this morning. Why don't we have some breakfast and we can talk about it later?"

"Breakfast? What time is it?" Brogan looked at the clock glowing by the bed. "Sonofabitch! I have to be to work in an hour." He dropped the towel and searched for his clothes. "I have to go. I need to change into my uniform and get downtown. Christ, I have to return the damn tux too."

Sareena followed him and couldn't help but admire the view of his tight ass hustling down the hall. While he jerked on his pants she picked her robe off the living room floor and slipped it on.

"I'll call a cab for you while you're getting dressed. I'd offer the use of my limo but I don't think you'd appreciate it."

"No! I definitely don't want to pull into my neighborhood in your limo. Maybe someday but not yet."

"I understand." She made the call from the kitchen phone to give Brogan a few minutes to pull himself together.

Once he was dressed, she slipped on a pair of sandals. "We'll take my personal elevator, it leads to a private entrance. There's no guard posted there so you won't be seen with me, although there are security cameras. Maybe you can turn your face away so no one will recognize you if they see the tapes. I'm sure if you move fast enough none of your police buddies will see you getting into the cab so no one will know you spent the night with me."

"Sareena, I'm not embarrassed to be seen with you, okay? It's just going to take me a little time to get used to it. A shitload has happened in the last twelve hours."

She took a deep breath and let go of her lingering irritation. Patience wasn't her strong suit. Just because she didn't have a problem seeing them as a couple didn't mean it would come as quickly to him. She had to back off and let nature take its course.

"Okay. C'mon, I don't want you to be late for work." She led him through the laundry room and into her private car that would drop him off near the servants' entrance.

When the doors opened at their stop, Brogan stepped out first and scanned the area. Her heart did a slow tumble in her chest. Even though he'd seen her turn into a jungle cat that could tear him apart with one swipe, he still felt protective of her. *How sweet.* Sareena waited for him to drop the arm blocking her from exiting the elevator but he left it there.

"Why don't you go on back up? I'm sure the cab will be here shortly, and you're not exactly dressed to be out in public."

"This is a private entrance and I'm covered from neck to ankle."

"But I keep remembering you in that same robe last night and I don't want anyone else to see you like that."

"Well, in that case—look out!" Sareena shoved him aside just as a knife slashed at his back.

The doors to the elevator slid closed without Brogan's arm to hold them open. In seconds, she dropped the robe and flowed into her cat form. Nudging the button with her nose, the doors opened in time for her to see Brogan scramble away from another attack. Her snarl of rage echoed through the tiny hallway as she leapt from the elevator.

Brogan and the man from last night wrestled across the tiled floor, grunting with the force of their blows. Sareena's tail lashed as she waited for an opportunity to pounce on the wretch who dared to harm her mate.

Finally her chance came when Brogan used his feet to throw the wife beater over his head. Sareena was on him like a terrier on a rat. She used her entire body weight to slam into him, sending his head crashing against the wall. Blood flew everywhere, its coppery scent inflaming her senses. Just as she raised her claw for the killing blow, Brogan jumped in and pulled the attacker away before she could slash him with her claws.

"Stop it! He's not worth it. Go!" he ordered.

Bloodlust raged through her and she growled with frustration. She wanted to kill the sorry piece of meat on the ground.

The wail of sirens whined in the distance and sent a thread of panic into her fiery thoughts.

"Get back to your apartment before the cops get here. I'll get you when it's safe."

Sareena shifted into her human shape and almost dropped to her knees. It was all she could do to press the elevator door button and stumble inside the car. A fog of exhaustion blurred her vision and tried to drag her down into its depths.

Her head pounded and she slumped down against the cool, metal wall. The ride to her floor seemed to take forever and every second that passed made her muscles ache that much more. She fought to remain conscious until she reached the safety of her home. Nausea rolled in her stomach as her vision faded in and out of focus.

Thank God she'd left her door unlocked because she didn't have the strength to fumble with it. Her white robe had streaks of blood smeared across it and she made a mental note to have Lana clean up the elevator and check for traces of blood that could lead to her condo.

It took every iota of willpower to wash off in the laundry room and not just lay on the tile floor and go to sleep. She didn't want the wife beater's scent on her or she would have done just that.

The bedroom was way too far away for her to make it. With the last ounce of energy left in her body she staggered into the living room and collapsed on the couch. Her brain registered Brogan's scent wafting up from the cushions seconds before she fell into oblivion.

5

SUNLIGHT WARMED HER face and the smell of fresh coffee woke her from the sleep of the dead.

No, not dead just damn close to it.

Her eyelids felt like they weighed a hundred pounds each but she forced them open. Lana stood at the side of the couch with a tray of coffee and a pitcher of orange juice.

"Lana, you're a goddess."

"I know," she said with a smile as she set the tray down on the table. "Overextended ourselves a little, did we?"

"I don't know if you did, but I sure as hell pushed the envelope last night."

"More like two nights ago. Last night you were unconscious on the couch. You didn't even stir when that policeman came banging on the door."

"Policeman?" Sareena perked up.

"Yes, Brody or Brogan or something. He's come by at least ten times since last night and he's called nearly twice that."

"What did you tell him?"

"I told him you were indisposed and you'd call him back when you were able."

"Did he leave his home number?"

"And his cell phone number and his work number and his pager. Now drink some of that orange juice as well as the coffee while I make up your eggs."

The icy juice felt heavenly against her parched throat as Sareena chugged down a tall glass.

What did Brogan want? Had seeing her in full feline rage destroyed any hope of a relationship with him?

Her heart jumped into her throat as someone pounded on the door.

"Come on, Nurse Ratchet, she can't still be sleeping. It's been over twenty-four hours!" Brogan's voice came through the door loud and clear.

Lana stepped from the kitchen and made to answer the door. Sareena waved her off and crossed to the foyer herself. Every muscle in her body screamed in protest but she was better off than she'd been when she came home yesterday.

"Don't shout, I just woke up." Sareena opened the door then stepped back as Brogan barged in.

"Finally! I've been a nervous freaking wreck. I thought you'd slipped into a coma or something." He yanked her to his chest and kissed her hard.

Shock held her in place for a few seconds before she melted into the kiss. God she hoped the orange juice she drank would disguise her morning breath.

"Are you okay? The last time I saw you, you were pale as a ghost and stumbling."

"I'm fine now. What about you?" She ran her finger lightly over the multiple bruises on his face. One eye was swollen and his nose looked puffy too.

"Just some bumps and bruises, I'll live. Thanks to you."

"I didn't do anything."

"You saw him coming at me with the knife when I'd missed him completely. If you hadn't shoved me out of the way I'd have been a goner."

"I'm just glad you're safe. Is that bastard behind bars?"

"Yeah, now that he's out of the hospital. They're sending him for a psych eval after his bond hearing. He tried to tell the doctors that the slashes on his stomach were from a huge cat."

"Really? And did anyone believe him?"

"Not after they read the part of my report where I stated he got caught climbing the fence and hurt himself as he flipped over it.

The consensus is that he's faking insanity to get out of his charges."
Brogan smirked then winced.

"Talk about crazy. A huge cat in the middle of the city. Who'd
believe that?" She nuzzled his neck, inhaling the scent of soap and
man. Delicious.

"I don't know, I think you could convince me of just about anything."

6

Six months later

"YOU'RE SURE ABOUT this? I don't want you doing anything that makes you uncomfortable." Sareena's gut twisted with nerves.

"Oh really? That's pretty funny coming from the woman who pulled out a vibrator and told me 'just relax.' I'm fine, honest."

"I just don't want you doing this for me. I want it to be your idea."

"'Reena, it was my idea. If you remember, *I'm* the one who suggested it."

"I know, but—"

"But nothing." He shut her up by placing a finger over her lips. "I want to meet the rest of your family. And I want to try my hand at running my own business. I only took a leave of absence from the force. If things don't work out I can always go back. My captain thought it would be a good idea to take a break until the heat died down anyway so it works out for everyone." He kissed her softly and stroked her hair.

"You wouldn't have any heat if it wasn't for me." Sareena leaned into his caress. Damn but Brogan had great hands.

The pilot of her private plane approached them. "Miss Wilton, we've been cleared for takeoff. We'll be leaving shortly."

"Thank you." She settled into the leather seat and fastened her seat belt while Brogan did the same.

"I'll never get used to this, you know. I've never even been on a plane before and here I am, getting ready to fly to freaking Europe on a private jet."

"And that's a bad thing?"

"Not bad, just different. Don't worry, I think I've mostly gotten over my hang-up about your money. As long as you don't try to make me a kept man I'll try to check my ego."

"I could always give it all away. You know I'd do that for you."

"Not that argument again." Brogan took her hand and kissed her knuckles. "You can do a lot more good by using your money to help people in need. I'm not so selfish that I'd sacrifice all the work you do for my pride. I know I love you for you and not your money. Even if that is what every freaking tabloid across the country prints."

"Screw them."

Her heart flipped over with a slow thump at his words. She'd never get tired of hearing him tell her he loved her.

The last six months had been both the most amazing and the most difficult of her life. Amazing because loving Brogan was mind-numbingly incredible. He turned out to be just as considerate out of bed as he was in it.

Unfortunately, balancing his job as a cop and her public image was a nightmare. His picture had been splattered over every tabloid in the city. He'd had to get an unlisted phone number because the darn thing rang all day and night. Every talk show and radio program in America wanted to hear about the cop who managed to snag the Wilton heiress.

His captain hadn't been happy when the paparazzi stormed the precinct house trying to get pictures of him at work. Brogan had been confined to desk duty, which nearly broke Sareena's heart. He was too good a cop to be taken off the streets because of her.

She shuddered a little, remembering when she tried to break things off with him.

"What's wrong?" he massaged her shoulders, sensing her tension.

"I was just thinking about the time I tried to dump you."

Brogan snorted and lifted the armrest so he could pull her closer. "Don't ever try that shit again. You almost gave me a heart attack. I can't stand the thought of losing you."

"It nearly killed me but I had to try. It was for your own good."

"Why don't you let me worry about what's good for me?"

"But you love your job. I hate seeing you punished because of me."

"Oh? I thought you enjoyed punishing me?" His smile bordered on a leer and shot sparkles of heat straight to her pussy.

"Only in bed."

The plane rolled down the runway, jostling them a little as it prepared for takeoff. Brogan used the movement as an excuse to press even closer to her. His hand stroked her breast covertly.

Instantly the barely banked fires of lust he stirred in her just by breathing flared to life. Her nipples hardened into little points and poked through her silk turtleneck.

"Damn, I wish I wore a low-cut shirt."

"I don't know, the way this one clings to your every curve works for me. And that long skirt you're wearing just makes me wonder what you have on under it."

Sareena shivered as his provocative words rumbled against her throat. His touch burned through her shirt and bra and made it almost impossible to hold still.

"The co-pilot will be coming back here as soon as we take off and you've got me all hot and bothered."

"It works both ways. At least you don't have an erection threatening to break your zipper."

She glanced down and saw he spoke the truth. His hard-on stood up like a tent pole in his dress slacks. Her hand drifted down to caress his length. He was hard enough to pound nails.

Another shiver trailed down her spine.

Sareena scrambled for a magazine to hide her erect nipples as the sound of the cabin door opening reached her super-sensitive ears. By the time the co-pilot made it back to the lounge area they appeared to be engrossed in their respective reading material. She hoped.

If the co-pilot noticed Brogan held his sports magazine over his lap and Sareena had her fashion magazine practically pressed to her chest, he didn't mention it.

"We've reached our cruising altitude and there's no turbulence as far as we can tell. It should be a pleasant flight to London."

"Wonderful, thank you."

Under the cover of his magazine, Brogan stroked her upper thigh. Tiny jolts exploded between her legs and her pussy dripped cream.

"You're welcome. Can I get you a drink or a snack?"

"We're all set for now. We may want a light dinner later but I think we're going to take a nap first." She fought to keep her breathing normal as Brogan continued to tease her. His fingers found the strap of her garter belt and traced it.

"Yes, ma'am. Shall I dim the cabin lights on my way back to the cockpit?"

"Yes, please." Sareena ignored Brogan's snort at the word cock.

"Enjoy the flight." The co-pilot left without the slightest flicker of emotion.

She waited until she heard the snick of the cabin door closing before she turned on Brogan.

"You beast! I could barely string two words together coherently. He's going to think I'm some sort of flake."

"Why do you care what he thinks?"

"Because I don't want to be thought of as an oversexed trust fund baby."

"I think you're far from oversexed. In fact, I think you're decidedly undersexed." He tugged on her long skirt, pulling it up inch by inch. "So tell me, Miss Wilton, what do you have on under this skirt?"

"A very damp thong."

He'd exposed the tops of her stockings and she heard his breath hitch at the sight of the black lace. She'd worn them just for him but hadn't expected to show them off before they'd landed in England.

"So, have you ever had an orgasm on a plane before?"

"Ah, no," she gasped as he followed the lacy strap of the garter with his finger.

"There's a first time for everything."

He drew a small circle over her clit, rubbing it through the wet silk of her thong. Sareena squirmed in her seat as he teased her. Flames of lust shot through her bloodstream and she arched her hips to get closer to his touch.

"I love how you respond to me."

"If you move my underwear, I'll show you one hell of a response."

"All in good time."

"Easy for you to say."

"Would you prefer I do something else with my mouth?" Brogan slipped out of his chair and knelt between her splayed knees.

Sareena had barely a second to thank God for having a private jet with plenty of room before Brogan tore her panties and her world exploded. His hot mouth descended on her pussy and lapped at her juices. Hot bursts of pleasure bubbled through her like the finest champagne, intoxicating her more than wine ever could. She had to bite her lip to keep from roaring out her pleasure.

His finger slipped inside her dripping channel as he licked her clit. The pressure in her core built to the breaking point with every stroke of his knuckle along her slit. She gripped the seat with all her might to keep from flying apart.

It didn't work.

One final stroke of his hot tongue against her clit and she exploded into a million pieces. Her pussy spasmed and her legs shook with the force of her orgasm. The plane might be flying over the Atlantic, but Sareena was among the stars.

"Dear God in heaven, that's a beautiful sight. I could watch you come apart for hours."

"Don't let me stop you." Her eyelids weighed too much for her to open her eyes. She was so relaxed she could melt into the leather seat and not move again until they landed.

Except Brogan practically vibrated with sexual energy next to her. She could smell his arousal mixed with her orgasm and it stirred her blood.

"You know the best thing about wearing a skirt like this?" she asked as she unzipped his fly.

"Easy access?"

"That too. But I was thinking more along the lines of coverage."

His cock sprung out into her hand as she pulled his pants and boxers over his raised hips. She couldn't resist running her tongue along his length just once before standing.

Gathering the yards of material of her skirt, she climbed onto Brogan's lap. Leaning forward she angled her body until she worked her way onto his stiff cock. Her heart almost burst in her chest as he filled her. Every inch of his length pressed against the slick walls of her pussy, setting her nerves aflame. His groan of pleasure washed over her and she squeezed him tightly, loving the feel of his hardness surrounded by her softness.

The folds of her skirt fell down over their legs, hiding their actions should the pilot or co-pilot emerge from the cockpit.

She fervently hoped they stayed put.

Brogan ran his hands under her shirt and up her rib cage. He circled her breasts, drawing closer to her begging nipples so slowly she almost cried. When he finally reached her tightened points she was ready to whimper with need.

"Do you know how sexy you are? How great you feel in my hands?"

"Do you know how fucking hot you are inside my body? How much I love feeling you in me?"

His rock-hard chest pressed against her back and his steely thighs bunched under her as he thrust slowly into her. She reveled in the feeling of all that power surrounding her. His large hands toyed with her breasts and she rested her head against his shoulder, pushing her chest out for more of his touch.

"I love you so much, Reena," he whispered against her, pushing down the fold of her shirt to reach her neck.

"I love you too, my Brogan."

"God, I never get tired of hearing that." He bit down on the tendon of her neck he'd exposed. Arrows of lust speared her at the touch of his teeth on her and she bucked as the wave of her orgasm overcame her.

Vaguely she felt him join her but she was too busy exploding to be sure.

• • •

HER BODY STILL quivered even after she'd cleaned up and returned to her seat. Just being near Brogan had that effect on her.

"So is there anything I should know before I meet your pops? I mean, are there any faux pas I should avoid? I'd kind of like to make a good impression."

"Are you nervous about meeting my family?"

"I just don't want them believing any of the crap they might have read."

"My parents know better than to believe any of that." And she was sure her father had already had Brogan investigated thoroughly. But Brogan didn't need to know that. "As long as you're kind to me they'll love you as much as I do."

"Like I could be anything but good to you. If I tried to smack you around you'd disembowel me," he teased.

"Then I guess you'd better take care of me."

"That might take the rest of my life."

"I can make it worth your while." She snuggled into his arms.

"Oh yeah? Convince me."

And as the plane sped through the night sky, she did.

ABLAZE

KIT TUNSTALL

1

BLACK SMOKE BILLOWED down the hallway, obscuring Nick's view through his face shield. His peripheral vision tracked two teenagers in the Westbridge Academy's conservative uniforms hurrying toward the exit, clutching hands and sobbing. He thought about stopping the girls to ask if they had seen anyone else left in the building, but the air of panic surrounding them indicated they wouldn't be responsive.

Seeing they required no assistance, he and his partner moved on, Paula taking the lead. As they progressed down the hallway, the smoke thickened, settling lower to the floor. He reached for his SCBA automatically as they checked each classroom, quickly but methodically.

At the last room in the hallway, where the fire had originated, Nick and Paula stepped inside, dropping to a crouch as they moved through the room, searching for anyone remaining. His low vantage point allowed him to avoid the thickest concentration of the acrid smoke and improved his visibility.

The room appeared to be a science lab containing several long black tables with three chairs at each. All of the tables were bare of the clutter of academic paraphernalia, indicating either everyone had grabbed their belongings, or no one had been in the room when the fire started.

Under that assumption, he didn't expect to find anyone but indicated with a hand signal to Paula that he was checking the adjoining lab, as procedure dictated. With Paula behind him, he entered the second room, and his heart stuttered when he saw someone lying facedown on the floor in the corner. Nick moved closer at a rapid pace, identifying the form of a woman when he knelt beside her. As Paula joined him, he rolled the woman onto her back and lifted her in his arms, not taking time to check her vitals. She settled over his shoulder easily. The woman was a negligent burden on his way from the building, and he emerged into fresh air seconds later, his partner close on his heels. Paula broke off to rejoin the group of firefighters gathered round the engine.

Nick went straight to one of the ambulances, where an EMT waited to care for her. He lowered the woman onto a waiting stretcher and stripped off his SCBA then pushed back his face shield, preparing to find his chief to inform him the building was clear. Nick's eyes fell on the face of the woman, and he caught his breath. Even the black smudges couldn't disguise her finely honed features. With olive skin and dark brown hair, she was a striking contrast to the crisp white sheet and pillow on the gurney.

Her eyes opened as the EMT slipped an oxygen mask over her face. The rich brown color reminded Nick of pools of molten chocolate. The bewilderment in them made his heart ache. Without removing his elkskin gloves, he took her hand and squeezed gently. "Everything's going to be fine, ma'am."

For a long second, her gaze didn't waver from his. Nick had the sensation she was peering into his soul. He squirmed at the thought, breaking eye contact when he caught sight of the chief. It was a struggle to release the woman's hand, much to his surprise. Glancing down once more, he saw her eyes had closed again. The sound of her harsh coughing remained with him as he made his way to Brady, the chief. Her frightened eyes haunted him, and it took all his willpower to push away thoughts of her and return to the business at hand. Never had he experienced such a connection in such a way, and the woman's image stayed with him as he rejoined the rest of the crew extinguishing the fire.

BREATHING HURT. COUGHING hurt even more, but Miri couldn't stifle the urge. The oxygen provided some relief from the burning, acrid sensation in her throat and lungs but didn't repress the reflex to clear the congestion. She was vaguely aware of the EMT hovering beside her, monitoring her vitals every few minutes, but couldn't manage to converse yet. Her throat was too raw. Even the thought of speaking made her wince.

The approach of a firefighter, stripped of his Nomex jacket, with a white T-shirt and red Nomex pants, distracted her temporarily from her misery. Miri's eyes widened when she recognized the black-haired, blue-eyed hunk as the man who had carried her from the building. Her stomach clenched with nerves—or the urge to vomit after a prolonged coughing fit—as he approached, a smile displaying his firm lips, set in a tanned face, to their best advantage.

He tapped the EMT on the arm. "How's she doing, Manny?"

"Pretty well." He pointed to the pulse oximeter attached to Miri's finger. "Her oxygen is ninety-eight."

"Will you be taking her to the hospital?"

Miri moved the oxygen mask. "No." She hardly recognized the hoarse voice emerging from her throat.

He turned his attention to her. "How're you feeling, ma'am?"

"Thirsty."

"I can take care of that."

She watched him walk away from her, heading toward the red engine with phfd emblazoned on the side in black letters. The loose fit of his pants hid his buttocks and legs, but the T-shirt clung to his defined arms like a lover, revealing each bulge and flex.

When he returned, water bottle in hand, Miri quickly dropped her eyes to hide the fact she had been staring. The instant attraction to her rescuer disturbed her. She wasn't the type to have her head turned so quickly, and definitely not just by physical attributes. She tried telling herself gratitude was the only thing she felt for the man, but knew it wasn't true.

"Here you are, Ms.—" He unscrewed the cap before handing her the bottle.

"Zorga. Miriam Zorga." She handed the mask to Manny, nodding to acknowledge his cautionary words of sipping slowly, and took a small taste. The water was like Heaven, though tainted by the flavor of smoke lingering in her mouth. After two more small sips, she looked up at the firefighter. "Thank you for the water . . . and for saving my life."

He inclined his head. "That's my job."

"Still, I want to repay you. May I buy you dinner Friday night?" Miri's eyes widened at the invitation. What was she thinking? She never dated a man unless she had known him for a decent length of time, knew his character, friends, interests and flaws. She did not go out with men she had just met, no matter how sexy. She certainly wasn't the one to issue the request. A retraction hovered on the tip of her tongue, but his reply cut it off.

"It's not every day a beautiful woman offers me dinner. How can I say no?" His blue eyes sparkled, as if he sensed she had been about to withdraw the invitation.

She couldn't graciously change her mind now. Miri forced a small smile. "Does Poplin Hills Country Club suit you?"

"If that's what you want." The idea didn't seem to thrill him. "I'll pick you up if you'll give me your address."

"No." She winced at the panic in her tone, hoping the lingering huskiness masked it. "We'll meet there. Seven thirty?" She held her breath, expecting him to argue. Hoping he would, giving her an out from the evening. She wouldn't feel at all guilty for rescinding the invitation should he prove to be forceful or controlling. To her disappointment, he simply nodded.

"I'll see you then." He started to turn but paused, looking down at her. "I'm Nick Martin, by the way." Then he was gone, fading back into the chaos of the scene on the front lawn of the staid private girls' school.

She blushed upon realizing she hadn't even caught his name before asking him to dinner. Hormones were to blame for her spontaneous action, which alarmed her further. She hadn't surrendered to the pull of hormones as a teenager. *It's about time you did*, whispered a sly voice in her mind—the voice she was careful to always repress and tune out. This time, it refused to be ignored, whispering all sorts of erotic suggestions about how the dinner date with Nick might end. Much to her surprise, she didn't want to ignore the voice this time.

MIRI GROANED AT the sight in the mirror. Her attempt at sexy had ended up closer to disheveled. Thick hair hung around her face in a tangled mass, refusing to lie sleek, as she had envisioned. The black silk pants she hadn't worn for years reminded her why she hadn't worn them with the way they clung to her thighs, accentuating the cellulite she hid under skirts and looser slacks. The red shirt dipped too low, exposing what should have been generous cleavage on a different woman, but merely accented what she lacked.

Miri glanced at the clock, biting her lip. She had twenty minutes until she was supposed to meet Nick. Availing herself of valet parking would give her five extra minutes to fix the disastrous sight she currently presented. In record time, she stripped off the slacks and shirt, and standing before the mirror in plain beige panties and a simple bra, she grabbed her hair and pulled it back. Her hands were adept at forming the bun she wore every day, so that took little time. She secured it with pins and turned to her wardrobe, once again examining her available clothing. Everything seemed wrong, which had already led her to the two sexiest pieces she owned, and look how they had turned out.

With a sigh, she selected an A-line brown skirt and camel turtleneck sweater with subtle threads of gold woven throughout. Adding gold hoops and a pearl necklace made the outfit dressy enough for the country club, though boring. She chose to look on the bright side as she scooped up a gold clutch and hurried from her small house. Boring was sure to be a turnoff to the all-male Nick Martin, who must be accustomed to dating beautiful women. If he had no interest in her, that saved her the effort of fighting her attraction to him. The thought provided little consolation as she pushed her beige Saab four miles over the speed limit through the sparsely populated streets of Poplin Hills.

• • •

SHE ARRIVED FIVE minutes late, to find Nick sitting at the bar, watching for her. She nodded to the maitre d' on her way through the spacious entryway, sparing no time to admire the antique teak, gold accents and deep red carpeting. The surroundings were familiar to her.

As she approached, Nick eased off his bar stool, drink in hand. He tugged at the tie around his neck, as if unaccustomed to such accoutrements. With a critical eye, Miri examined him, noting he was sexy in the black suit but obviously uncomfortable. Her choice of restaurants was clearly a failure.

"I'm so sorry I'm not on time," she said in a rush when reaching him. "I'm never late . . . " She trailed off, deciding not to elaborate on why she was tardy.

He shrugged. "Don't worry. The beer is cold, and this is a nice place to wait." His expression betrayed the small white lie. Miri bit back a gasp at the electricity flaring between them when he took her hand. "All that matters is you showed up."

She cleared her throat, resisting the urge to tug her hand from his. The contact discomfited her. Not because he was a stranger, but because she liked it too much. "Are you ready for dinner?"

He nodded as the maitre d' appeared at their side, as if psychically summoned. Nick didn't release her hand while they followed the man to a round table draped with a red tablecloth. Gold candleholders shone in the muted illumination from the crystal chandelier above the table. The flames from the red candles provided a cozy glow to accentuate the overhead lighting.

She breathed a sigh of relief when he had to let go of her hand as she prepared to sit at the table. The light-headedness his touch had inspired almost faded, though she still felt giddy. Inner alarms screamed warnings about his effect on her, but Miri tried to ignore them as Nick pulled out her chair and seated her. Once again, his touch made her breathless.

Awkward silence fell between them as the maitre d' departed after promising their server's attention shortly. She stared across the table, struggling not to stare into his sinfully blue eyes while trying to avoid the appearance of rudeness by ducking his gaze. She couldn't strike a balance and ended up looking away.

"Do you come here often?" His mood was difficult to discern. He didn't seem nervous, merely out of his element. Nick's voice didn't betray anything other than mild curiosity.

She nodded. "I have a lifetime membership." Miri didn't share the complete history of how it came to her. Her mother's numerous sordid marriages weren't a topic for first-date discussion. "It was a gift from my stepfather. He owned Poplin Hills Country Club a few years ago." Stepfather number four, to be precise, and the only one she had ever loved as a father.

His brow furrowed. "Richard Grazier was your stepfather?"

She nodded, struggling to maintain an indifferent façade as she studied him subtly, searching for a hint of avarice. More than once, she had disappointed a suitor who thought her stepfather had left her a large inheritance. His death had been several years after the divorce, and Miri had refused to accept anything from him other than companionship at that point. His other children and current wife had been relieved.

"It was hard on the town when Mr. Grazier passed. Everyone loved him."

Her heart softened at his sympathetic tone, and she struggled to make an intelligent response while hiding the tears in her voice. Thankfully, the arrival of the waiter prevented a reply, allowing her a minute to compose herself as Nick ordered a steak. Her order of grilled tilapia came automatically, and the server moved away.

The sommelier arrived within seconds, handing the wine menu to Nick. "What will you have this evening, sir?"

Miri almost grinned at his deer-in-the-headlights look. It was clear he wasn't a wine aficionado. Smothering her mirth, she said, "I don't believe we'll need a bottle tonight, Jules. Would you please bring me a glass of sauvignon blanc?"

Jules turned to Nick. "For you, sir?"

"Beer's fine." Nick seemed unbothered by the wrinkling of the sommelier's brow as he left the table.

Again, the conversation lapsed. Miri asked a few meaningless questions, as did he, while accomplishing nothing but killing time. Out of desperation, she asked about his family. That was a topic she rarely broached with a stranger, for fear of having to give reciprocal information, but something needed to move along their exchange.

His posture relaxed, and he began telling her about his large family, all currently living in Boston.

As Nick spoke of his relations, Miri tried not to let envy plague her. As she laughed along with him at his shared remembrances, she couldn't help contrasting his childhood to hers. Nick's had been full of family and love, while hers was one long stretch of loneliness, with no siblings to share the trauma of uncles and stepfathers constantly coming and going, and a mother who was more concerned about her sex life than her daughter's welfare.

As their meal arrived, she asked, "Why are you in Oregon if your family is in Boston?"

"I wanted to see something besides Boston. I ended up here after traveling a few years." He shook his head. "It's funny. I thought I wanted to break away from the family traditions, but I ended up a firefighter just like my brothers and father, in spite of myself. It just took me a few years longer."

Her eyes widened. "Everyone in your family is a firefighter?"

"Just about." Pride shone in his eyes. Before she could ask anything else, his expression dimmed. "My oldest brother isn't a firefighter now. He married a woman who hated the whole idea, so he gave it up." It was clear what Nick would do in a similar situation. Miri would hate to be the woman to ask him to give up his career.

As they ate, they managed to fill the meal with stilted, meaningless conversation. By dessert, Miri had chalked up the date as a disaster and was admonishing herself about rash behavior when the bill arrived.

After settling the check, Miri rose to her feet, not waiting for Nick to pull out her chair. He rose just after her, putting his hand on her lower back as they left the restaurant. She searched for a painless way to close the evening while getting across the point that she didn't want a repeat. It probably wasn't a concern. What man would want a second date with her after this calamity?

Outside, she handed a slip to the valet, noticing Nick didn't. They stood in silence as the young woman brought forth her Saab. At the curb, Miri turned to him, extending her hand. "Thank you for allowing me to repay you for saving me, Nick."

His lips twitched, as if repressing laughter. "My pleasure, Miri." He took her hand, caressing the palm with small circles of his thumb.

With a decisive nod, she pulled her hand from his and slid inside through the opened car door. Miri looked up at him, trying not to let her eagerness to escape show. "Well . . . good night."

He nodded but made no effort to walk toward his own car, wherever it might be. She waited for him to speak or move, so she could close the door and drive away, but he just stood there. "Good night," she said again, allowing a hint of exasperation to show.

"I'll follow you home to make sure you get there safely."

"There's no need—"

He tapped on her windshield, already setting off in the direction of the self-parking area. "I'll catch up with you," he called over his shoulder.

She gritted her teeth and resisted the urge to run over him as he stepped in front of her car. No, she didn't want to dent the pristine grill, and blood would never come out of the beige paint.

As he jogged away, she slammed the door and shifted into drive, hitting the accelerator with a vengeance. All the way to her quiet home, she seethed with anger at his high-handedness. If he was pulling this stunt to get her to invite him in, he was in for a disappointment. Yes, he was too sexy for words, but she didn't like his attitude. He was too blunt for her tastes. She had cultivated a sophisticated life, courtesy of the time she had spent as Richard's stepdaughter. Nick would never fit into her existence. She couldn't even imagine him in her immaculate brick home, decorated in neutral colors with pastel accents.

She squirmed as an unwanted mental image came to her of Nick sprawled across her periwinkle Egyptian-cotton sheets with his hair tousled, his chest gleaming with sweat and the flush of passion still in his cheeks. Okay, there was one place he would complement her décor, but she refused to let her self-control slip enough to allow him into her home, much less the bedroom.

2

By THE TIME Miri parked in her garage, Nick's red Dodge Ram had caught up with her. He stopped at her curb and bounded out without invitation to meet her at the door leading into the kitchen.

She pasted on a cool smile, valiantly ignoring the pool of heat that formed in her stomach when he touched her arm. "Thank you for the escort. It was unnecessary but appreciated."

He chuckled. "You don't lie well, Miri."

A blush swept through her cheeks. "Pardon?"

"You don't appreciate my chivalry. You're too busy trying to figure out what my angle is." He lifted an arm, resting his palm on the door behind her and bringing himself much closer.

Her spine stiffened. "You're mistaken, Mr. Martin. If you'll excuse me, I'm tired."

"Liar." His breath brushed her cheek. "You're thrumming with need. How long has it been since a man touched you here . . . " He brushed a hand across her hip. "Or here . . . " His hand moved higher to cup her stomach before inching up to just below her breast. "Or here?"

Breathlessness made it difficult to speak. "I . . . I'll scream . . . "

"No, you won't, because you want this. You wanted it from the moment you saw me." Nick leaned closer still, his lips brushing against her cheek. "Want to know how I know?"

She thought she shook her head but couldn't be certain. Every nerve in her body responded to his touch, and her brain couldn't seem to coordinate movements.

"It was the same for me." His voice lowered an octave. "From the moment I looked into your eyes, it was like a fist in the gut. I've thought about you all week."

Miri summoned a reserve of mental clarity. "I haven't thought about you at all. I want you to go now, or I'll have to call the police."

He ignored her, leaning closer still, almost touching her lips with his. "You want me. Why fight it?"

"How can I want you after that disaster of a date? We have nothing in common." She chewed her lower lip, finding it difficult to concentrate with his proximity. "We could never have anything besides a physical connection."

"We have sex in common. Why does it have to be more complicated than that?" He kissed her then, just for a second, but it was long enough to melt her insides. "I don't want a relationship. I saw what love did to my brother. That's the last thing I want."

Finally, they had something other than the physical in common. "I don't want to fall in love either." After seeing the way her mother moved from lover to lover so casually, Miri had decided at a young age she would rather be alone than have a string of affairs. She had maintained her resolve to avoid relationships, never meeting a man worth compromising for.

But it had been so long since a man had held her. Her last lover had been a memory for three years now, cast aside because he wanted a deeper emotional commitment than she would give.

"Great. We know what we want from this. What's the harm?"

She shivered at his breath against her lips. "I don't have one-night stands."

"How about two nights . . . or a week?" His husky laugh danced along her nerve endings, exciting them to a fever pitch. "Take it one day at a time, and we'll move on when we're no longer hot for each other."

She stared into his eyes, swimming in the molten desire reflected there. Her brain said no, but her body softened against his, and Miri licked her lips. She cursed her weakness, even as she put a hand on his chest. "Do you want to come in?"

• • •

HE SWALLOWED UP the space inside her home. *Feng shui* had failed in this instance.

"You really like beige, don't you?"

Her neutral color scheme suddenly seemed boring next to Nick, and she had to resist the urge to hide the pastel pillows spread over the beige sofa. She owed him no excuses for her tasteful home, she reminded herself. "It's elegant."

Nick shrugged, dismissing the topic. "Coffee?"

She exhaled a breath she hadn't been aware of holding. It had been so long since a man had violated her sanctuary that she had forgotten how the process worked. Had she expected him to leap on her, take her on the floor and leave? Miri shook her head at the thought, squashing the ripple in the back of her mind that liked the scenario. "Of course. I have Seattle Sunrise or Mocha Mulberry."

His brow quirked. "Never mind. I'm strictly black, plain."

"Your loss. May I offer you an iced tea?"

Nick scanned her apartment. "Do you have beer?"

She shook her head. "I rarely drink at home."

"Tea is fine."

She turned to the kitchen, leaving Nick to settle on the sofa. As she peered through the opened top of the Dutch door, she saw him tossing her cushions haphazardly in the corner. Miri gritted her teeth to avoid saying something. She wasn't fitting the man into her life. Simply her bed.

Her hands shook at the thought, and she slopped a bit of tea from the pitcher onto the floor when removing it from the fridge. With a smothered curse, she ripped a paper towel from the roll on the counter and cleaned up the spot.

The dispenser on the refrigerator hummed, but no ice dropped into the glass when she pressed it against the sensor pad. Frowning, she bent at the waist to examine the dispenser just as the ice burst free, exploding from the chute into the glass, on the floor and at Miri.

She slammed the glass onto the counter with more force than necessary and bent to pick up the cubes. How many more signs did she need to know this was a bad idea? What had she been thinking, agreeing to a fling with Nick Martin, a man she had known less than a week? She couldn't allow libido to overrule common sense. Once he had his tea, she would explain she had changed her mind and send him away.

With that decision made, Miri's hands steadied, and she was able to get another glass, fill it with ice and put it on the counter. Not a drop of tea spilled from the pitcher as she filled the glasses, and she grasped them firmly before returning to the living room.

Nick hadn't waited for an invitation to make himself comfortable. He'd kicked off his shoes, removed his jacket and tie and rolled up the sleeves of his light blue shirt. His sock-covered feet screamed at her from their perch on her antique coffee table. She stared at them when putting his glass of tea on a coordinating coaster.

"Thanks." He patted the cushion beside him. "Sit with me."

She eyed the recliner and sat beside him with a soft sigh. Had he read her intentions to maintain distance between them?

Nick took the glass and gulped the tea in three long swallows. Miri watched his throat move, mesmerized by the cords flexing. Her mouth watered as she imagined trailing her tongue across his flesh.

To distract herself, she took a sip of tea and choked on it. Nick came to the rescue by patting her back, managing to knock the rest of the tea down the front of her sweater. She gasped as liquid soaked her front and then gasped again when Nick's bare hands brushed down her breasts in an effort to remove the ice cubes. She surrendered the glass to him, unable to speak for a moment.

"Come on. You need to get out of that. It's soaking wet." He took her hand, and Miri stood when he did and followed him down the hall. "Which room?"

She opened her mouth to tell him he had done enough, that he should leave now, but a small, "The door at the end of the hall," issued from her. What? Why was she so timid, going along with this? She wasn't that horny, was she?

Her nipples hardened at that moment as heat pooled between

her thighs when she ran into Nick's back. Her body reeled from the contact, forcing her mind to admit maybe she was that turned on. She wanted him more than any man who had ever been invited into her bedroom. Why was she fighting it?

He pushed open the door and stepped in ahead of her, whistling through his teeth. "Nice." His eyes were on the blond sleigh bed, complete with a beige velvet comforter that invited stroking. "I may never leave, darlin'."

"Tonight only. We agreed."

Nick turned to her, wearing a wolfish grin. "Actually, we agreed for however long it lasts."

Had she agreed to that just by inviting him in? Miri lifted a shoulder, dismissing the disagreement. He might or might not agree, but they were on a night-by-night basis, with no guarantees.

"Let me help you with that. I'll bet that virgin wool is scratchy when wet."

Miri stepped away from him, hoping her cool expression hid the heat spiraling through her as her mind conjured up an entirely different use for virgin wool on wet places. "I can handle it."

"I know, but it's more fun if I do it." Nick cocked his head, winking. "C'mon."

She stood still, holding her arms loosely at her sides. The first feather-soft touch of his fingers at the waistband of her skirt made her stomach quiver. She sucked in a breath as he pulled the sweater slowly from the skirt, an inch at a time, until her waist was bared. He moved the sweater higher, revealing her stomach, which quaked continuously as his fingers stroked the exposed area.

"Your skin is so soft. Like silk. I can't wait to taste it." Nick spoke with an arrogant certainty that he would taste whatever he liked. She didn't contradict him, not wanting to. Now that she had given in to this insanity, she intended to enjoy it fully. What good were morning-after regrets without a helluva night before?

He pulled the sweater over her head, and Miri trembled at the hunger in his gaze. It made her feel vulnerable and desirable all at once. Had any man ever inspired such feelings before? Maybe her previous interludes had been so tepid because she knew all about the men selected to be lovers. There was mystery with Nick, heightening her anticipation. She didn't know what he would do next.

His lips twitched. "A beige bra too, Miri?"

She shrugged. "I like beige."

His fingers unfastened the back clasp with confidence, letting the cups lower to just above her nipples. "You need some color in your life, darlin'."

She shook her head but offered no further protest, too entranced by the way his fingers danced across the silk cups, easing them away from her small breasts with a finesse never equaled by any preceding him. Miri hardly noticed the bra as it dropped to the floor but didn't miss his fingers caressing her nipples. They hardened again, straining to meet his fingers, begging for attention. A mingled gasp-groan escaped her when he lightly pinched one. "Nick?"

He met her eyes. "Yes?"

"Kiss me."

She had barely uttered the second word when his arms were around her and her body melted against his. Miri tilted her neck to meet his descending head, and their lips touched. She was almost surprised sparks didn't flare when their flesh met. His lips were firm and demanding but also giving. She molded hers to his, sighing at the electricity humming between them. How could a kiss be so earth-shattering?

It only got better when he parted her lips with his and slid inside, playfully pushing his tongue against hers before slipping over the surface. Miri caught his tongue with hers, pinning it briefly before he broke away.

The kiss changed, getting deeper and more passionate. Nick's hands ventured from her back to her buttocks, cupping and squeezing them as he fitted her pelvis against his. His cock pressed insistently against her pussy, making her dizzy with need.

Nick's mouth moved from hers and took a leisurely trip across her cheek to her ear. Miri gasped when he twirled his tongue around the tiny hoop in her lobe, darting through the jewelry to lick a sensitive spot. She put her arms around his waist, pressing him closer. He breathed a short laugh into her ear before sucking the lobe and earring into his mouth to bite gently.

When he lifted his head, Miri surged forward, determined to see if his neck was as tempting as she had imagined. Nick jerked at the first stroke of her tongue down the column of his throat then groaned when she sucked skin between her teeth to nibble.

"Why do you scrape back your hair? I bet it's gorgeous."

She would have answered that it was practical for work, but her mouth was too busy devouring his skin. He tasted sweet, with a hint of salt, and the woodsy fragrance of his cologne contributed to his allure. She didn't hesitate in her appointed task as he unwound her hair from the bun, letting the dark brown locks fall to the middle of her back.

"God, Miri, I could lose myself in here." Nick brought a handful to his face, rubbing the strands against his cheeks. "I can't wait to see you on the bed, with your hair spread out on the pillow."

"Umm." Miri kept kissing his neck while her fingers undid the buttons of his shirt to the waistband of his pants. After parting the lapels, she let her mouth venture lower, licking a path across his chest, keeping a hand there to touch the lightly furred skin, running her fingers through his chest hair as her tongue swept over his nipple, eliciting a moan. His hand tightened on her hair, dragging her closer, and Miri surrendered to instinct.

She swirled her tongue around his nipple in small circles, gradually increasing the radius while still stroking his chest with her hand. Her other hand hooked into his waistband and one finger was bold enough to slip inside to caress his waist.

She cried out with surprise when Nick swung her into his arms to carry her to the bed. He didn't bother to push back the velvet comforter to reveal the nine-hundred-count cotton sheets underneath. The velvet cradled her back as Nick's body hovered over her front. Her breasts fit perfectly against his chest as he aligned his body over hers. She wriggled, teasing her nipples with the hair on his torso. "You're wearing too many clothes."

He cupped the back of her head, bending her neck to take control of her mouth. "You too," he said, before touching his lips to hers. The kiss was slow, with each stroke of his tongue branding her as his. She was aware of the possessiveness in his actions and reveled in it but refused to focus on the implications of giving him more power in the liaison than she should.

He eased away from her long enough to strip off his shirt, remove his belt and unfasten his pants, leaving the zipper and button of his trousers open. Miri lifted her hips as he fumbled for the zipper at the back of the skirt, easing the passage of the garment.

Nick touched her thighs, stroking the bare flesh. "I didn't figure you for a garter belt girl."

She squirmed as he ran a thumb over the beige garter belt before rubbing the silky hose on her thigh. Should she ruin the illusion and tell him she had resorted to an old-fashioned garter belt and thigh-highs because her last pair of pantyhose had ripped? No. "I need a surprise or two. Keeps things interesting."

"That it does." His hand moved higher, past the garter belt and bare skin, to her panties. They were beige too, but he made no comment.

Miri arched her hips when he ran his thumb down her slit, exciting every nerve centered there. Moisture accompanied the motion, and the panties seemed to chafe unbearably against her pussy.

Nick grew bolder, penetrating the elastic side of the panty to caress her pussy. "You're so wet."

"I want you." She was going to go insane if he didn't move along soon. She groaned as his thumb slipped inside her, probing her entrance. "Please."

"Not yet."

She gnashed her teeth when he pulled away again, this time to remove her panties. She reached for the clip on one of the garters, but his hand stayed hers. "I'll take care of it." Nick dispensed with the garter belt and panties quickly, leaving only the thigh-highs.

Miri lay there watching him, wondering what he planned next. Should she take the initiative? She wasn't shy, but there was something so manly about Nick that it precluded her feeling confident enough to demand what she wanted. He might have a dominant personality, but more important, he made her want to submit to his whims.

She reached out, running her hand up and down his bicep. "What do you want me to do?"

"Nothing. I just want to look at you." Nick nudged her thighs wider so he could kneel between them. His gaze never wavered from her pussy as he parted it with one hand. The cool air on heated flesh induced a shiver in Miri, and she held her breath, wondering if she would feel his tongue on her.

Instead, a finger from his other hand circled her clit slowly as he bent forward. His tongue rasped wetly across one of her swollen nipples, teasing her unbearably. He sucked the bud deeper into his mouth as his fingers mimicked the movement to plunge deep into her pussy. Miri arched her hips, straining for more of his hand.

Nick complied with her unspoken request by thrusting his fingers in and out of her while circling her clit with firm strokes. His tongue laved her nipple, and she squirmed under the passionate onslaught. She was so hungry for him, just aching everywhere. It no longer seemed foolish to rush into a fling. Now she couldn't get there fast enough. "Please, Nick. I need you."

He lifted his head from her breast but took his time withdrawing from her pussy, stroking her for another minute before relenting. She was slick with need when he stood up to remove his pants. The sight of his thick cock flooded her pussy with moisture. Miri imagined stroking him, tracing her fingers down the throbbing veins of his shaft and caressing the mushroom head as it spasmed against her hand. She watched impatiently as he pulled a condom from his pocket to sheath his cock before returning to her.

Nick took up the same position between her thighs, stretching out atop her. He didn't allow his full weight to rest on her as his hand parted her pussy to guide his cock inside her. Miri cupped his buttocks, pulling his cock in as deeply as she could. Her body accepted the length of him with surprising ease considering how long it had been since she had taken a lover.

She arched her hips, meeting his first thrust. The pace was slow, inciting a surge of desire that built in ever-increasing pulses. Miri's nails formed half-moons in the flesh of his buttocks as he thrust in and out of her and was eagerly met by her each time. Nick's hand slipped between their bodies, his thumb seeking out and stroking her clit in time with his thrusts.

His cock was deep inside her, seeking to learn every inch of her pussy while his fingers memorized her clit. Miri cried out when Nick buried his mouth against her neck to bite her with more vigor than tenderness. His roughness excited her, much to her surprise. She was used to polite lovemaking, not the uninhibited variety that Nick seemed so adroit at.

She closed her eyes, struggling to contain a cry of pleasure as her pussy contracted around him. Convulsions swept through her, emanating from deep in her womb and squeezing his cock to milk every last drop of satisfaction from him. The world looked fuzzy when viewed through the haze of passion obscuring her vision, and her breathing was heavy. It was difficult to draw in a deep breath as she hovered on the edge of coming, just before plunging forward. A cry escaped her as her body went rigid with release.

Spasms shook her, making her pussy contract even tighter around his cock, which spasmed in time with the tremors racking her body. Miri tried to drag him inside her by digging her nails even deeper into the skin of his buttocks as afterglow started the process of making her muscles relax.

He stiffened against her, thrusting frantically a couple of times before staying deep inside her. Nick seemed to make no effort to conceal his husky groan of fulfillment as he let loose his satisfaction. His cock released in spurts that filled her with contentment, renewing milder spasms inside her core. Their bodies shook in time with each other for what might have been seconds or hours, uniting them as one for that short time.

When it was over, he didn't withdraw from her. Nick turned on his side, bringing Miri with him, and tucking her body close to his. He brushed a kiss across her forehead, murmured, "Thank you," and held her.

How did she respond? She wanted to weep with the pleasure he had given her. Never had it been so good. What was it about Nick that completely fulfilled her, when no other man had?

As he slipped into sleep, emitting soft snores, Miri cautioned herself to be careful. Nick was dangerous to her ordered life and sheltered heart. If he could breach her body so easily, what could he do to her carefully controlled emotions?

3

M IRI AWOKE ALONE, finding a note and the slight indent his head had left on the pillow the only proof he had been there. That, and the minor aches of gratification. The twinges were more pronounced when she leaned forward to retrieve the note.

Sorry I can't be here when you wake up, but I had an appointment I couldn't cancel. Be ready at seven. We're doing things my way tonight.

Nick

She frowned at the note, questioning the veracity of his vague appointment. Had it been an excuse to leave, to avoid the awkward conversation that might have awaited him if he had been there when she awoke? His high-handed tone didn't please her either. How dare he issue a dictate? She should make plans with someone else tonight, to be gone when he came around. That would show him she wasn't at his disposal.

Miri knew she wouldn't stand him up as she climbed from the bed, ill-at-ease from her nakedness. The T-shirt she normally wore to bed lay over the beige armchair in the corner. For however long this fling lasted, the old T-shirt could stay there. He was too intoxicating to cut short this . . . whatever it was . . . prematurely.

Refreshed by the previous night, she strolled to the French doors and opened them, squinting as sunshine flooded the room. Still naked, she took a step onto her balcony to survey the neighborhood. It wasn't quite eight, but several neighbors were engaged in weekend chores as children played on the streets.

She leaned against the wooden rail, hugging her arms over her breasts, wondering what prompted her to stand outside in the nude. The others in her conservative, upwardly mobile neighborhood would be shocked if they looked up at her balcony and saw her like this. They'd be even more shocked, might even shun her, if they knew the local high school science teacher had spent all night in bed with a man she hardly knew.

A giggle escaped Miri, and she clapped her hand over her mouth, alarmed by the blithe sound. It brought a return to sanity, and she hurried inside, closing the French doors behind her. For a moment, she had been a free spirit, not unlike her mother, Marnie. What was she thinking?

Last night's decision to end things with Nick at a one-night stand had been a good one. If she was going to be crazy enough to see him again, even for one more night, she had to keep a rein on her impulses, for fear that she become too much like her mother. Shaking her head with disgust at the very idea, Miri padded into the bathroom, intent on showering and slipping into clothes as soon as possible. Naïvely perhaps, she believed she could conceal the secret thoughts plaguing her mind simply by hiding her body under garments.

AGAINST HER BETTER judgment, she was waiting for Nick by six forty-five, pacing the house, pausing every few minutes to stare at the grandfather clock in the entryway, mutter under her breath and mentally chastise her foolishness once more.

Her internal cautions to be sensible did nothing to slow her racing heart when her doorbell rang at seven. With features schooled in a composed arrangement, Miri opened the door to Nick and forgot how to breathe. The black T-shirt hugged his arms and torso indecently, revealing every flex and bulge as he moved. The faded jeans, now a worn gray, clung to his legs like a second skin. Her hands itched to test the fabric to see if it was as soft as it appeared. She knew from experience that underneath she would find rock-hard flesh.

"You look delicious," he said, stepping over the threshold without waiting for her to issue an invitation. Nick leaned forward to kiss her, lightly stroking her lips with his tongue. Straightening, he towered over her again, so close she could feel his body heat.

She longed to melt against him but held herself erect by sheer willpower. "Thank you." Did he really consider this pale yellow sheath delicious? Bought to wear to an Easter service she had planned to attend with an ex-lover, the dress had gone unused when they had split days before the holiday.

He nodded. "Too dressy though. Do you have jeans?" Before she could respond, he said, "Go change."

Miri glared at him. Now was the time to nip his bossiness in the bud. "Don't be so patronizing. I've been making my own decisions for a long time, so I don't need your input on my wardrobe."

Nick's eyes widened. "Sorry, darlin'. I meant nothing by it. I want you to be comfortable. Where we're going, jeans are the norm, but it's up to you."

Put like that, her anger faded. "I'll be right back." Miri returned to her room, half-expecting Nick to follow for a repeat performance of last night. To her disappointment, as she slipped on her sole pair of blue jeans, still stiff with newness, he never made an appearance. She deliberately loitered over selecting a top, hoping he would come in, but he didn't.

With a sigh of disgust at her actions, she chose a beige square-necked tunic made of a gauzy fabric, suggesting more than it truly showed, while simultaneously slipping her feet into loafers. When she found Nick in the living room, he whistled. She extended her arms, doing a complete circle. "Does this meet your approval?"

"You bet, darlin'." He stood up and put an arm around her waist on the way to the door. His hand slipped inside her back pocket, and he winced. "Those jeans sure are stiff, unless your ass is that firm."

His words should have appalled her but instead she had to stifle a laugh. "They're new. I've only worn them once, on a field trip with the seniors last year."

He made no further comment as they left her house until Miri headed in the direction of her Saab. He tightened his grip on her pocket, steering her left to a gleaming red motorcycle parked at the curb. "We'll take my Concours."

Miri was already shaking her head even as he continued to bring her with him across her front lawn. "I've never ridden one before."

"It's about time, don't you think?"

"No, I—"

He ignored her objections by thrusting a helmet into her hands. "Try this on for size, Miri."

"Nick, I'm not riding on this—" She gasped when he pushed the helmet on her head, squashing her bun.

He pushed up the face shield and leaned forward to steal a kiss. "Live a little." His eyes twinkled. "Unless you're scared?"

Hell, yes, she was scared, but not about to admit it. Miri firmed her trembling lips, nodded just once and cinched the strap of the helmet under her chin. "Let's go."

Nick's laugh was rich with joy and too contagious. She had to bite her tongue to keep from chuckling along with him. At least the moment of mirth tempered her nerves, and she was almost relaxed by the time Nick put on his helmet and directed her to sit on the seat behind him after he climbed on.

Her hands shook when she grasped his shoulders to steady herself while mounting the seat. The position was odd, and she clutched him tighter when he started the motorcycle. The Kawasaki seemed to roar like an injured beast, and she was two seconds from backing down from his challenge when he shifted into gear and took them onto the road.

Miri's eyes widened with shock when the vibrations of the seat transmitted to her pussy. Without thought, she shifted positions to feel more of the power, loosening her death grip on Nick's neck in the process.

She spared a glance for the road, deciding she didn't like the way the lines whipped by with nauseating quickness but otherwise enjoying the ride. It was difficult to remain in fear for her life when the engine's vibrations kept her constantly aroused, just shy of an orgasm.

Nick detoured from Main Street to an area of town she never frequented. If any place in Poplin Hills could be considered seedy, it was the strip of establishments on Route 7. Her apprehension grew when he slowed down the bike to turn into Hooch's, a local tavern with colorful clientele. She'd never been inside, but rumors abounded of drunken brawls, marriage-ending events and other horrors taking place there every night of the week. No decent citizen would step foot inside.

All those thoughts ran through her mind when Nick parked by the door beside a beaten-up black motorcycle, but she didn't utter a word when he helped her from the bike and removed her helmet. She had taciturnly agreed to let Nick set the rules for tonight. It was too late to argue now. She just hoped they survived the night without anyone connected to the school seeing her at Hooch's.

As Miri took a seat at a table shrouded by shadows in the corner of the room, she swore she could still feel the vibration of the engine through her body. Her damp pussy throbbed in time with her heart, seeking release. Would anyone notice if she pushed Nick down across the table and had her way with him right there? Surveying the dim interior, clouded with smoke, thick with partiers, she couldn't say with absolute certainty they would. It was the sort of place where one could do just about anything without having the other patrons look askance.

"What would you like?"

"Chard . . . beer, please." When in Rome . . .

Miri's gaze remained on Nick's tight form as he moseyed up to the mahogany bar to place their orders. Her eyes narrowed when a blonde sitting on a stool gave him an enthusiastic greeting that included a wet kiss on the lips. Was she jealous of the bimbo? How could she be, considering she had no emotional ties to Nick?

Nonetheless, the sting of jealousy bit into her when the blonde climbed off the stool to plaster herself against Nick. Miri bunched her hands into fists atop her thighs, fighting the urge to march over and rip every bleached hair out of the slut's head.

Her strong reaction jarred Miri back to reality. She wasn't the kind of woman to get into a barroom brawl, especially over a man she had spent just one night with. Her anger switched to simmer as Nick brushed off the woman, got their drinks and returned to the table. She struggled to hide any hint of how she felt behind an aloof smile when he sat down.

"You didn't say tap or bottle, so I took a guess." He pushed a mug of draft beer across the scarred black table.

She lifted it, took an enthusiastic gulp and managed to hide a grimace of distaste. "Who was the woman at the bar?" Her frosty tone pleased her.

A hint of red might have tinged his cheeks. It was difficult to tell with the low lighting. "Um, a friend."

"You should have invited your *friend* to join us. I hate for her to be alone."

Nick shifted, looking uncomfortable. "I'm sure Chloe won't be lonely long."

"Hmm." She took another sip of the beer, finding it easier to tolerate with each drink. "What do you do here, besides drink?"

"Dance, play pool." He shrugged. "Hang out."

She wasn't accustomed to hanging out. Miri liked plans for everything. She always knew which movie she was going to watch at the theater before going, always reserved activities well in advance when going on vacation and never changed her mind about anything at the last minute. Drumming her fingers on the table, she scanned the bar again, noticing one of the pool tables was free. "Teach me how to play pool." What she really wanted to do was request he take her home and fuck her until she forgot her own name, but held back. They were having a civilized fling, which included the pretense of dating.

"Sure. Go hold the table, and I'll get the balls from Belle."

Miri took her mug with her to the table and stood by it with a hand on the edge, not sure if she was holding it properly. This time, Nick picked a spot several stools down from Chloe as he conversed with the mid-forties woman behind the bar. Soon, he returned with pool balls.

As he racked them, he asked, "You've never played?"

"No." The closest she had come had been the times Marnie left her in the car while she went in to drink at various bars. Miri shuddered slightly, remembering the numerous nights she had fallen asleep in various old cars, waiting for her mother to stumble out at closing time. "It never appealed to me. Until now."

"Fair enough. I'll let you break."

"Break?"

"Grab a cue and go to the other end of the table."

When Miri had selected a green cue from the wall and stood on the opposite end from Nick, he rolled a white ball to her. She had seen enough on television to know to chalk the cue. After finishing, she figured out where to put the ball and assumed breaking was the act of scattering the balls after he took away the rack holding them.

The cue was clumsy in her hands as she maneuvered it into position to hit the ball. Before she could make her shot, he moved behind her, standing so close she could feel his cock pressing into her buttocks. "Now what?" The breathless question sounded coy, not logical, as she had intended.

"Don't clench the cue so tightly." He put his hand over hers, loosening her grip while repositioning her hold. His other hand rested briefly on her hip before taking possession of her free hand, which he placed on the table, positioning it exactly. "Rest the cue here, but lightly. You want to be unrestrained when you shoot." He kept his hands over hers, demonstrating the way she should shoot. "Keep your motions fluid."

To her disappointment, Nick withdrew to let her make the shot. As soon as he stopped touching her, she forgot everything he had shown her. The cue barely touched the ball, sending it only a couple of inches off its straight course, without getting anywhere near the triangle of balls at the other end of the table. She groaned, ready to quit.

"My turn." Nick took a cue and held it with confidence born of practice. Miri's eyes didn't stray as he leaned over the table to make his shot. The way his buttocks clenched in the tight jeans dried out her mouth. The beer she gulped did little to provide relief but kept her from uttering a moan when he completed his shot, making his body one streamlined work of art. The kind meant to be touched, not hung on a wall and admired from a distance.

The cue ball scattered the others when it slammed into their midst, causing three to drop into pockets immediately. He looked over his shoulder. "It's still my turn, but why don't you go ahead?"

She shook her head, in no hurry to end his turn. He was delicious enough to watch all night. "Play by the rules."

He started to walk past her but turned to pull her against him and press his mouth to hers. Miri's first thought was of protesting the public kiss. Her second was all about the kiss itself. She wrapped her free arm around his waist, trying to pull him closer. His mouth devoured hers as his tongue feathered against her lips.

When he pulled away, his grin was full of smug arrogance and a healthy dose of satisfaction. "Darlin', I've always found it more fun to break the rules." He moved past, leaving her with a lingering squeeze on her bottom.

The balls seemed to disappear with lightning speed as Nick set about putting them into the pockets. She watched raptly each time his muscles bunched or flexed, studied his expression for clues of his mood and felt the moisture in her pussy spread. By the time he knocked the eight ball into the corner pocket, a light sheen of perspiration misted her body and she was light-headed with arousal.

"Another?" he asked, rounding up the balls from under the table, where they had dropped after going into the pockets.

She shook her head. "Where's the ladies' room?"

"Down the hall." He pointed to a sign across the room. "Are you sure? You didn't get to play much."

"It's fine." She abandoned her beer and rushed to the restroom, shaking with the effort not to make a fool of herself. Her body ached for his. She was hotter than she had ever been, dripping with need. A few minutes of privacy was all she needed to collect herself. She hoped.

The restroom was as dim as the rest of the bar but not as smoky. There were two stalls, and she chose the handicapped one because it was closer. Miri locked the door and leaned against it, taking deep breaths that did nothing to calm her. This night had been nothing but foreplay, and she was ready for the main event. The only thing that had stopped her from begging Nick to leave was she didn't think she could wait to get back to her place.

The main door opened, and she tried to halt her rapid breathing. Her inhalation turned to a gasp when Nick peeked over her stall. "What are you doing? This is the ladies' room."

He grinned, unrepentant. "Open up."

She shook her head, even as her fingers obeyed his command and turned the lock. A flutter of common sense had her reaching for the door as he swung it open. "You can't . . . we can't."

"Remember the rules, darlin'." Nick entered the stall with her, locking the door. He was too close for rational thought as he pinned her against the side of the stall, pressing his mouth to hers. "Break them," he said, right before kissing her.

Propriety dictated she push him away, but her body had other ideas. Miri clung to Nick, running her fingers through his hair with one hand while resting the other at his waist. A moan escaped her when Nick's hand slid under the hem of her tunic to caress her stomach. His tongue thrust inside her mouth, and she met it eagerly, parrying his attempts to explore all of her.

One of his hands moved higher, cupping her breast through her bra, while his thumb rubbed over her swollen nipple, inflaming it with the lacy fabric. She nipped his tongue, earning a pinch that served only to heighten her arousal. Her hips arched of their own accord, bringing her dripping pussy against his cock, separated only by the fabric of their jeans. The barrier was too much, and she wanted to strip off their clothes and have him pin her to the wall.

Nick broke the kiss to sweep his mouth down her throat,

pausing to bite the bend of her neck with just enough pressure to elicit a moan. Miri tightened her fingers in his hair, trying to halt his descent as he slid lower. He ignored her temporary resistance, and she stopped fighting when he pushed her tunic above her breasts. His tongue swept into the valley of her cleavage, modest as it was, and he inhaled. "You smell like flowers," he said against her skin, sparking flicks of heat with every breathy word.

"You smell like sex." The blunt words shocked her, but he didn't seem taken aback by her uttering them. And it was true. Nick smelled, tasted, walked and talked S-E-X. She couldn't help responding. Urgent hands tugged his T-shirt up so she could caress his abdomen, which fluttered under her hand. His cock pressed more insistently against her pussy through the jeans, and she parted her thighs wider to allow it to nestle deeper.

To her surprise, he shifted her suddenly, pressing her against the wall and supporting her on one of his thighs while she braced her hands on his shoulders. His movements were smooth and quick when he released the back clasp of her bra and pushed the cups above her breasts, along with the tunic. Once freed, her breasts strained for his touch, and Miri's nipples tingled with warmth.

Nick's mouth was gentle but with a hint of roughness when he took possession of one nipple. The bead disappeared into his mouth, where he flicked his tongue over the tip, causing her to stifle a cry of passion. Miri dug her nails into his shoulders, pulling him closer still while writhing against his thigh, seeking relief for the inferno blazing inside her pussy. "Nick, I can't take this." They had to leave, find the nearest bed and satiate each other.

He lifted his head to stare into her eyes. "Yeah, you can, darlin'. Trust me." Then his hands moved to her waistband, dispensing with the button and zipper to plunge his hand inside. His fingers stroked her pussy through the silky panties she wore, and Miri tossed her head from side to side, desperate for relief, as his fingers teased her clit through the silk. "Please, Nick. Let's get out of here."

"Easy." His hand left her pants, and he lowered her back to her feet. Miri experienced a dart of disappointment, despite it having been her request to stop and find somewhere else more private. Her discontent changed to confusion when Nick got on his knees before her.

Her eyes widened when he pulled down her jeans and panties. Somehow, she managed to remain coherent enough to kick off her loafers and step out of them.

There was no mistaking his intentions as he leaned forward, tongue extended. She twined a hand in his hair, not sure if she wanted to push him away or pull him closer. He didn't allow her to choose, lunging forward suddenly, tongue seeking out her heat. Miri closed her eyes with a gasp, leaning against the stall wall for support as Nick's tongue sought out all her secret places, paying special attention to her clit, swollen with need.

The moist swipes of his tongue probing her opening made Miri ball her hands into fists to keep from shouting. Nick pressed his tongue deeper inside her pussy. She shifted with restless energy, needing more than his intimate kiss. She wanted him inside her.

Nick seemed to have read her thoughts, because he brought a hand between her thighs. His tongue abandoned her opening, leaving her temporarily bereft, until two of his fingers plunged inside to take its place. It wasn't his cock, but the digits were almost enough to satisfy her. When Nick swirled his tongue around her clit, she cried out while mindlessly thrusting against his face as spasms in her pussy built in intensity.

She was on the brink of release when the outer door opened. Miri's eyes snapped open, and she froze as footsteps went past their stall, though Nick continued to lick her pussy. She pulled on his hair, trying to get his attention, but he remained focused on his task. "Nick," she said so quietly she barely heard it herself as the door to the stall beside them closed and the woman engaged the lock.

She couldn't help seeing Nick kneeling on the floor and must know what they were doing. Shame burned through Miri, firing her cheeks, but another sensation fought for supremacy. It was the wild impulse to ignore the other woman's presence, and it was winning. Nick's passionate ministrations, continuing without pause, helped it along toward victory. With a sigh of defeat, she closed her eyes, struggled not to breathe too heavily and let his tongue work its magic.

The woman was in the process of washing her hands when the orgasm swept over Miri. Try as she did, she couldn't keep in a moan of satisfaction. Every muscle in her body quivered with release, and she slumped against Nick, who was still caressing her with slow strokes, coaxing every drop of pleasure from her.

The outer door closed, bringing Miri back to a semblance of awareness as Nick got to his feet. Her actions should shock her, and they did, but she was too limp with gratification to make an issue of what they had done.

He kissed her gently on the mouth before saying, "That was intense. There's a real wanton underneath that schoolmarm exterior, Miri."

"Only with you," she admitted, leaning against him with her arms on his shoulders. His hands moved between their bodies to free his cock from his jeans. Miri kept her head against his chest as he ripped open a foil packet taken from his pocket and covered his cock.

Her thighs parted wider when he shifted into position, aligning his cock with her pussy. With a soft gasp, Miri welcomed him fully inside. After the last orgasm, she didn't know if she could survive another, but he set about proving she could, using his cock and hands to stroke her to a fever pitch. As her pussy contracted around him, she tossed her head, biting hard on her tongue to hold in a cry.

Nick filled the silence with a groan as he came, pulling her so tightly against him that they were almost one person for a moment, especially when their heartbeats thundered in time with each other.

When it was over, he held her for a long moment before pressing a kiss to her neck. "Your place or mine?"

She was exhausted and opened her mouth to tell him she couldn't do this again tonight, needing time to recover, but her answer caught her by surprise. "Yours. I want to see where you live."

"It's your standard bachelor pad, but it has a bed."

"That's all we need."

As he'd said, his apartment was standard fare—white walls, brown carpet and a single bedroom, which they didn't make it to. As soon as Nick closed the door, he swept Miri into his arms and carried her to the overstuffed leather sofa. She stretched out on the sumptuous cushions, supporting her head on an arm bent behind her. She smiled up at him as he stood over her. Her eyes focused on the bulge in his pants, and she licked her lips.

Nick settled onto the couch, straddling her, making his cock dig into her stomach. He braced his hands on either side of her head and leaned forward to kiss her. Miri opened her mouth when his lips touched hers, changing the kiss from casual to intense by sweeping her tongue inside his. She brought both hands forward to splay across his chest, pulling him closer.

Nick groaned when she sucked his lower lip into her mouth, and she grasped handfuls of his shirt to keep from vocalizing her own pleasure. Her pussy ached with need, despite the pleasure he'd already given her, and she arched her hips, finding no gratification in empty space.

Frustrated, Miri tore her mouth from Nick's before he could pin her tongue with his. "I want you." It was liberating to be so blunt with her emotions. So liberating, she tried it again. "I want your cock inside me."

Nick seemed surprised by her words but nodded. "Sure, darlin'. Whenever you're ready." He winked.

Miri couldn't hide a grin of satisfaction at his startled look when she shoved against his shoulders. He went tumbling off the couch, and she followed, now straddling him as they lay on the floor. She tugged at his T-shirt. "Now would be appreciated."

He groaned. "Can I have a minute to catch my breath? That was a helluva ride."

"No, but it will be." She ignored his requests to take it easy as she pulled at his shirt until it was over his head. When he was bared from the waist up, she let her hands roam over his chest, raking her nails across his nipples. She enjoyed his sharp inhalation so much she scratched the tender nubs again.

"Damn." He didn't sound angry. Rather, surprise and something more colored his tone. Enjoyment, perhaps?

Miri bent her head so she could focus her attention on the button and zipper of his jeans. They yielded to her determined hands with a rasp, and she opened the pants to reveal her prize. Nick's underwear posed a slight deterrent, and she had to tug at the waistband of his jeans and briefs a few times until he cooperated by lifting his hips.

In her impatience, she got the pants no lower than his knees. Seated across his shins, she shifted slightly to maximize her mobility. Then Miri looked up at him, finding Nick watching her with amused indulgence. She wanted to wipe that expression off his face, wanted him to feel the same need she felt, just as urgently. She hated being vulnerable, but if she was going to be, she refused to experience it alone.

"I'm going to fuck you now," she said, almost conversationally.

He folded his hands behind his head. "Is that right?"

She nodded just once.

His grin held more than a small measure of self-satisfaction. "Wouldn't you be more comfortable on the bed?"

"I'll be plenty comfortable on your cock," she retorted.

A hearty laugh escaped him. "By all means, go for it. I'm not going to stop you."

"No, you aren't." He still wasn't feeling the same urgency, but that was about to change. Miri leaned forward, catching a brief glimpse of his stunned expression just before his face disappeared from her line of sight. He jumped when her lips touched the head of his cock, but she spared no mercy for him to adjust to the erotic intrusion. In a smooth motion, Miri engulfed his cock in her mouth, somehow accommodating all of him.

He tasted like come and latex, along with something uniquely him. It wasn't completely unpleasant, and she soon forgot her initial reaction to his flavor when his cock convulsed in her mouth. She began to suck, working her head up and down, and knew she had provoked the response she wanted when he started pumping his hips.

Miri had her hands braced on his thighs, but she brought up one to hold the base of his cock, squeezing lightly. Nick groaned when she moved her mouth in a circle around his shaft, applying more suction to the head.

His thrusts increased in speed, and he sounded hoarse when he spoke. "I'm about to come, darlin'. You're too good."

She bit him on the head, scraping her teeth across the sensitive flesh. When he uttered a wordless protest, she lifted her head to smile at him. "You aren't coming yet."

He growled, glaring at her. "Are you playing with me?"

Miri didn't respond verbally. Instead, she let her gaze settle on his cock while her hands dispensed with the tunic. Nick reached up to help with her bra, and she smacked his hand lightly. "This is my show, Nick."

He laughed, though it contained more strain than amusement. "I guess I'll just watch."

"For now." She unfastened the bra and tossed it onto the floor beside the tunic. Her sense of order winced at the mess, but desire overrode her natural prissiness, and she turned her attention to the jeans. Her hands shook with anticipation, making it slow work to strip her jeans and underwear down below her knees. Though they restrained her legs, she had no time to waste getting them off.

"Condoms?"

Nick pointed downward. "Right pocket of my jeans."

Miri reached behind her awkwardly, feeling for a bulge in the denim. When she found the pocket, she plunged her fingers inside and pulled out three condoms. With haste, she tore one off the strip. It resisted opening so she used her teeth. Her urgent need was disquieting, but she was too immersed in it to back off, cool down and think about all the reasons why she shouldn't be attacking Nick—least of all, she wasn't like this. Clearly, she was when with Nick.

His cock jerked at her feathery touch when she rolled the condom down the shaft. Miri paused to caress his head, applying a small amount of pressure to the sensitive V until he lunged upward, his teeth clenched. Satisfied he finally felt the same driving desire as she did, she scooted higher up his body.

If not for the jeans hindering her legs, she could have been on him in seconds. It took close to a minute to position her pussy atop his cock and get a sense of balance. When she was centered, Miri sank down on him, and they both moaned when his cock filled her.

She dug her nails into his chest where she'd braced them and began arching up and down. "That feels so good." Miri circled her hips while clenching her pussy around his cock.

"You've got that right, darlin'. I could stay in your hot little pussy for hours."

A bead of sweat dripped into her eyes, but she didn't bother to wipe it away. "I can't wait that long."

"Me neither," he admitted with a grunt while driving forcefully inside her. His cock spasmed, making her womb quake in response. Miri was on the edge of coming, and when she scooted forward a smidge and arched her back, his cock rubbed right against her clit as she rode him. Their frantic thrusts pushed them closer to the edge, and she suddenly found herself falling over it.

The heat of his liquid satisfaction spread to her through the condom as he climaxed, and it triggered more convulsions in her pussy. She tightened her muscles around his cock and crested the peak of her orgasm, gradually slowing the speed of her thrusts until the last bit of tension faded, and she collapsed on top of him, breathless.

They didn't speak, and she was grateful not to have to make conversation. At that moment, she was still out of control, a sensation that terrified her. She needed time to gather her composure, which was impossible with his cock slowly waning inside her. After the way she had just behaved, she couldn't face him and act normally. It was better to hide her face against his chest and try to forget how wild she had been. That was easier to plan than execute with her body still glowing from the amazing release, and her inhibitions temporarily freed from restraint.

She knew, lying atop him, that she couldn't let this happen again. If he could make her lose control this way, she could easily end up like her mother. Miri couldn't allow herself to lose her hard-won self-respect on the altar of desire.

But when his cock hardened a few minutes later, and his hands cupped her breasts to rub her nipples, it never occurred to her to refuse him. In a matter of moments, she was swept away again, forgetting her previous resolutions.

4

NICK WAVED OFF the last of the guys trying to talk him into going to the bar while dialing Miri's number. He hadn't seen her in the three days he had been on duty, hadn't even called her, but hadn't been able to think about anything except her during that time. The last two weeks of their affair had flown by, it seemed, and he still hadn't gotten enough of her.

It scared the hell out of him, but here he was, calling her after only three days of self-imposed silence, when he had been trying to make it a full week. Would she be happy to hear from him or irritated he had gone so long without speaking to her?

He grimaced as the phone rang, reminding himself she hadn't tried to call him at the station either, though it would have been a simple matter of looking up the number in the phone book. Perhaps she was managing to compartmentalize their casual fling better than he was.

She answered on the third ring, rasping, "Hello."

"Miri?"

"Yes. Nick?"

"You sound awful." He winced at his honesty.

"Thanks." She coughed before continuing. "I picked up a bug at school."

"I was going to bring by Chinese food, but maybe I'd better bring you soup instead." Smooth invitation. He shook his head at the way the words had emerged, leaving her little choice.

Silence filled the line for a moment. "I'm sick."

"I won't catch anything. Hearty New England stock, remember?"

It was clear from her tone she was trying to get rid of him, so why wasn't he accepting that gracefully?

Again, she hesitated, finally saying, "I'm not feeling up to anything . . . if you know what I mean?"

His voice lowered, becoming more reassuring. "That's fine, darlin'. I'll bring food, DVDs and pampering."

Her reluctance was evident, along with her weariness, when she spoke again. "Fine."

Nick didn't like the surge of relief that swept through him, nor the way his stomach clenched with anticipation at seeing her. He forced himself to sound neutral when replying. "Great. Do you want Chinese food or chicken soup?"

"Egg-drop soup sounds good."

"Right. I'll see you soon, darlin'." Nick hung up before she could retract her acquiescence, sensing she was on the verge of telling him not to come over. He didn't want to scrutinize too closely why he was so desperate to see her or why his experiment of imposing some distance between them had failed. Nor did he want to think about why he couldn't get her out of his mind or how it had hurt to know she thought he only wanted to come by for sex. It was a logical assumption on her part, since every date they'd been on had ended with them tangled in the sheets of one of their beds, so there was no reason for him to feel wounded.

No reason he wanted to examine anyway.

MIRI MADE LITTLE effort with her appearance before Nick's arrival, deciding to let him see her complete with red nose, swollen eyes and an old robe she'd had since college. This sudden move from casual sex into relationship realm alarmed her, maybe because she wanted to move to the next level as she never had before. When a man got too close, she'd had no trouble sending him on his way but didn't feel the same compulsion to do so with Nick.

Her insides had warmed in a disconcerting way when he'd said he was going to come by just to pamper her. No one had ever brought her soup or taken care of her when she was sick. It was disconcerting to have her casual lover showing such tender concern.

When the doorbell rang, the thoughts were still swirling through her mind as she tried to decide what was the best way to get rid of Nick and her own treacherous longings.

All thoughts of sending him on his way flew out of her brain when she opened the door to see Nick holding a large teddy bear under one arm and a bag of Chinese food in his hand. The bear held a heart that said "Get Well." Before she could school her reaction, she was reaching for the bear and cuddling it against her.

"You like it?" His boyish need to please was evident in his expression and the way he shifted from foot to foot.

Miri nodded, incapable of speech for a moment. Nick slipped past her to set the Chinese food and a bag of DVDs on the coffee table before turning back to take her in his arms.

Sick as she was, her body responded to his proximity, and it was strange to have him press a chaste kiss to her forehead instead of receiving the passionate greeting she had expected. Somehow, she ended up cuddled against him, with the bear forming an awkward barrier between them. Tears burned behind her eyes, and Miri blinked rapidly to dissolve them, not certain why she wanted to cry.

"C'mon. You should be resting." He guided her to the couch, seating her on the middle cushion. Looking sheepish, he touched the bear briefly. "Silly, huh?"

She shook her head. "It's wonderful." Her voice was wet with suppressed tears, but at that moment, she was unable to hide her emotions and hoped he would chalk it up to her illness. "Thank you."

Nick shrugged, as if trying to push aside his embarrassment. He didn't respond except to remove a Styrofoam container from the plastic bag and hand it to her. "Egg-drop soup." A plastic soup spoon followed before he arranged two boxes of food and chopsticks on the table.

Miri made a production of opening the soup and examining the contents before taking a small spoonful, desperate to avoid his eyes lest he see the vulnerability in hers. She only looked up when he called her name, jiggling two rental cases.

"I wasn't sure what you liked, so I picked up a chick flick and an action movie. Which will it be?"

She pointed to the action movie, in no mood to have her already raw emotions exposed further by any heartrending issue the chick flick might explore. Nick put it in her DVD player before joining her on the couch.

As they watched the movie, eating, no words passed their lips. When Miri had eaten as much of the soup as she could, she put the lid on and leaned back against the cushion, carefully resting her head on his shoulder. Nick put aside his food to take her into his arms. A spark of electricity arced between them, but his demeanor was one of caretaker rather than lover as he held her.

She relaxed into him, enjoying his embrace more than she should. It was a foreign experience to have someone else care about her well-being, to take care of her. That it would be Nick, the man she was supposed to be having a fling with, made it even stranger. He wasn't supposed to be the sensitive type. All brawn with a massive dose of sex appeal—that was his persona. He wasn't supposed to upset her preconceived notions and make her start to fall for him.

Her eyes, drooping, snapped open at the thought. Miri tensed, almost pulling away, as if she could escape her emotions just by putting some distance between them. Three days of silence on both their parts hadn't done anything to diminish her desire for him, so why did she think withdrawing from his embrace would do anything?

"Miri? Are you okay?"

Slowly she nodded, allowing her body to relax again. "I was falling asleep."

"Go ahead. I'll make sure you get to bed."

The words themselves were sexy but delivered in a nurturing manner. Miri tried to force her thoughts from her emotions to concentrate on the movie, but it was a long time before she was successful.

• • •

BY THE END of the movie, Miri was snoring softly against him. Nick looked down at her upturned face, noting the lines of worry around her eyes, and wondered what haunted her.

She sighed in her sleep, snuggling closer. A glance at the clock revealed it was nearly ten, which meant he should get going. In other circumstances, he would have stayed with her for a few hours, but tonight he didn't feel the urge.

As he got to his feet, lifting her into his arms effortlessly, Nick acknowledged that that wasn't true when his cock swelled against his jeans. He had the desire, but her needs outweighed his wants. Never before had he experienced this curious blend of tenderness and passion for a lover. Not one of the women he had been involved with in the past had ever evoked a need in him to take care of her.

Carrying her to her room, staring down at her, Nick faced an unpleasant truth. He was in love with Miri. It didn't give him the surge of terror he expected. Instead, as he placed her under the covers and brushed a kiss against her cheek, satisfying warmth spread through him, radiating from his heart, not his cock. For the life of him, he couldn't remember right then why he had fought so long against feeling something real for a woman.

"I love you," he said in a whisper, trying out the words, liking the way they sounded. Her eyes opened briefly. She locked gazes with him for just a second before her eyes slammed closed again and her snoring increased. It was just long enough for him to catch the glint of panic in her eyes.

5

AS SOON AS Miri opened her eyes the next morning, Nick's words swirled through the layers of her subconscious to lodge in the forefront of her mind. With a smothered groan, she rolled out of bed, desperate to escape her emotions. Panic was there, as it had been last night, but there was more. Was that giddy tickle in her chest happiness or simply the remnants of her cold?

Miri hurried into the bathroom, trying to deny she felt anything other than fear at Nick's confession. Her eyes revealed something different than her brain wanted to see. They were soft pools of darkness, tinged with a warm glow. Her lips tried to curve into a smile, and she had to school her expression into her most severe look, one usually reserved for recalcitrant students.

Dammit, she was pleased with Nick's words. Somehow, he had wormed his way into her life, burrowing into her heart in a way no man had ever done before. Her walls had dropped, her defenses had let her down . . . and she didn't care?

"I love you." Her lips formed the words hesitantly, and her voice was a rusty rasp in the enclosed space of the bathroom. She waited for some reaction, like the ceiling to fall on her, but nothing happened, other than a lightening in her chest.

Padding from the bathroom, forgetting about her morning ablutions, Miri continued practicing the words under her breath. Each time she said them, they came easier, until she almost thought she could say them to Nick when they next met.

• • •

HER FLEDGLING COMFORT with Nick's confession and her own response lasted until the next afternoon, when her phone rang. Not given to moments of intuition, it was with strange foreboding that Miri answered the telephone, every instinct screaming to ignore the out-of-area number. "Hello?"

"Miri, darling."

Her stomach churned as soon as her mother's voice came over the line. "Hello, Marnie." She'd used her mother's given name since she was eight, when Marnie had decided she looked too young to have men know she had a daughter. "How are you?" To what did she owe the phone call? Marnie kept in touch infrequently, usually only if she wanted something, like money.

"Deliriously happy."

Ah, a new man. "Oh?"

"I'm getting married."

Miri's lips curled in a cynical grimace. "You're already married."

Marnie laughed. "Oh, darling, not for long."

"What happened with Herb?" Or was it Howard? After the number of uncles and stepfathers who had paraded through Miri's life, she couldn't keep them straight.

Her mother sighed, sounding impatient. "He's so boring. He doesn't understand me at all. Can you believe he wanted me to work with him? I can't think of anything duller than sitting in an office all day."

"So you went shopping for a new husband?"

Marnie's tone sharpened. "I didn't plan it. It just sort of happened, but I couldn't stop how I felt. Craig is the one."

"Hmm."

Not picking up on Miri's skepticism, Marnie continued. "He's never been married, has no children, owns a chain of restaurants and has the most beautiful yacht. We're going to spend six months sailing around the world for our honeymoon. It's a ninety-footer, complete with a full staff—"

Miri tuned out her mother's enthusiastic description of the yacht and other material goods. It was just another match made in material heaven. One thing she could credit her mother with was Marnie's ability to trade up. She could certainly pick her targets. The thought of using men so callously turned Miri's stomach, though she had little sympathy for the men who had married her mother. They should have realized what they were getting into. Loving Marnie was no excuse to be blind to her faults.

Nothing good ever came from love. It was a lesson Miri had learned repeatedly over the years, but a moment of weakness had nearly undermined her. Whatever fragile emotional attachment she had almost allowed to grow had to be firmly squashed. Her mother's phone call and latest marriage was a timely reminder of what Miri had known most of her life. She was better off alone than allowing herself to love anyone as passionately as she could love Nick. She would lose herself in him, and for what? An emotion that couldn't possibly last. She had to protect herself, and that meant hardening her heart.

NICK POUNDED ON Miri's door relentlessly, knowing she was home. He had seen her car in the garage when he peeked in the window. Her avoidance of him over the past five days was about to end. He was going to force a confrontation, damn her wishes and his own fear of rejection. Limbo was worse than knowing how she felt about him, even if her feelings weren't mutual.

Finally, she opened the door, a trace of annoyance in her expression. "Nick? What's so urgent?"

He didn't wait for an invitation, instead pushing past her. She followed him, emanating arctic silence as he turned to face her in the living room. "Why have you been avoiding me?"

Miri frowned, giving every appearance of ignorance. "I don't know what you mean. I missed three days of school and have been struggling to catch up with everything."

"You haven't had time to return even one of my calls in the last five days?" He snorted. "Yeah."

"I had other priorities."

Her cool façade, such a contrast to the inferno burning inside him, was infuriating. He took a step closer, absurdly pleased by the way she stood her ground, though he wouldn't have minded some acknowledgement she wasn't as unaffected as she pretended. "Liar."

Her eyes widened. "Excuse me?"

"You're running scared." Nick shook his head. "It won't work. You have to face me sometime."

Miri turned partially away from him. "I have no idea what you're talking about."

He touched her shoulder, and she tensed at the light contact. "I know you heard me."

She shrugged him off. "Heard what?"

He pressed her back against his chest. "I told you I loved you."

Miri shook her head. "No."

"I did." He turned her resisting body so she was facing him, though she avoided his gaze. Nick lifted her chin, forcing her to look into his eyes. "I do. I love you."

Fear flared in her eyes. "You're crazy. You don't know me."

"I know all I need to."

She pulled away. "No, you don't. You don't know anything important about me. Did you know my mother has been married seven times . . . about to be eight? There was also a parade of countless uncles in my life, always a priority over me." Tears leaked from the corners of her eyes, and she brushed them away with an impatient gesture. "Do you want to know how many of them had grabby hands? How many times she ignored me when I told her?"

His stomach clenched with anger. "Give me their names. They'll never hurt you again."

She shook her head. "None of them ever really hurt me, not nearly as much as knowing my mother needed a man—any man— more than she needed to live up to her responsibility to me."

Nick reached for her, not allowing her to shove away his hands. He pulled her stiff body into his arms. "I'm sorry you had to go through that."

"It doesn't matter now. It taught me an important lesson. I don't want to love a man, and I don't want one to love me." Her expression was a perfect sheet of ice when she looked up at him.

"I don't want your love, Nick. You're wasting your time trying to convince me."

He shook his head, refusing to believe. "You don't mean that. It's natural to be frightened after the experiences in your childhood, but I wouldn't hurt you."

"I know, because you'll never have the chance." Miri withdrew from him and pointed to the door. "You need to leave now."

"Miri—"

"Go. I don't want to see you again."

Nick stared at her for half a minute, searching for a crack in her veneer but finding none. His shoulders slumped, and he took a step toward the door. "You'll change your mind. You just need time to think things through."

Miri turned away from him. "I won't. I don't want you, and I definitely don't love you."

He winced at the pain her words caused. Nick had the fleeting urge to rage at her, but it faded quickly. Nothing he could say would reach her right then, emotionally frozen as she was. He could only hope she might come to her senses and open up to him in the coming days. His happiness—and hers—depended on it. He walked away without looking back, not wanting her to see the tears misting his eyes, wondering if she was as close to weeping as he was. In her frigid state, he doubted it.

6

MIRI POURED A cup of coffee, deliberately avoiding the gaze of Janine, the French teacher, the closest thing she had to a best friend. She hoped Janine wouldn't look up from the TV as Miri slid into a seat at the table in the staff room.

"Finally, a minute alone." Janine turned from the TV, giving Miri an assessing glance. "Spill."

Assuming a cool expression, Miri looked up from the newspaper spread across the table. "What?"

"Something's up with you. A man?"

"No."

Janine laughed. "Yeah, sure. Only a man can make you as testy and disagreeable as you've been lately."

Frowning, Miri met Janine's eyes. "I don't know what you're talking about."

"I'm talking about that delicious firefighter you were banging for a short time. Suddenly, you no longer say a thing about him, and you're a regular grouch. Clearly, a lack of sex is to blame."

"Well, aren't you full of insights today?" Miri glared at her.

Janine nodded, asking matter-of-factly, "Did he dump you?"

Miri inched up her chin. "No. As a matter of fact, he's madly in love with me." Why bother with the pretense? Janine was the only person who had even an inkling of how her childhood had been, so she would be the only one who could understand why Miri had rejected Nick.

Her green eyes sparkled with excitement. "That's fabulous. Are you keeping it hush-hush until you have a firm commitment?"

"No. I broke it off."

"What?" Janine's outburst carried throughout the room, briefly rousing the interest of Gertrude, the gym teacher, before she returned to a thick manual of physiology. "Are you out of your mind? You finally find a man worth keeping and you discard him?"

Miri drew into herself, wrapping her hands around the coffee mug to draw some warmth from it, upon finding none from her so-called friend. "You know I don't want a man, not long-term anyway."

Janine's voice lowered to a whisper when she leaned across the table, coming closer. "You aren't going to turn into your mother by daring to have a relationship, Miri. You don't really want to be alone for the rest of your life, do you? If so, it's a very bleak future you're contemplating."

She got to her feet, abandoning the coffee. "I'm happy as I am. I didn't ask for your opinion, and I'd appreciate you keeping it to yourself." Without allowing Janine the opportunity to respond, Miri swept from the staff room, refusing to look back or acknowledge the icy ball in her stomach that had formed at Janine's words. No, it wouldn't be bleak to be alone. It would be safe and predictable. No one could hurt her as long as she kept them all at arm's length. She regretted the friendship she had allowed to blossom with Janine and vowed it would end right then.

IN KEEPING WITH her decision, she met Janine with a chill tone when the other woman stopped by her classroom a little after four. "Yes?"

"I need to tell you something—"

"I accept your apology." She stuffed papers into her eel-skin briefcase, keeping her profile turned from Janine.

"I'm not here to apologize."

Her distraught tone finally caught Miri's attention, forcing her to look up. "What's wrong?"

"There's been a fire at the country club . . . the roof collapsed." Janine's eyes were wide with apprehension, and her hands trembled when she reached out to Miri. "Two firefighters were killed, and three more have been taken to the hospital."

"Nick." Was he working a thirty-six-hour shift this week, or was it one of his three days off? She didn't know. Miri didn't question her reaction as she dropped her briefcase and scooped up her purse, fishing for car keys as she ran to the door. Janine shouted something behind her, but she didn't take time to figure out what it was as she ran through the building to the parking lot. She had to get to Nick. *Please let him be alive.*

THE HALLS AT Poplin Hills General were crowded with friends and family members of the firefighters, making it difficult for Miri to push her way through the throng to the front desk. Three nurses engaged in various tasks ignored her for a long moment until she thumped her hand onto the counter to get their attention.

The oldest one looked up from her paperwork. "May I help you?"

"I'm here . . . is Nick . . . " She took a deep breath, struggling to compose herself so she could force out the question, almost afraid to hear the answer. "Is Nick Martin here?"

The nurse glanced at a clipboard before looking up. "He's in room 115."

Miri turned from the desk, heading down the hallway.

"Miss, you can't go back there. Only family—"

She broke into a jog, hoping to outrun the nurse's admonishment and make it to the room before anyone stopped her. The woman's voice faded as Miri moved farther away from the desk, and she dared to hope she would make it to the room.

She passed 113 and 114 before seeing a man in a blue security uniform moving toward her from the opposite end of the hall. Miri increased her pace and pushed her way into 115 as security called to her.

Her breath caught in her throat when she saw the body lying in the bed, wrapped in bandages from almost head to foot. His leg was suspended in traction, and what visible skin there was around the bandages bore blisters. She walked forward, bracing herself. The person lying there was in bad shape.

"Nick." His name was a choked whisper, and she sagged forward, wanting to touch him but afraid of hurting him. "Oh, Nick, what have I done?"

"Miri?"

She jerked with shock at his voice and spun around to find Nick standing behind her. Her mouth dropped open, and she drank in the sight of him, noticing the bandages on his arm and across his forehead. She threw herself into his arms. "You're alive."

He held her close. "I wasn't inside when the roof collapsed. I got my injuries going in with the second squad to help get out my buddies."

Sobs shook her body, and she clutched his shirt. "I thought you were dying or dead. I was such an idiot." Miri raised her head. "I could have lost you, and you never would have known—"

The door opened, admitting the guard. "You can't be in here."

Nick waved his hand. "We'll leave in just a second."

Miri turned her head in time to see the guard's stern expression fade. "Never mind. I didn't realize she was with you, Nick." He turned to the door, leaving a heavy silence in his wake.

Finally, Nick cleared his voice. "You were saying?"

She hesitated, finding her courage had deserted her at the penultimate moment. During the frantic drive to the hospital, all she could think about was how could she go on without Nick, but now that he was safe, she found it impossible to remove the last fragment of the wall protecting her heart. Instead, she asked, "Who is the man in the bed?"

"My chief, Brady Holland. I'm waiting with him until his wife arrives. She works in Portland."

"Will he make it?"

Nick sighed. "We don't know yet."

Still clutching his shirt, Miri looked up at him. "What you do is dangerous."

He nodded. "Yes. I love it, but I'd give it up if you asked me to.

I finally understand how my brother could walk away from his career for his wife."

Tears trickled from her eyes, and she buried her face against his chest. "I couldn't ask that of you."

He pushed up her chin, forcing her to meet his eyes. "Haven't you figured out by now I'll do anything for you? I love you, Miri, more than I've ever loved being a firefighter. More than I've ever loved anything. I want to spend my life making you happy, if you'll let me."

The wall crumbled with what she swore was an audible crack. Miri's muscles refused to support her, and she slumped against him, letting his T-shirt absorb her tears. "I love you, Nick." The words were strange on her tongue, but she meant them with every ounce of her being. When she dared to look up, she found Nick's lips trembling and couldn't tell if his eyes were glazed with tears or if the mist was from hers. "I love you." This time, the words were easier to say. "I don't know how it happened or when, but I do love you. Can you forgive me for pushing you away?"

"It doesn't matter what happened in the past." His words carried significant meaning, not just for their history but also for her own. "All that matters is the future."

She stretched on her tiptoes to kiss him, finding herself optimistic about the future for the first time ever. With the thawing of her heart, she was free to imagine a dizzying array of possibilities in their future, and none were bleak. How could they be with Nick by her side?

FANTASY BAR

TRISTA ANN MICHAELS

DEDICATION

This story is dedicated to four wonderful ladies. First, Lydia, who came up with the name Fantasy Bar, the two words that started a firestorm of inspiration. To Ester, our lady bartender and inspiration behind the interesting idea of ordering your sexual fantasy by ordering a drink. To Sarah, for her input on plot and for always reminding me to rate my chapters, so she has a heads-up to the content, even though most of the time I forget. And Sharon, my partner in crime, for letting me "borrow" some of her outrageous sayings and continually keeping me in stitches. You guys are the best and I love each and every one of you.

1

"OH, MY GOD, Kira! What happened?"

Kira Vordak stumbled into the room and slumped onto the edge of Mirage's velvet settee. Her back burned and needles of pain shot through her limbs. Her shirt clung to her bloody flesh, but she was pretty sure the wounds had stopped bleeding. With trembling hands, she removed her overcoat and swallowed back a sob.

"Oh, shit, Kira." Mirage tugged at the blouse and hissed as the material broke away from the dried blood. The shirt slid down her arms and fell to the Oriental rug. "You stay right here. I'm going for the doctor."

"No!"

"No? Forget it, girl. Your back is a mess and needs to be stitched. It's way beyond my capabilities. But the second the doctor leaves the room, I want to know who did this to you."

The door slammed and Kira laid her head in her hands, the fatigue and pain finally catching up with her. The rush of adrenaline she'd been relying on had vanished, leaving her weak and trembling. For the first time in hours, she felt safe. She knew no one could find her here. No one knew of her connection to Mirage and the Fantasy Bar on the small planet of Klindor.

She'd made sure to remain well hidden in the back of the transport from Meenus Prime, hoping and praying no one recognized her. She still couldn't believe her stupidity. How in the hell had she gotten into this mess and more importantly, how the hell was she going to get out of it?

The door opened and she sat up straight then winced.

Lightheadedness overtook her and she leaned precariously to the side, no longer able to keep herself upright. Mirage caught her, offering her shoulder for support.

"Help me get her to the bed," the doctor ordered after a brief inspection. "It looks like she's lost a lot of blood and we need to get these cuts closed."

Kira wearily watched the doctor as he opened his bag. His eyes were shadowed, but his hair was thick and black, just brushing over wide shoulders corded with muscles that flexed as he moved. His face was masculine and tinged with a hint of Mediterranean. Certainly not someone she would consider a doctor. She always pictured them with glasses and thin builds.

He moved to touch her and she closed her eyes, bracing herself. His warm fingers brushed across her shoulder, reassuring her. "I'll be as gentle as I can."

She nodded and waited, her shoulders tense with nerves.

"Oh, God, there's so many," Mirage sighed. "Kira, what did this?"

She was so tired, so weak, she couldn't open her mouth to speak. Instead, she remained silent while the doctor cleaned and sealed her wounds.

"Looks like a whip," the doctor replied quietly. "See the jagged edges?"

"Oh, God," Mirage sniffed and placed her hand over Kira's when she flinched at the doctor's gentle probing.

"She'll be sore for a few days but she should be fine."

"Thank you, Jaimee," Mirage said as she walked the doctor to the door.

"You're welcome. Call me if you need me."

Kira watched as the handsome doctor touched her friend's cheek with such tenderness it made her heart ache. To have someone touch her like that was her deepestwish, but she doubted it would ever come true. Especiallynow.

"How are you feeling?" Mirage sat on the edge of the bed and gently ran her fingers along the red and swollen tears.

"I've been better." Kira tried to smile but it quickly faded. Her eyes drooped heavily and her words were sluggish. "I feel strange."

"Jaimee gave you something to take care of the pain and to help you sleep. What happened?"

"I was leaving the university. I had a late class in intergalactic business trades and I stayed to grade papers. When I was heading home someone caught me from behind. He bound my hands and feet, gagged my mouth. I was so out of it from the hit to my head, I couldn't put up a fight. I never even saw his face, Mirage, never knew who he was until . . ."

"Until?"

Kira swallowed her sob and squeezed her eyes closed, trying to block out the images, the pain. "Until I killed him."

JERROD SCOLLIN STALKED back into the brightly lit bedroom after stepping outside for some fresh air and a few much needed moments to collect himself. The stench of dried blood and death permeated the small space. He'd been an investigator for the high regent of Meenus Prime for almost ten years and he'd never become accustomed to that smell. Even now, it rolled his stomach.

Trying to turn his mind to other things, his trained eye took in the scene. Clothes and linens lay scattered about in disarray. Blood splattered the bedsheets and headboard. The lifeless body of his best friend Micas Lordakin lay across the foot of the bed.

He'd been informed of his death prior to his arrival, but that didn't prepare him for actually seeing it for himself. He'd been shot in the chest four times at point-blank range. His eyes still stared at the ceiling, focusing on nothing. Wasn't it just last weekend they had been planning their yearly trip to Vingosa?

Think about your job, Jerrod, he scolded himself and pushed his grief aside.

There had been no forced entry, and as far as Jerrod knew, Micas didn't have any enemies. Considering he was shot in the bedroom, he would bet Micas knew his killer.

"Find anything, Simas?"

Simas turned from his study of the blood-soaked bed linens. A lock of blond hair fell across his forehead and he brushed it back in aggravation. "It's not his blood. It's female."

Jerrod frowned. "Female?"

"Yes."

What the hell were you doing, Micas? "Can you determine what happened?"

"Not from what little there is here. I've run a scan. Whoever it belongs to isn't in the system."

"That just means she's not a criminal." Jerrod wandered around the room, looking for something, anything that would answer the questions running through his mind. What had gone on here? Had Micas been involved in something illegal? Had he brought home a prostitute that later turned on him? Had she been injured and was that why her blood was all over the room?

With a tired sigh, he dragged his hand down his face. So many fucking questions!

"Sir?"

Jerrod spun and looked at the young investigator standing behind him. Daniel. He stood a good three inches shorter than Jerrod and had to crane his neck slightly to look at him. He was new to the force, just out of the academy, but Jerrod heard he had excellent potential as a profiler. "Did you find out anything?"

"Yes, sir. The doorman said he saw the same woman Micas arrived with two days ago leave last night. She seemed upset so he followed her to the transport dock. She boarded a ship bound for Klindor."

"Klindor?" Simas mused from his position kneeling by the bed. "Interesting destination."

Jerrod nodded. "Especially for a woman alone. She was alone?"

"Yes, sir. As far as the doorman knows."

"Now why do you suppose the doorman would follow her?" Simas stood and placed his hands on his hips.

"The guy said she was hot. He wanted to get her alone and sample her wares, if you know what I mean."

"Her wares?" Jerrod asked.

"Yes, sir. He said Micas indicated the woman was a prostitute when he arrived with her the other night. He brought her in through the back entrance. She was slung over his shoulder and bound. Micas told him it was 'all part of the S&M package.'"

Simas swore softly and Jerrod glanced at him. Immediately, a veil dropped over Simas' expression. For a second, Jerrod wondered what the outburst was about, but he returned to the investigation. "Thank you, Daniel," Jerrod mumbled then turned to sit on the only clean spot at the foot of the mattress.

"Micas was into S&M?" Simas whispered. "Did you know about this?"

Jerrod shook his head, his mind reeling from the possibilities. He'd known Micas since they were kids. They'd grown up together, playing in the same abandoned mines and flying the same spaceports. His friend had a wild side and sometimes even a cruel streak, but Jerrod had had no idea it ran to this extreme. S&M was one thing—and sometimes quite fun—but it was obvious from the amount of the woman's blood on the bed it had gone beyond fun and turned quite deadly.

"What are you thinking?" Simas asked.

"Daniel." Jerrod raised a hand and waved the young man over. "I need a physical description of the woman. Did you get one?"

Daniel related what the doorman had told him while Jerrod quickly recorded it in his mini-computer. "Blond, green eyes. About five feet, seven inches tall, maybe one hundred and twenty pounds. He also said she had nice legs."

"Nice legs?" Simas smirked. "That'll narrow it down."

Jerrod flipped his computer closed in aggravation. "That will be all, thank you."

"Yes, sir."

Jerrod headed to the main living area, Simas following close on his heels. "You didn't answer my question."

Jerrod frowned. "What question?"

"I asked what you were thinking."

"I'm thinking of going to Klindor to try and find the woman."

Simas pointed to the computer. "Based on that description?"

"It's all we have, Simas. You got any better ideas?"

"Not at the moment."

"Besides, how many women arrive alone on Klindor? She shouldn't be too difficult to track down."

"Why don't you let me go?"

"Why?" Jerrod asked. Simas never wanted to go out in the field. He preferred to work the scene, handle the evidence. What had brought about the sudden change?

Simas shrugged, not meeting his stare. "I thought since you'd just returned, you might want to stay here."

"No. I'll go. I have a higher clearance than you. I can get into places you can't by flashing my badge as an employee of the Planetary Senate."

"True, but Klindor isn't officially a member of the Senate."

Jerrod's frown stopped Simas' argument. "I said I'd handle it, Simas. Klindor may not officially be on the voting roster, but they try to stay on the good side of the regent. They won't be a problem. Besides, I need you here. I want you to search this apartment from top to bottom. Find me something." With a pointed look that brooked no argument, Jerrod pulled his coat collar around his ears to ward off the winter chill in preparation of stepping onto the private landing pad just outside Micas' apartment.

"Even if we don't like what we come across? Micas was your best friend, my mentor and possibly the next regent elect. What if this was self-defense, Jerrod? Do you have any idea what kind of a scandal that will raise? How do you explain the next leader of the Senate being shot because he was trying to kill a prostitute?"

"That's why we need to find the woman."

2

ON YOUR KNEES, *whore," the man hissed out, the words followed immediately by the sting of the whip slashed across
her back.*

*She bit her lip, the metallic taste of blood filling her mouth.
Again the whip landed across her flesh and she cried out, bending
her body to escape the harsh leather.*

*She lay facedown in the same position she'd been in for what
seemed like days, her hands shackled to the bedposts. Black material covered her eyes, preventing her from seeing her attacker, but
she could smell him. His nasty, evil scent invaded her nostrils, making her want to vomit.*

"On your knees!"

*She couldn't get on her knees. Not the way she was lying and he
knew it. He only wanted to yell at her, scream demands he knew
she couldn't possibly meet just so he would have a reason to beat
her again. She couldn't take much more. Blood trickled down her
back and onto the sheets. She had to find a way out of here.*

"Kira?"

She awoke with a start and couldn't seem to pull enough air into
her lungs. Grasping her throat, she tried to relax, tried to take a few
deep breaths to slow her frantic heartbeat.

Sitting up, her nervous gaze darted around the suite, checking
dark corners. The maroon walls reflected the soft light coming from
the fireplace and created flickering shadows. A human form appeared amidst the dancing designs and she gasped as fear trickled

down her spine. With growing trepidation, she jerked her head toward the door.

"It's just me." Mirage stepped farther into the room. Her blue silk dress clung to her petite curves and gave her gray eyes a turquoise hue. "You okay?"

"Yeah." Kira sighed and placed a trembling hand against her chest. Relief surged through her and she sagged against the pillows. "Just nightmares."

Mirage sat on the mattress, her tiny hand resting on Kira's thigh. "They'll pass soon. It was self-defense, honey. You didn't have a choice."

"I know. That's what I keep telling myself. But the nightmares continue."

"It'll get better, I promise. After all, no one knows that nightmares fade better than I do. Have you let the university know you're okay? I'm sure, since you didn't return to your classes, they're wondering where you are."

"It doesn't do for the professor to miss class, does it? No. I haven't contacted them. I'm not even sure what to say. I'm sorry I brought this here."

Mirage shook her head with a frown. "Don't be. We're friends. No matter what. You'll stay here as long as you need to."

"I can't just sit up here, though. I could tend bar."

Mirage bit her lower lip in a move Kira recognized as uncertainty. "Are you sure that's a good idea?"

"No. But I am half-owner, so it wouldn't be unreasonable that I would be here. It should be safe enough. It's been a long time since I've tended bar. I hope I remember how."

"I know. Not since the last time you were here, which was what? About four years ago?"

"Yeah." Had it really been that long?

Mirage smiled. "I remember where we first came up with the idea for this place."

Kira chuckled at the memory. The whole thing had started out as a joke, a silly idea from four drunk women who were bored out of their minds. But with Mirage's imagination and Kira's business savvy, it soon took off and developed a life of its own.

Fantasy Bar was now the most popular and profitable business on Klindor.

It was the only bar where you could order a drink and have it become your sexual fantasy.

Mirage patted Kira's thigh. "Let me take a look at your back."

Kira sat forward, allowing her friend to exam the quickly healing slashes.

"Jaimee said they would remain red and sore for a while longer, but you can move around and do whatever you feel comfortable doing. Have you kept up with your birth control injections?"

With a start, Kira realized that no, she hadn't kept up with them, but it might not be a bad idea. Fantasy would be a great place to exorcise some demons. She shook her head. "It's been at least a year. I wasn't seeing anyone so I just didn't see a point."

"I'll have Jaimee give you one. The injection he uses takes effect immediately." Kira tensed as Mirage gently ran her fingers over the welts, checking for any sign of infection. "They look as though they're healing nicely. Still a little red though, so be careful," Mirage said.

Mirage stood and walked over to the lounge chair by the fireplace and picked up the outfit that was lying across the arm. "I laid out some clothes for you. I thought the green would go exceptionally well with your eyes."

"Thanks," Kira said with a slight smile. After Mirage studied her for what seemed like forever, Kira frowned. "What?"

"Should we color your hair?"

Kira ran her hand down her long blond locks. She hated the idea of changing the color, but it might not be a bad idea, just in case. She'd killed a prominent man, well known in high society and government circles. She'd never kept track of the news, but she'd seen enough to know who the man was.

She still didn't know if she should turn herself in or not. Would they believe her story or would they hang her from the tallest tree after the joke of a trial? Changing her looks might be smart, at least until she decided what to do. "What do you think of red?"

Mirage titled her head to the side, her lips pursed in concentration. "Just a little red, I think. Not too much."

"Well," she sighed and threw the purple satin sheets aside. "Let's get this over with."

JERROD STROLLED INTO Fantasy Bar, his eyes scanning the dark interior. He'd heard of this place as far away as the Neptune Moon. If you ordered a Blowjob, you not only received the drink but an actual blowjob. Same with Slow Screw, which he could see going on in the far corner.

A male patron had the barmaid bent over, her hands resting against the deep red wall, her hips moving in rhythm with his as he pumped his cock into her pussy. Another couple off to the left was engaged in the same fantasy, only positioned differently. With this couple, the woman's back was against the wall and her legs wrapped around the man's waist.

Jerrod's cock twitched at the erotic displays around him. He'd come in here for a drink and to check the place out, not to participate in the hedonistic activities. He'd had enough of one-night stands. He'd wanted something more for quite a while now. Something deeper than just sex. He seriously doubted he'd find it in a place like this, though.

As he made his way farther into the room, he took in the French influence throughout the two-story bar. Whoever decorated had been to Earth. His mother had loved the Napoleonic era and had redone her whole house with pieces from that time period. He recognized much of the furniture as replicas. A smart move. It would be foolhardy to decorate a bar such as this with actual antiques.

Along the wall to the right was the long mahogany bar. It was packed save for a few open stools here and there. At the table to his right, two blowjobs were taking place. It was quite a show, a dark-haired woman taking every inch of a man into her mouth and down her throat. Beside them, two men licked at the large cock of another man. He just shook his head and moved on.

Stepping through the mass of bodies laughing and undulating against one another, he moved toward the bar and sat down at one of the stools. He was tired and this would be his last stop for the night. So far, he hadn't had much luck. A woman had arrived here alone, but where she'd gone once she exited the transport was a mystery.

"Can I help you?"

Raising his gaze, he found himself staring into the most beautiful pair of green eyes he'd ever seen. They were fathomless, turned up slightly at the corners, holding just a hint of amusement. Could she help him? Is that what she'd asked? He wasn't sure he'd heard her right over the pounding of his heart roaring through his ears.

She was a beauty, and he couldn't stop staring at her, which probably accounted for the adorable grin now gracing her china-doll face. What the hell was she doing in a place like this?

She raised an eyebrow. "Need time to think about it?"

He shook his head, trying to clear the fog that had settled in his brain. He smiled, slowly letting his gaze memorize every inch of her oval face and full lips. "No. I think I know exactly what I want."

"And that would be?" she asked with a soft chuckle.

Something in the sound tugged at a part of his chest that had been long buried, waiting for the right girl to come along and uncover it. For a second, it startled him. How could a laugh do that? A smile? "Your name, for starters."

Her head tilted to the side as she laid her hand against her hip. "Sorry, not on the menu."

"Not even a hint?"

She slowly shook her head, her lips twitching ever so slightly. He could stare into those eyes all day, and all night for that matter. They were deep green, like the summer grass of Earth, framed with long, elegant lashes.

"How about I just call you Gorgeous then?"

"Flattery will get you—"

"Everywhere?" he asked, raising an eyebrow.

She chuckled. "Nowhere."

He clucked his tongue. "My loss."

"What can I get you to drink, charmer?"

"I'll take a Vegan Ale."

She nodded. "Vegan Ale it is."

Turning, she sashayed to the other end of the bar. The soft sway of her hips caught his attention, and he couldn't seem to look away. The green material clung to her, outlining her perfect curves. Not chubby, but not too skinny either. She had hills and valleys his hands itched to explore. But would one night with this gorgeous woman be enough? Something deep inside told him no, he didn't think it would be.

He hadn't had that kind of reaction to a woman in a while. Matter of fact, he wasn't sure when he'd ever had that kind of reaction. He wanted her body, yes, but for some reason he wanted her name more. He wanted to talk to her, find out why she was here, for she certainly didn't fit.

Glancing around the bar, he tried to block out the erotic images all around him. Coming into this place had been one hell of a bad idea. But then he locked gazes with his gorgeous redhead again and realized maybe it wasn't a bad idea at all. Maybe it was the first thing he'd done right in years.

Kira drew in a steadying breath and tried to concentrate on pouring the Vegan Ale. The man was sexy as hell. He certainly didn't look like the type that would need to come to a place like this for sex. He could probably get any woman he wanted. If circumstances were different, he could certainly get her.

From the second she'd seen him cross the floor, she'd known in her gut there was something different about him. Something she couldn't put her finger on. Normally the atmosphere of the bar didn't affect her. She could ignore it or participate if she chose, but ever since this man had smiled at her, participating was all she could seem to think about—or at least participating with him only. No one else she'd seen tonight—or the past several years for that matter—interested her.

Glancing to her left, she caught him watching her. His intelligent, sapphire gaze held hers hostage. Her whole body tingled from the current skimming through her, making her heart race. What was it about him that did this to her? Turned her normal self-control into nothing but a jumbled mass of nerves?

He looked to be about thirty-six, just three years older than her. He had short black hair with just a hint of wave to the thick locks. A day's worth of stubble completed his masculine face. She loved a man with stubble, especially when he would scrape the rough hairs against her flesh.

Long fingers rubbed his chin and she admired them, wondering what they would feel like against her skin. He had strong hands. Masculine hands, and for a second she tried to imagine if they would be gentle or firm. From out of nowhere fear and uncertainty traveled up her spine before she trampled it down. She didn't want what had happened to her to make her skittish of men. They weren't all that way.

She doubted he would be cruel. He held a look of gentleness in his eyes, a playful look. As she stared like a fool, thinking about his lips, ale spilled over the side of the glass and over her fingers. "Damn," she mumbled, shaking the liquid from her hand and searching the bar for a dry towel.

Dax, their oldest bartender, handed her his. "First rule of bartending here at Fantasy," he whispered in her ear. "When a customer affects you that badly, you fuck him."

"Real cute, Dax."

She tossed the towel at his chest and he caught it with a grin. Taking a deep breath, she grabbed the glass and turned back to her gorgeous customer. She'd have to face him sooner or later. Might as well be now.

His eyes twinkled with laughter as she walked toward him. Inwardly, she cringed, the heat of a blush spreading up her cheeks. Why did he have to see that?

"Here you go," she said with as steady a voice as she could muster.

"Thank you." He smiled and a dimple formed in his cheek.

Ah God. A man with a dimple. Those adorable indentions were her weakness.

"You're welcome. Anything else?" Like an Oral Sex, perhaps? A Screaming Orgasm? What was she thinking? She was here to bartend, not participate in the hedonistic activities.

"I could try again for your name. On the menu yet?"

Her name? She shouldn't give him the name she normally went by and racked her brain for an alternative. "Tired of 'Gorgeous' already?" she teased.

He grinned behind his glass, his eyes crinkling in mischief and smoldering desire. "I don't think I would ever get tired of gorgeous."

She bit at her lip. There was an underlying meaning to that but she ignored it. "I don't recall seeing you here before," she said. For all she knew he could be a regular. After all, it had been four years since she'd been here.

He swallowed a sip of his ale. "I haven't. It's my first time."

"Ah," she sighed with a nod. "A Fantasy virgin."

He smirked and glanced around the room. "A virgin wouldn't remain a virgin for long in this place."

"Yeah, if you're not used to it the atmosphere can be a bit . . ." She waved her hand, mentally searching for the right word. "Arousing."

"All this doesn't affect you?" he asked, his eyes widening in slight surprise.

She shrugged. "Not anymore."

"So if this doesn't affect you, what does?"

Her heart jumped at the dimple in his cheek and the way his eyes seemed to devour her. She must be out of her mind. The last thing she needed to do was stand here and flirt with someone she didn't know. She was here to hide, not get into something she wouldn't be able to finish. But for some reason she couldn't make herself walk away from him. "Fishing for information?"

"Fishing is what I do best. Have I caught a bite or am I just dangling in the water?"

Taking a deep breath, she glanced over his shoulder to the far corner. There were two new couples engaging in a sexual fantasy there now, the four of them huddled together, pleasing each other in ways even Kira hadn't seen in a while.

What would it hurt to have a little fun? Maybe if she stayed with her gorgeous customer a while longer, she might figure out what it was about him that made her so frazzled.

Meeting his gaze dead on, she grinned. "It takes a lot to affect me. I'm very hard to please."

God, I am such a liar. The man's sapphire gaze affected her. The way he tilted his head and studied her, amusement dancing in his eyes, affected her. The way he licked his lips just then affected her.

"Hard to please, huh? Sounds like a challenge to me." His lips spread into a devilish grin that made her heart lodge in her throat. "And I love a challenge."

She just smiled. The sultry look in his gaze made moisture gather between her legs. It would be so easy to lose herself to this man. Even in here. She didn't care. She'd done the whole public sex thing before. Just the thought of him pleasing her made her nipples tingle, and she could tell by the look in his eyes that he knew exactly what she was thinking.

A man behind her yelled, trying to get her attention. Damn. She glanced over her shoulder to the waving customer. "Excuse me, I need to get back to work."

"I'll be right here. Just in case you want me to take you up on that challenge."

"You wish," she replied devilishly.

Jerrod sipped on his drink, his gaze studying her as she moved up and down the bar. *Hell yeah, I wish.* Occasionally, she looked in his direction and he winked. She immediately turned away, her cheeks deepening to an adorable shade of red. It seemed odd that a woman who worked in the midst of all this sex would blush, but he loved it.

With an aggravated sigh, he realized he'd forgotten to ask her about the female fugitive he was searching for. Oh, well. He had all night and at the moment he was perfectly content to just sit there and watch her.

Suddenly, he wasn't so tired and he began to plot out an idea to get her interested in more than just bartending. Maybe he should do a body search. He grinned at the idea.

It was getting late—too late to roam the streets questioning people. Tomorrow he would continue his search. Tonight, he'd pursue the nameless minx.

KIRA DIDN'T KNOW how much more of the erotic scenes she could tolerate. Everywhere she looked couples were having sex. She'd forgotten just how arousing working here could be.

Her mystery man wasn't helping matters either. He kept staring at her like he knew exactly what she was thinking. And wanting. Turning back toward the crowded floor, she put her back against the edge of the bar and surveyed the dark room. Slow, sexy music played in the background while couples danced and swayed against one another.

Two tables away, one of the male customers grabbed Lyanne, their youngest and most popular barmaid, and pulled her down on his lap. She leaned her head back and giggled while the man buried his face in her neck.

"Seron," Lyanne moaned and wiggled on his lap. "I've missed you. Where have you been?"

"All that matters, my sweet, is that I'm here now and I want you."

Kira smiled slightly at the two of them. From what she'd heard, Seron was a regular here and always went for Lyanne.

With a growl, Seron stood and laid Lyanne back across the table, lifting her short, pleated skirt around her waist. Lyanne liked to dress like a young girl in a private-school uniform and apparently Seron liked it as well. He freed his engorged shaft, letting his pants drop around his knees before plunging deep between her legs. Her scream of pleasure could be heard above the usual chatter of the bar patrons and several of the customers stopped what they were doing to watch. Including her dream guy.

If the couple having sex did so in the open, it was nothing un-
usual for other customers to join in and most did in one way or
another. Kira stared as her mystery man stood and made his way
over to the couple. His brown pants clung to his firm ass and ac-
centuated his trim waist. His white shirt opened partially, giving
just a hint of the hard chest beneath.

Never taking his eyes off Kira's, Jerrod popped the buttons of
Lyanne's shirt and slid his large palm over her breast. With a groan,
she thrust it further into the air.

Kira frowned, unsure how she felt about him putting his hands
on another woman. It didn't feel right to her, and she wanted to tell
him to stop, but at the same time, she couldn't look away.

His sapphire eyes met hers, silently challenging her as he leaned
down to circle Lyanne's nipple with his tongue. Kira's breathing
hitched, her nipples beading into hard pebbles. He sucked Lyanne's
breast further into his mouth, his daring gaze never leaving Kira's.

He was doing it on purpose, trying to arouse her, daring her to
join in the play. She could tell by the way he watched her, the way
he held her stare and wouldn't let go. Kira's gut told her he wanted
her, but did she dare go to him?

Seron lifted Lyanne's legs over his shoulders, and she moaned
her pleasure, her hips moving in time with Seron's. Kira gasped,
mesmerized, as her dream man unzipped his slacks and removed his
magnificent shaft.

Oh, jeez.

Her gaze remained glued to his fingers as they worked up and
down his thick length. She swallowed hard, fighting the urge
to take it into her mouth, to swallow every last drop of cum he
spewed forth. Her eyes moved back to his. They smoldered, boring
into hers with intensity that stole her breath. There was that challenge again, that dare she was finding harder and harder to resist.

"Give it to me," Lyanne sighed, her eyes locked on his cock. "Put
it in my mouth." Seron grunted his approval, his eyes glazing over
in pure animal lust.

No!

Possessiveness raced through her, sending a jolt of shock through her veins. For some reason, Kira didn't want Lyanne touching him. Any part of him. Pushing away from the bar, she walked toward him, choosing to act on the feeling instead of trying to analyze it. Grabbing his arm, she turned him away from Lyanne and dropped to her knees.

Jerrod inwardly smiled in triumph as he watched her walk toward him and turn him from the other couple. Her eyes glowed with the same possessive passion and need that gripped him and his heart beat a hard, excited rhythm. He'd hoped his silent challenge would work—that she felt the same tug in her chest that he did. There was something between them, something he couldn't explain but wanted desperately to explore.

Deep down, he knew now wasn't really the time for this. He was here on business, investigating, but all thoughts of his job left his mind as her tiny hands gripped his shaft. Damn, he'd never been so hard in his life. He knew he'd explode the second her succulent lips enveloped him, and he ground his teeth to keep from losing control.

"I was hoping you would join me," he rasped.

She glanced up at him, her small hand circling, teasing the head of his cock until he thought he would scream.

"So all that was just for show? To get me interested?" Slowly, her hand moved up and down, her fingers squeezing just under the purple head.

He sighed, fighting the pleasure that skimmed through him with every movement of her hand. "Did it work? Are you interested, Gorgeous?"

In answer, she closed her lips around his cock, and Jerrod sucked in a breath. Her mouth was hot and wet and felt so damn good. In one swift move, she took him deep in her throat. He groaned, his hips jerking forward.

Through heavy-lidded eyes, he watched her take his shaft deep in her mouth, her cheeks sunken in from the sucking motion. He touched the side of her face, brushing the soft skin of her cheeks with the back of his fingers. Her surprised gaze met his and for a fleeting second he wondered why such a move would shock her. Had she never experienced tenderness before?

He supposed in a place like this, she probably wouldn't and that bothered him, more than he wanted to admit. Backing away from her, he pulled his cock from her mouth and reached down to grab her shoulders, tugging her to her feet.

She watched him questioningly as he grabbed a chair and sat down. With a hard jerk, he ripped her pants down in one swift motion. She gasped and for a second, he thought she might shy away. Fear clouded her eyes, and he reached up to touch the side of her face. "I won't hurt you."

A small smile lit up her face. "I know. Dax wouldn't let you."

She nodded her head toward the bar. The massively built Dax kept a close eye on the small group, making sure nothing got out of hand. She kicked her slacks aside and straddled his lap, her wet pussy rubbing along his raging hard-on.

"Damn, I want you," he growled against her lips. "What is it about you, Gorgeous? Did you put something in my drink?" He grinned slightly. "Put a spell on me, perhaps?"

"Maybe you did that to me. This place doesn't affect me, remember?"

His palms gripped her hips, moving her in a slow rhythm along his shaft. "Haven't you figured out yet, this place has nothing to do with it."

He tried to kiss her, but she jerked away at the last second and wagged a finger before his nose. His brow creased in a frown as he stared at her. "No kissing. That's not what this is about."

"What's it about then, Gorgeous?"

"Sex. Pure and simple."

He grinned. "Woman, you are so in denial."

Kira lifted her hips and slid down his length, effectively silencing any other argument he might have. She knew she was in denial, but she couldn't let it get that personal. She just couldn't. Not now.

She groaned as his thick cock stretched and filled her. Slowly, she began to move back and forth, each rock of her hips taking him deeper. This would be quick. She'd been so turned on when he entered her, she knew she wouldn't be able to last for long.

His palms cupped her breasts through her top and a ragged sigh escaped her lips. It had been so long since a man had touched her like this. It almost made her forget the last week of torture.

There had been no sex. The man hadn't raped her, just hurt her. It had seemed the louder she screamed and the more blood there was, the more excited he'd become. But he'd never fucked her, just masturbated and shot his cum all over her, while in the background someone laughed.

Someone laughed? Who had laughed? Had there been someone else there? The memory was just beyond her consciousness, just out of her reach, and she couldn't grab it.

Closing her eyes, she tried to block the memories and concentrate on what was happening now. She would figure everything out later. The feel of this well-endowed man deep inside her, his lips warm and wet against the flesh of her neck, made her forget it all. She whimpered and arched her back, her fingers gripping his shoulders through his shirt.

She lifted herself, dragging his cock almost completely out of her, then slowly slid back down his length, teasing them both. He growled, his fingers digging into the flesh of her hip. Again, she teased him, and he threw his head back, his hips lifting off the seat. "Damn it, Gorgeous!"

His palm slapped the cheek of her ass, not hard, but enough to heighten her already out of control passion. It had been years since she'd done this—let herself go in the middle of the crowded Fantasy Bar. The people watching only turned her on, made her hotter, bolder.

Oh, God.

She was so close. She could feel the walls of her pussy squeeze him, dragging him deeper. His grunts and groans mingled with hers as her whole body tensed then exploded into a wave of pleasure so strong she screamed.

She had no idea how much time passed before she felt him yell and jerk, his own body lost in the bliss of release. Laying her head against his shoulder, she sighed, her muscles relaxing as she slowly came down from the high. A high she never dreamed she could reach. Was it him or was it because she'd been without for too long?

It has to be the abstinence. I refuse to let it be anything else.

His arms tightened, held her closer and for a moment she allowed herself to curl into him. She felt safe in his arms—protected—and after the last few days she wanted to hold onto that feeling. If only for a little while.

Out of breath, he buried his face in her neck and mumbled, "There's no way in hell I'm leaving this bar without your name."

Kira stiffened. Oh, God. The name again. "I don't know yours either," she whispered, stalling for time.

She sat straight and met his gaze. His sapphire eyes were almost black with fading passion. "It's Jerrod," he said with a smile, making his dimple deepen.

His hand was buried in her hair, sifting through its thickness. She closed her eyes, the gentle motions of his hand relaxing her. He placed a soft kiss on the sensitive spot behind her ear. "Name, Gorgeous. I'll figure it out one way or another. You might as well tell me."

"I see Kira hasn't lost her touch," Dax snickered from behind her, and she tensed, turning to glare at him. For the first time since she'd known him she felt like slapping the smirk from his face.

Jerrod chuckled, a smile of satisfaction spreading his lips. "Thanks, Dax."

So much for coming up with an alias.

4

JERROD ROLLED OVER and tried to block out the high-pitched beep of his communicator. *It's too damn early for this.* The incessant beeping continued, and he buried his head deeper under the covers. For several minutes he remained there, trying to ignore it.

Sunshine streamed in through the crack in the blinds, sending streaks of yellow across the hardwood floor. Vaguely, he wondered what time it was and peeked at the clock on the bedside table. Damn. Didn't he just get into bed?

The beeping continued, and he ground his teeth. Rolling to his back, he threw his arm over his eyes and sighed. Whoever was calling wasn't going to stop.

With a growl, he threw the covers off and rolled out of bed. The streams of sunlight warmed the floor and it felt good against his bare feet. Stepping to his portable computer, he lifted the screen and punched in his code before sitting down. Instantly, Simas' face appeared.

"Damn, Jerrod. You look like hell."

Jerrod snorted. After only about two hours of sleep how the hell else was he supposed to look? "Good morning to you as well, sunshine."

Simas chuckled. "Sorry."

"Have you found anything yet?"

"You mean besides a diversity of sex toys and bondage paraphernalia?"

"Shit," Jerrod sighed and rubbed his forehead.

"You know, everyone is entitled to their little quirks and tastes, but this," Simas held up a belt, complete with handcuffs and two dildos. Jerrod quirked an eyebrow at the erotic images the toy brought to mind. "This is just a tad bit strange, even for Micas. I'm not even sure I know what the hell this is."

Jerrod grinned. "Think about it for a minute or two, Simas, and you'll figure it out."

Simas tossed the handcuffs aside. "That's all right. I think I'll remain ignorant."

Jerrod chuckled and shook his head. Thinking about sex toys brought his mind to Kira. There were a few toys he wouldn't mind using on her, as well as his mouth and hands. She'd disappeared last night after their little foray into exhibitionism. He'd tried to find out from Dax where she'd gone, but he'd gotten nowhere with the tall giant. If nothing else, he was protective of the women who worked there.

He'd hung around for a couple of hours in the hopes that she would come back out. While he waited he questioned some of the waitresses. As far as they knew, no one new had been around looking for a job, but if they heard of anyone, they'd let him know.

"Jerrod!"

At the sound of his name, he snapped his head up and stared at the screen. "I'm sorry. Did you say something?"

Simas frowned. "Yeah. I asked if you'd found out anything about the woman?"

Squeezing his nose to try and relieve the banger of a headache he felt coming on, he nodded. "The transport pilot said there was a woman who matched our description who disembarked, but he has no idea where she went. He thought she might have been hurt, but she refused his help."

"All that blood on the bed was hers. I'm shocked she was able to walk out of here at all."

"You'd be amazed what people would do to survive."

"So you think that's what this was? An S&M session that got out of hand?" Simas asked.

"Maybe."

"Sure you don't want me to come up there? You look awfully tired, Jerrod."

Jerrod frowned. Something wasn't right here, but he couldn't put his finger on what. Maybe he was too tired to do this right.

"No," Jerrod said with a sigh. "Stay there and continue looking and keep me informed."

"Will do."

Jerrod flipped his screen down and stared at the wall. How was it that he'd been best friends with Micas but had had no idea of this fetish of his? Light bondage could be fun sometimes, Jerrod had even dabbled a little in it himself, but to physically hurt a woman was something else entirely. That was just sick and certainly not the type of behavior befitting a future candidate for high regent.

Maybe that was why he'd kept it hidden from him. Micas must have known he'd never approve and would certainly never have let him get away with violence against a woman. Apparently, there had been more to his friend than met the eye. The only thing that concerned him was what else he would discover.

KIRA MADE HER way through the streets of Klindor, Dax close behind. He'd refused to let her go out alone. Even in broad daylight, crime was high. Klindor hadn't been this bad when they'd first opened the bar, but with all the gaming halls and bars that had opened since, the planet had deteriorated fast.

Dragging in a deep breath, she grimaced. The thick air was damp and moldy. She hated the smell of this place, but scenery-wise, it reminded her of the swamps of Louisiana back home on Earth.

It was terribly hot and muggy. She tugged at her damp shirt and perspiration slid down her back and between her breasts. She needed clothes. Unfortunately, there weren't many places here to get them. They would have to be ordered, so she headed to the only shop in town where she could take care of that.

Mirage had said to bill everything to the bar, that way Kira could keep her name off the order. She was glad she'd thought to open herself an account under another name when they first started the bar.

She'd done it that way to keep the university from finding out one of their professors was half-owner of a hedonistic bar. It would be even worse if they knew she sometimes worked there as well.

She enjoyed it. The exhibitionist in her loved the thrill, the excitement of having sex within a crowd. All her life she'd been fascinated with the idea, but she never actually went through with it until the first night the bar was opened.

She'd become hooked and always spent her summers here, until she was offered the job as assistant professor at the university on Meenus Prime four years ago.

It was affiliated with Harvard, an extremely old university from Earth, and it had been an incredible opportunity. She'd jumped at the chance to finally be recognized for her business knowledge. Last night was her first time back in several years. And she'd certainly jumped right back into things.

She sighed and shook her head, thinking about the gorgeous man who'd driven her crazy. Just remembering the feel of his hands on her, the look in his beautiful sapphire eyes, made her skin tingle. Never in her life had a man affected her like he did. Scowling, she realized she'd even become jealous. Jealous? Why on Earth would she be jealous?

This is so not the time for this.

Finally spotting the store she needed, she put her hand out to open the door, but a firm, tan arm snaked out to block her way. She gasped and came to a complete stop.

"Good afternoon, Kira."

Jerrod.

She'd recognize that voice anywhere if for no other reason than the immediate surge of desire that ran through her veins. Turning her head to her left, she caught his stare and was held hostage by his twinkling eyes. Warm sunlight beamed down and highlighted the streaks of gray within his hair. She loved that salt-and-pepper look. It had been so dark in the bar last night she hadn't noticed it.

She'd been too enthralled with his thick shaft and how good it had felt buried deep within her.

Clearing her throat, she moved back a step and stood ramrod straight. "Jerrod." It was the first time she'd been approached by a customer outside the bar and she wasn't quite sure how to act. The patrons knew what happened in the bar stayed in the bar.

He raised an eyebrow in amusement. "I was just thinking about you and then suddenly, there you were."

She swallowed and glanced around uncomfortably. "Really?"

He took a step toward her, bringing his body close. Too close. She could smell his musky scent, feel the heat radiating off his skin and her whole body sparked with unseen energy. Sexual energy.

Damn. What the hell is the matter with me? I'm a fugitive. "It's nice to see you again. But if you'll excuse me, I have errands I need to take care of."

"It's nice seeing you again?" His eyes narrowed slightly, and she got the impression he didn't care for her cold attitude. Well, neither did she if the truth were known. She desperately wished she wasn't in trouble and could pursue something with this man. He tugged at her heart in ways no one else ever had. And she'd only just met him.

"So that's it?" he asked. "We have incredible sex and then I get the cold brush-off?"

Kira sighed. "What happens in the bar stays there. I don't have relationships with patrons outside Fantasy."

He shrugged. "I'm not asking for a relationship, just a drink. This Klindor sun is killer, so I thought you could use something cold."

"Oh." She licked her lips nervously. "I'm sorry. I'm a little on edge today."

"Perfectly understandable." His lips spread into a charming smile that made her insides melt. "It's just a glass of Earth tea, Kira. I promise I won't jump your bones."

His hand touched her back and sharp pain slammed through her. She gasped and shrank away from him. Immediately, her gaze met his worried one.

She mentally scrambled for something to say. "I leaned too close to the furnace last night and burned my back. It's still very sore."

"Did you have someone look at it?" he asked.

Nodding her head, she glanced toward Dax who stood off to the side, watching her closely. With a trembling hand, she pushed a curl behind her ear. Physically, she wanted to touch Jerrod, run her fingers through his hair, kiss his lips. Kissing was definitely out. It made the sex at the bar too personal—it needed to be kept on a strictly physical level.

Emotionally, she was terrified. In reality she was on the run and shouldn't trust anyone she didn't know. And that included this man, no matter how badly she wanted to.

He brought the back of her hand to his lips, sending a shot of awareness straight to her stomach. "Come on, Gorgeous. Take pity on me."

She gave a very unladylike snort then watched his eyes crinkle in amusement. "I can assure you, pity is the very last thing I would feel."

Actually what she felt was heat, radiating up her arm on a wave. His fingers held hers as he watched her over his knuckles. "You know you want to," he taunted with a grin.

She couldn't help the chuckle that escaped. She was making a huge mistake. She just knew it. "Why is having tea with me so important?"

His gaze never wavered. "I don't know. But I'd like to find out."

Oh, God. She gulped. *I am in such deep shit.* She pulled her fingers from his grasp and sent him a firm look. "Tea only."

He smiled, deepening his dimples, and her resolve chipped away a little more. He held his elbow out, inviting her to slip her hand inside. She did then glanced at Dax over her shoulder. He nodded and continued with them down the street.

Jerrod looked behind him as well and shot her a look of amusement. "Will it be the three of us then?"

She grinned back. "Afraid so."

"Do you really think you need protection from me?"

Jerrod's blood pounded in his ears when she sent him a playful look out of the corner of her eye. "Maybe he's here to protect you."

"Now there's a thought."

She laughed and the sound floated through his senses, again tugging at that spot long buried. How the hell did this happen? He'd never dreamed he'd meet a woman like this here.

"What are you doing here?" he asked without thinking.

He felt the muscles in her arm tense and wondered what brought it on. He knew her story about the furnace had been a lie. What would they need a furnace for in this heat? The investigator side of him knew she was hiding something, but he couldn't imagine what.

She pointed to a table beneath a large, overhanging tree. It sat on the edge of the dock, just outside the tiny restaurant. "This looks like a good spot."

She grabbed a seat, Dax close by at the table behind them. At least he wouldn't be sitting at the same table. As he sat across from her, images of the night before flashed through his mind. She'd felt so perfect in his arms. So right. Was he out of his mind? Was everything moving too fast?

"You never answered me," he said.

Her eyes widened and her face paled just a hair, but before she could reply a waiter came over to take their order.

"I'll have the orange tea," she replied with a smile.

"Same here," Jerrod said. "And one for that gentleman there."

"Yes, sir."

He turned back to Kira and watched her fiddle with the napkin. "Well?"

"Oh, sorry. I'm from Earth."

A small smile tugged at his lips. That wasn't what he'd asked her. "Where on Earth?"

"Louisiana."

"That explains your accent."

She stared at him in surprise. "I have an accent?"

He nodded with a smile. "It's faint, but it's there."

"I thought I had gotten rid of it. Are you from Earth also?" she asked.

"I was born there, in England."

Her eyes filled with censure. "You don't have an English accent."

He grinned. "I wasn't raised there. My father moved us to Vorhala when I was three."

She nodded and resumed fiddling with her napkin. Jerrod reached across and placed his hand over hers, stilling it. "Why are you so nervous, Kira?"

Her gaze remained glued to his hand over hers. He felt the slight tremble in her fingers and frowned. What had happened to her to make her so jittery?

She jerked her hand away and looked out toward the swampland next to them. Turning back to him, her eyes held mischief, and he knew in his gut that she was about to lie.

"You're mistaking an inability to keep still for nervousness."

His lips quirked at her ability to quickly cover herself. "I thought they were one and the same."

"No." Her eyes narrowed slightly. "They're not."

Okay, Kira. I'll give you that one. "You know, you never answered my original question."

She frowned. "You asked me where I was from."

He shook his head. "No, Gorgeous. I asked why you were here."

She reached out and straightened the fork and spoon to her right. "Same reason as everyone else. I'm here to a make a little money." At his look of disbelief, she shrugged. "Okay. A lot of money."

Jerrod laughed and held up his hands. "Okay, I give. If you don't want to tell me that's fine."

"What about you? Why are you here?"

He took a moment to think about his answer, unsure he wanted to tell her the truth just yet. Although for the life of him he wasn't certain why it really mattered. Just something in his gut that told him to tread slowly with her. "I'm looking for something."

She snorted. "Aren't we all."

5

Later that evening, Kira made her rounds about the bar, stocking shelves and putting everything in order. With a mumbled curse, she stopped dead in her tracks, causing Mirage to run into her back.

Kira hissed at the pain but kept her eyes on Jerrod as he walked in. His T-shirt hugged his chest, outlining his pecs and firm abs, and her heart raced at the powerful grace of his movements as he made his way over to a dark corner table. The bar had just opened. What was he doing here so early? Hadn't they just had tea a couple of hours ago? God, the man was going to be a thorn in her side.

"Oh, God, sweetie, I'm so sorry. You okay?"

She turned to face her friend, trying to block out the way Jerrod's bronzed skin glowed like gold under the bar lights. "I'm okay. It was my fault."

Brushing past Mirage, she stomped back to the bar. Her friend's softly spoken "oh" made her turn with a frown.

"What?"

"Well, I was about to ask what made you stop so quickly, then I saw him."

Mirage's face spread into a saucy grin and Kira scowled. "I don't know what you're talking about."

"Yes you do." Mirage glanced over her shoulder at Jerrod. "He's gorgeous and I understand the two of you put on quite a show last night."

Kira shrugged, the heat of a blush spreading across her cheeks. "It had been awhile since I'd had a good fuck. Where did you run off to last night?" She spun and continued on to the bar, Mirage fast on her heels.

"I had something I needed to take care of."

Kira shot her a grin. "Like the doctor?"

This time it was Mirage's turn to blush and Kira's grin widened. "I knew it!"

Mirage shook her head. "It's not what you think."

"Mirage. Would it be so bad if it was?"

"Yes. It would."

Kira's eyes widened. Her friend's blue eyes were downcast, studying something on the bar. Tonight she had her hair piled on her head, a few tiny ringlets framing her face, and Kira saw the love bite just below her ear. When was Mirage going to just admit she loved Jaimee? "Please tell me you don't still have that love-and-marriage hang-up."

Mirage narrowed her eyes. "Stop trying to change the subject. I believe we were talking about you and hot stuff over there." She pointed over her shoulder with her thumb and Kira quickly grabbed it, pulling it down before he saw her.

"Would you stop that?"

"What on Earth has gotten into you?"

"You know what," Kira sighed. "He could be anybody and right now attracting attention is the last thing I need to do. Regardless of how gorgeous the man is." *Or how I feel when I'm with him.*

"I could find out who he is."

"People never use their real names here. You know that."

"You did," Mirage teased with a smirk.

"That was Dax's doing! Which reminds me, I haven't chewed him out for that yet."

"Like that will bother Dax." Mirage studied Jerrod for several minutes. "You know. He looks really familiar."

Kira raised an eyebrow, her nerves jumping. "Familiar how?"

Mirage shrugged. "I'm not sure, but it'll come to me sooner or later." She turned and moved to lean her hips against the back of the bar. Kira shifted to face her, putting her back to Jerrod and the corner table. Which was fine by her. The more she looked at him, the more unnerved she became. Unfortunately, Mirage continued to study him, her brow creased in thought.

"Would you stop staring at him like that? You're going to bring him over here."

"Honey, I've got news for you. If he comes over here it won't be because of me."

"I'm supposed to be hiding out, remember?" Kira hissed in exasperation. What was her friend doing?

Mirage's expression softened. "I know, sweetie. But I also know that sex like that, well . . ."

"What do you mean 'sex like that'?"

"Dax saw the two of you. He saw the connection that you have, whether the two of you realize it or not."

Kira frowned, determined to turn this conversation away from her and Jerrod. "Like the connection between you and Jaimee? I saw the way he looked at you the night I arrived." Mirage rolled her eyes and Kira grinned. "It's not so fun being on the receiving end, is it?"

Mirage pointed to the bar behind Kira. "You have a customer."

With an amused shake of her head, Kira spun around and found herself not two feet from the man she most wanted to avoid. Jerrod. She glanced at her friend and caught the devilish smirk on her face.

Damn you, Mirage.

"Hello, Jerrod. What can I get you?"

"You mean besides you? Alone?"

The grin on his face made her skin tingle. Erotic images of her flat on her back and him buried between her thighs ran through her mind, and she swallowed back a groan. All it took was that smile and she melted, desperate to be in his arms.

"Hmmm, I don't believe I have a drink called 'you alone,'" she replied with a cheeky grin.

"I wasn't talking about a drink, Gorgeous."

"I am."

Jerrod chuckled. "Okay, I get the hint."

"It's a good thing. I would hate to have to get Dax after you."

He tilted his head to the side, studying her. "Would you really do that?"

"Do you really want to know?"

His grin widened and her heart skipped a beat.

"I'll take a Buttery Nipple, preferably yours." When she shot him a glare he winked. "But in the glass is fine for now."

She strolled to the far end of the bar to fix his drink and he followed her, taking a seat at one of the stools close by. Uneasiness swept through her at the way he studied her, his eyes ever watchful, curious.

"It's awfully quiet here tonight."

His softly spoken words almost made her jump, and she took a deep breath to steady her shaking hands. "It's early yet. It'll pick up before too much longer."

She slid the glass across the bar, causing the drink to slosh over the side and onto the deep cherry wood. "Sorry," she mumbled.

"It's okay, Gorgeous."

It made her uncomfortable when he called her that. It wasn't that she didn't like it—she did. Which was a bad thing. "My name's Kira."

A look of startled confusion crossed his features. "I know. But I like calling you 'Gorgeous.' It suits you."

His gaze held hers, seeming to reach clear through to her soul. She glanced away and surveyed the small crowd gathering around the pool table on the far side. Later, she was sure, the table would be used for something other than pool. Bodies would cover the green felt top. Men and women alike would undulate against each other, moan and scream their pleasure.

Kira swallowed as a wave of lust slammed through her. She could see her and Jerrod making use of that table. On her back, her legs hooked over his shoulders as he pushed his thick cock into her over and over.

"Kira?"

"What?" Her startled gaze jerked back to Jerrod, and she blushed at his knowing grin.

"You all right?"

"Yeah, fine." *Kira, you are such a liar.* "I better get back to work."

Grabbing the towel lying on the counter, she quickly wove her way through the growing throng of people to the other side of the bar.

Jerrod's lips twitched in amusement. He wondered what she'd been thinking about while she stared at the pool table. He certainly knew what he'd been imagining. He hadn't been able to stop thinking about her all damn day. Nothing felt right until he came in here and saw her. Just the sight of her, the knowledge she was close by, put him at ease and that more than anything startled him.

One of the other waitresses walked over and with a seductive smile introduced herself as Sky. She was pretty in a young, perky kind of way. Not the classic beauty that Kira possessed. Sky's black hair looked blue under the lights, her brown eyes were framed by black lashes, long and curling upward. He returned her smile then took a sip of his drink.

"Would you like anything other than your drink?"

"Not at the moment, maybe later."

His gaze wandered back toward Kira, who now stood at the pool table talking with a couple of younger men. Something tugged in his chest. Something he didn't like. Why would he care if she talked with other men?

"Got the hots for Kira, huh?"

Startled, he returned his attention back to Sky. "What do you know about her?"

"I'm fairly new, so I don't know her that well. I just know she's half-owner."

Jerrod choked on his sip. "Half-owner?"

"Yeah. Her and Mirage started this bar about six years ago. She's not here much."

"Not here much?" His curiosity was piqued. "What does she do when she's not here?"

"I think she's a professor or something." She shrugged her dainty shoulders. "She just returned a couple of days ago, so I haven't had a chance to really talk to her."

Jerrod's drink froze halfway to his mouth, his heart pounded in his chest. A couple of days ago? He remembered how she'd acted when he'd touched her back earlier in the day. Was Kira the woman he was looking for? The woman who killed Micas?

Ah, hell!

6

SLOWLY STROLLING AROUND the dark bar, Kira nursed her fourth Sexual Frustration. An apt drink for how she felt at the moment. Every time she glanced toward the far end of the long bar, Jerrod was watching her. His gaze raked over her body, sending sparks of awareness to every pore on her flesh.

This is insane!

Avoiding his sensual gaze, she turned her back to him and gulped down the rest of the drink. The alcohol burned her throat, making her wince, but she welcomed the heat. Anything to keep from attacking Jerrod, throwing him on the pool table and having her way with him, running her hands over his tight, hard flesh, inhaling his masculine scent. Just like the threesome there now.

A group had gathered, watching the two women and one man pleasure each other. Threesomes were one of the more popular fantasies. Although she'd never participated in one with two women, observing never failed to turnher on.

Her whole body was on fire and all she could think about was Jerrod's face between her legs, doing to her what the man was doing to the woman spread before him now. The other woman was positioned below and between his legs, his cock moving in and out of her mouth.

Two more women came up, one on each side of the woman on the pool table, their mouths suckling the girl's breasts. A man came behind each of them, lifting their skirts and exposing their wet pussies. One man unzipped his slacks and fucked the woman before him with quick, deep strokes. The other was more patient, taking his time to prepare the woman before slowly sliding deep into her ass.

There were now seven and more joined in. The scent of sex permeated the air, making her nostrils flare. She should turn away but she couldn't. It was like a train wreck, and she wanted desperately to participate. She shook her head. No she didn't. She wanted Jerrod and only Jerrod.

Despite her desire, she remained frozen, unwilling to encourage him. She couldn't shake the feeling she should stay away from him. He was dangerous. Unfortunately, she couldn't put her finger on why.

She caught him, out of the corner of her eye, slowly stalking toward where she stood, like a lion stalking his prey. She didn't look at him. She couldn't. She knew if she did he would see the obvious longing in her eyes, the desire to have something she knew she couldn't.

He came to a stop next to her and she could feel his heat, his breath on the side of her neck. "Do you like watching them?" His whisper sent a shiver down her spine.

She shrugged. "I see this kind of thing every day. It doesn't affect me one way or the other," she lied.

"Liar." His finger brushed over her extended nipple, and she sucked in a breath. "Your reaction gives you away, Kira. Why do you fight it?"

Jerrod was dying. He wanted her so bad he could taste it. It wasn't just physically though. He wanted her in his arms, in his life. He wanted to know everything about her—her likes, her dislikes. But most of all, he wanted her to trust him enough to tell him the truth. Her arrival on Klindor, coupled with a sore back she lied about, was too much of a coincidence. The investigator in him knew something was up, but the man wanted desperately to ignore the mounting evidence.

Leaning over, he buried his face in her long hair and inhaled her vanilla scent. "Do you taste as sweet as you smell, Kira?"

His palm slid up her thigh and under her short skirt, cupping her mound. She wasn't wearing any underwear and her wetness coated his palm. Brushing his finger along her slit, he smiled at her soft moan.

"Jerrod, we . . ."

He pushed a finger into her dripping pussy and her knees buckled. He caught her around the waist, holding her close. "You're a woman of many secrets, aren't you, Gorgeous?"

She nodded then shook her head no. He didn't want to believe this woman was the one he was looking for. Surely a coincidence. Please let it be a coincidence.

He slowly moved his finger in and out, stretching her as he went deeper. "Oh, yes, Jerrod," she whimpered and he almost lost it. To hell with the investigation. At the moment, he just needed to taste her.

Finding a free spot on the other side of the table, he sat her on the edge then lifted her skirt. Her long legs were the color of cappuccino, firm and muscular. He'd never liked women with reed-thin thighs and Kira's were just perfect. Exactly the way he liked them.

She fell to her back and he grabbed her hips, pulling her closer. With her skirt around her waist she was open to him, to anything he desired. And he desired her.

Leaning down, he spread her labia with his fingers and circled her clit with his tongue. He inhaled, dragging her scent into his lungs. Damn, she did taste as good as she smelled. Her hips undulated against his face, her hands sank into his hair, pulling him closer. He was about to burst. His cock throbbed to be buried inside her delectable pussy. She was so wet, so hot. And so damn good.

Another man came forward and lifted her shirt, putting his mouth on her breasts. She arched her back and moaned.

Jerrod wasn't sure he liked another man touching her, though for the life of him, he wasn't sure why. He'd never been jealous in his life, but damn if the emotion didn't suddenly almost bring him to his knees.

Grabbing her hands, he tugged her away from the other man.

Jerrod scowled at him over her shoulder and the man lifted his hands in surrender, shifting to horn in on someone else.

He turned back to Kira and caught her startled expression. "I didn't like him touching you," he said simply.

Her lips lifted in a slight smile, and she touched the side of his face with her palm. He turned his head and kissed it, letting out a ragged sigh.

"Are you running, Kira?" His gut clenched, waiting for her answer. Her eyes widened in fear then clouded over, a brick wall firmly in place.

She licked her lips. "Why do you ask that?"

He shrugged. The middle of a bar, his cock rock hard and aching to be inside her was not the right time or place for this—he knew better. He needed to get her alone. "Just a sixth sense." A long silence passed between them. "I can help you," he whispered.

Kira stared at him, her insides waging a war. She had no idea who he was. She couldn't tell him, but she wanted to so badly. There was something about him that made him seem like he would be easy to talk to, easy to trust.

What would he do if he knew she had killed someone? Would he stare at her in disgust or fear? Or would he turn her in? She couldn't risk it. She wouldn't. Until she decided what she was going to do, she couldn't get attached to this man. There was no point.

He moved his lips close to hers, his hands gently framed her face. She still sat on the pool table, his hips sandwiched between her thighs. His tenderness and the . . . was that love in his eyes? Fear? "Let's get out of here. Go somewhere and talk. Whatever it is, Kira, I can help you."

"No." She shook her head, her lower lip trembling. "You can't help me."

"Why don't you give me the chance to try? Damn it, Kira. You can't keep running."

Her stomach rolled with nausea. *Oh, God. What did he know?* "I'm not running."

"Kira," he sighed in exasperation.

"Let me down." She shoved at his chest, hard, but he didn't move.

"No."

"I'm not running, Jerrod. I'm here to help Mirage. Now let me down."

When he continued to stare at her, she shoved again. "Do I have to yell for Dax?"

With a sigh, he stepped back, allowing her down. Without looking back, she fled up the stairs to the office level. She heard Jerrod behind her, yelling for her to stop. She glanced over her shoulder and saw Dax step between him and the bottom of the stairs. Jerrod ran a hand through his hair and scowled. "Damn it, Dax!" he snapped.

Shutting the door behind her, she wobbled to the desk and sank into the chair. Her lower lip quivered, and she swallowed down the tears that threatened. She had to get out of here. It was the only thing to do.

She thought back to his comment about not liking the other man touching her, the jealousy shining in his eyes. In some ways, the idea of belonging to only him sent a wave of warmth through her, but she quickly pushed that nonsense aside. She didn't have a clue what tomorrow would bring. For all she knew, she could lose her freedom in the snap of a finger. She had to get a grip on her emotions and forget Jerrod.

Mirage burst through the door and Kira jumped, placing her hand over her chest. "Jeez, Mirage. You scared the crap out of me." Mirage was pale, her eyes wide with fear. "You all right?"

"I just remembered where I know him from."

"Who?" Kira asked, dread gripping her heart.

"Jerrod."

Kira sat straighter, every hair standing on end. She had a feeling she wasn't going to like what Mirage was about to say.

"I've seen his picture in the papers. Don't you read the papers, Kira?"

She shook her head. "No, you know I never read the news. Why? Who is he?"

"He's Meenus Prime's lead investigator and best friend to the man you killed."

"What?" she croaked. *Oh, fuck!*

"We've got to get you out of here. Now."

7

JERROD STROLLED ALONG the dock, his hands clenching and un-clenching at his sides. Kira had once again gone into hiding. He'd tried to get into Fantasy and see her that morning, but Dax had said she was still sleeping.

He'd actually thought about using his position, flashing his badge and demanding to be let in, but changed his mind. If Kira was the woman he was searching for, the last thing he wanted to do was scare her off—if he hadn't already.

Once he realized he wasn't getting in to see Kira, he went back to his room at the local hotel and sent Simas a message to contact him as soon as possible.

Five minutes later Simas called him back. "You want me to re-search Fantasy Bar? What the hell for?"

"Just do it, Simas. I have my reasons. I'm particularly interested in a woman by the name of Kira."

"All this for a woman?"

"Possibly the woman we're looking for," Jerrod growled, and Simas immediately nodded his head, agreeing to get started right away.

So now here he was, walking along the dock, staring at the swampland that bordered Klindor City. This town was a lot like the old city of Earth called Las Vegas, but gambling had been outlawed there, which had put the city and several more like it out of business.

Some of Earth's gamblers and casino owners had moved here, building even larger casinos and brothels atop floating docks.

Klindor had flourished, but it had also become home to some dangerous people.

A hot wind blew, and Jerrod adjusted the sunglasses on his face. It was almost time to call Simas back. Hopefully, he'd found something. Jerrod just hoped it wasn't what he thought it might be. He'd become attached to Kira and the last thing he wanted to do was arrest her for murder.

KIRA THREW A few more outfits and a couple of sweaters in the bag then zipped it closed.

"Do you think you have enough?" Mirage asked.

"For a couple of days. Once I get there I'll get more clothes."

"I slipped some extra money in the hidden compartment underneath."

"Mirage," Kira said, shaking her head. "I'm fine. I have enough money. Besides, you've already given me most of your clothes."

Mirage frowned and handed her the green sweater that went with the slacks Kira wore. "You won't be able to touch your account on Earth, so you'll need some extra 'just in case' money. Don't argue with me."

"Yes, mother," Kira sighed.

"It's not funny. I'm terrified for you. It's not a coincidence that he's here."

"I know it's not. But maybe I should tell him what happened." If he'd found her here, he would find her wherever she went. But if he knew she was guilty, wouldn't he have already arrested her?

"You killed Micas Lordakin, right-hand man to the high regent, not to mention candidate for the next election. They would never believe he almost killed you. He's Meenus Prime's quintessential golden child."

Kira sighed. "You're probably right."

Mirage walked over and placed something in her hand. "Here's the key to my house on Portaka 3. It's right on the beach and secluded. You should be safe there until we figure out what to do."

"You really shouldn't know where I'm going."

Mirage waved her hand. "Don't worry. I'll be fine. And so will you. Now hurry, the transport leaves in twenty minutes."

Kira hugged her friend, her eyes closing against the tears that threatened. How in the hell had her life become such a mess?

"I'll see you soon," she whispered.

JERROD HAD NO sooner walked into his room than his communicator began to beep. He flipped his computer screen open and hit the enter key. Immediately, Simas' image appeared.

"What did you find?" Jerrod demanded.

"I've got two things I need to discuss with you. Neither one you're going to like."

"First things first. Did you find out anything aboutKira?"

"Yes. I checked into the bar, but neither of the women that own it is named Kira. After some digging, I found out that your Kira used an alias on the deed."

"Wonder why?" Jerrod mumbled.

"I can almost guess. Kira is none other than Kiranda Vorkin. Professor Kiranda Vorkin."

Jerrod sat straighter, trying to think. "Why does that name sound familiar?"

"She's the newly promoted, youngest, I might add, head professor of the Intergalactic Trade Department at the university on Meenus Prime."

Jerrod nodded, inwardly impressed. He'd heard of her. She was considered a brilliant mind when it came to business. "Sounds like she used an alias so the university wouldn't know about it."

"That's my guess. I also contacted her department. They said she hasn't been to work in almost two weeks, which would put her disappearance at about the time Micas took the woman to his apartment."

Jerrod sighed. This wasn't looking good.

"Before we go any further, there's something you need to see."

"What?" Jerrod asked with trepidation.

"I'm sending it through now."

Jerrod made the window with Simas' real-time image smaller to allow room for the digital video coming through. As the file downloaded, Simas continued to talk. "We found a hidden camera in the ceiling of Micas' bedroom. Everything he did to the woman is on there, including his death. You were right, Jerrod. It was self-defense."

Jerrod remained silent and hit the play button. With growing dread, he watched as Micas beat a woman repeatedly. He never raped her but took her blood and coated his cock, then masturbated until he came all over her bloody back. Bitter bile rose in his throat, and he grimaced. How in the hell had he missed this?

"You all right, Jerrod?"

"Yeah," he croaked, unable to take his eyes from the sick images.

"There's five more of these videos. All the women but this one died."

He'd heard Simas, but he'd stopped listening, paying more attention to the woman on the screen. She was fiddling with her bindings and was almost loose.

Finally one hand was free, and she lifted the black cloth from her eyes. Her nervous glances kept straying toward the door, watching for her captor to return. There was no sound on the tape but he could imagine her anxious whimpers, her frightened sobs. He gritted his teeth, trying to block the sound.

She was free, and he gripped the arm of the chair as she searched frantically for something to use as a weapon. Opening a drawer, she pulled out a gun then pointed it at Micas the second he walked in the room. When Micas stepped toward her to take it away, she fired, knocking him back onto the foot of the bed. Just like Jerrod had found him. Her hands were shaking so badly he was amazed she'd even hit him.

He still hadn't seen her face. She hadn't looked up fully to the ceiling, but there were other parts of her body he recognized. The thighs in particular. His instincts screamed it was Kira, but he needed to see her face to be sure. Finally, she glanced toward the ceiling and the hidden camera. His gut clenched at the frightened look on her face, the tears streaming down her cheeks. To him there

was no doubt. Even though the image was slightly blurred, he knew
it was Kira.

Damn it all to hell!

"Have you shown this to anyone else?" Jerrod demanded.

"No. There were two other investigators there when videos were
discovered, but I'm the only one who knows what's on them."

"Sit on them for a couple of days." Jerrod stood and started to
close the lid to his computer.

"Not until you tell me why."

Jerrod sighed. How the hell did he explain this? He wasn't
even sure what he was going to do. "If this were to get out, Simas,
whether it was self-defense or not, the woman would be ruined. She
doesn't deserve this."

"It's Kira, isn't it?"

"Yeah. I won't let Micas destroy everything Kira has worked for.
Not like this."

Simas scowled. "Damn it, Jerrod. What the hell were you thinking falling in love with her?"

Jerrod frowned at his friend's image. "I didn't say I had." Had
he?

Taking a deep breath, Simas ran his hand down his face.

"Look, Simas. I honestly don't have a clue how I feel. I only
know I need to talk to Kira before I go any further. I need two days.
Not because I'm your boss, but because I'm your friend."

Simas nodded, although his eyes shone with reluctance. "You've
got them."

"I NEED TO see Kira," Jerrod demanded as Dax tried to block him
from entering. This time, he wasn't going to take no for an answer.

"Sir, I told you . . ."

"I know what you told me, damn it." Jerrod opened his wallet
and showed his badge. Dax's eyes widened, but his resolve to keep
him out remained if his stiffening body was any indication. "I want
to see Kira, Dax. Now. You can't keep me out and you know it."

"She's not here," a soft voice replied from behind Dax.

Jerrod peered around the tall giant and scowled at Mirage. She wrung her hands but her chin was high, her stance determined. "Where is she, Mirage?"

She nodded to Dax and he stepped aside, letting Jerrod enter.

"She left. She had business to attend to somewhere else. I don't know when she'll be back."

"I need to know where she went and I think you know why."

Her chin went up another notch. "I told you, I don't know."

He stepped closer and placed a hand on her shoulder, his voice soft as a whisper. "I know what happened, Mirage."

"How?"

"We found a hidden video. He'd recorded the whole thing. I know it was self-defense."

Her shoulders sagged and she glanced at him with uncertainty. Desire to help her friend and desire to keep her safe were more than likely waging a war within her. "She almost didn't make it here," she whispered. "He beat her so badly—her back will never be the same."

"I know."

"How do I know that you're not going to cover up his activities and put this all on her?"

Jerrod sighed. He didn't have a clue how he would convince her. "I'm not going to let anything happen to her, Mirage. I promise. I'll make sure the high regent knows what happened. But it's imperative I talk with her now."

8

Kira walked along the beach. The deep blue ocean lapped onto the sand, covering her bare feet. The water was warm, more so than the oceans of Earth. The thermal core of the planet kept the liquid heated to perfect bath temperature.

An offshore breeze blew, whipping her hair into her face. She brushed it back and glanced over her shoulder toward the house embedded in the cliff.

Mirage had incredible taste and had designed her house to blend into the scenery. And blend it did. If you didn't know what to look for, you'd never know it was there.

It became one with the cliff face—only the glass was visible and then you had to really look for it. The roof was dirt and grass with a small path down the side of the hill to the entrance.

Once inside, one was greeted with a six-foot waterfall that fell from the rock wall into a small pool surrounded by tropical plants indigenous to both here and Earth. Gray metal lights hung from the stone ceilings, casting a soft glow against the tile floor. Colorful rugs were thrown about to add color and warmth. To the right were the two bedrooms, each with large windows that overlooked the surf below.

The glass lightened to a soft gray during the day but darkened to black at night so the light from inside wouldn't be visible to someone on the beach.

The perfect hideaway.

Turning back toward the ocean, she inhaled the salty air and closed her eyes. The waves crashing against the shore relaxed her and she smiled as the warm water slapped against her calves.

She felt safe here, but she couldn't keep her mind off Jerrod. Last night she'd dreamt of him. His hands caressing her skin, his lips nibbling at the sensitive spot behind her ear. Their bodies fit so well together and she'd awoken with a need she came nowhere near to appeasing. Just thinking about it made tingles run along her flesh, and she shivered.

She never should have had sex with him. She would compare every man from now on with his gentleness, his passion. She knew in her heart no one would ever measure up.

What men? I'll spend the rest of my life hiding.

She spent a couple of hours that morning investigating Jerrod. The Galactic Net was quite a source of information. Anything and everything you could ever want was right there at your fingertips. It turned out Jerrod was quite the investigator, several times receiving the Golden Star for capturing galactic fugitives no one else seemed to be able to catch. It had even been rumored he might run for regent elect himself. If there was ever a man out of her league it was Jerrod Scollin.

Taking a deep breath, she made the decision that she couldn't live like this. She had to do something. Maybe she should just suck it up, turn herself in and pray for the best.

"Penny for your thoughts."

She stiffened, her breath catching in her chest at the softly spoken words. Her eyes opened to stare out at the waves. A storm loomed just beyond the horizon, but the electricity in the air was nothing compared to the fear that snaked down her spine.

Please let me be hearing things.

Slowly, she turned and almost fell to the sand in a heap.

Jerrod.

"I think you and I need to have a talk, don't you?"

An overwhelming desire to run gripped her, and she stumbled back a step.

Jerrod shook his head, his mouth set in a firm line. "Don't, Kira." He took a small step toward her, his outstretched hand a lifeline she wanted desperately to grab. "I can help you, sweetheart. Just trust me."

Could she trust him? She wanted to so badly but was still so afraid. "Why should I? You were his friend."

His hand dropped and guilt clouded his eyes, making them darken to navy. "He may have been my friend but I would never have condoned his actions."

She swallowed. "How did you find out it was me?"

"There was a video camera in the ceiling. It caught the whole thing."

"Oh, God." She felt sick. Jerrod had been witness to her humiliation, her shame and desperation. She took a deep breath, trying to calm her stomach.

"Kira," he whispered and took a step closer.

She shook her head and jumped back. How did she know he wasn't just like him? "Don't. How did you find me?"

"Mirage."

A muscle jerked in her cheek and she clenched her hands. Had Mirage sent her here on purpose, knowing Jerrod would only be a few hours behind? Why would her friend do that?

"She just told you?"

The corners of his mouth lifted in a slight smile. "She tried to keep your whereabouts from me, but I assured her I could help."

"And she believed you?" she asked incredulously.

"Yes." He nodded. "She only wants what's best for you, Kira."

"And she thinks you're what's best for me?" Anger now rolled through her. She felt as though she was on a roller coaster—emotions up and down, uncontrollable. She felt helpless.

"Right now I'm all you've got, kiddo. Whether I'm best or not, I'm it."

She stared at him, her eyes pleading for him to understand. "How do I know I can trust you? I don't even know you. How do I know you won't do the same sick things?"

He raised an eyebrow. "We've had sex, Kira. Did I hurt you at all then?"

"We were in public. In a damn bar!"

He opened his mouth then closed it, his eyes narrowing, his forehead crinkling into a frown. "I want to help you out of this mess." He spread his arms and sighed. "I don't know what to do to convince you of that. You just have to take a chance."

"HERE, SWEETHEART."

Jerrod handed Kira a cup of hot coffee. His chest tightened when her small, trembling hands gripped the mug. Right now he could kill Micas with his bare hands if he weren't already dead. What the hell had made him do those things, and more importantly, why the hell hadn't Jerrod seen it?

"How are you holding up, kiddo?" He sat on the sofa beside her. Lightning flashed, illuminating the living room and the uncertainty in her eyes.

"I've been better." She gave him a faint smile and took a sip of her coffee. She grimaced, making Jerrod smile apologetically.

"Sorry," he said. "My assistant usually makes the coffee."

"I can see why." She chuckled softly and set the cup on the table.

She was so beautiful, so fragile. He hadn't stopped thinking about her since the first time he saw her. It wasn't just the sex. There was something about her, something that drew him to her, gave him peace. He wanted to know everything about her, but even more than that, he wanted her to trust him, open up to him.

"How in the world did you and Mirage come up with a place like Fantasy Bar?"

She eyed him in surprise then her brow creased in thought. She was so cute when she did that. He wanted to smooth out the tiny lines with the tip of his finger.

"It started out as a joke. We were laughing over some of the crazy names of drinks and wondered what it would be like to have a place where sex was based on your drink order. Mirage and I made the idea a reality." She shrugged. "There's really not a whole lot more to tell. We just hit the market with something fresh and new that took off."

"It was a brilliant idea. Have you thought about opening more of them? The small planet of Eden would be a good place. Or even Sincta 5."

"We've talked about it. We believe Dax would be the perfect person to open the next one, but he's a little reluctant. He doesn't want to leave us."

"Can't say I blame him." Jerrod grinned and a blush spread up her cheeks. He took a sip of his coffee. She chuckled when he grimaced and set the cup back down. "Maybe you should make the coffee next time."

"Definitely." Her smile faded and she wrung her hands, nervously twisting the small pearl ring on her finger. "Why me? Why did he do this to me? He didn't know me from Adam." Her eyes widened as an idea dawned. "Do you think he knew me from the bar?"

"No." Jerrod shook his head. "I checked. Micas had never been to Klindor."

"What makes you think he didn't use an alias?"

"He had plans to run for regent. He wouldn't have risked going there. It was too public." The second he said it, he realized how lame that was. "What the hell am I saying? He made every mistake there is with you, an alias wouldn't have been out of the question."

"What mistakes and why would he have made them?"

Jerrod wasn't sure what to tell her. He had a theory, but they would probably never know if he was right. "I have an idea."

"Want to share?"

Taking a deep breath, he stood and paced to the counter separating the kitchen and living room. He leaned on the waist-high tile countertop and stared at the bowl of Portakin fruit. Picking up a small purple berry, he twisted it between his fingers. "I believe Micas wanted to get caught."

"Why? Because of the mistakes?"

"Yeah."

"Maybe he just didn't know what he was doing."

"No." Jerrod dropped the berry and ran a hand through his hair. Guilt once again slammed through him. "He knew what he was doing. His first mistake was that you're high profile. You would have been missed. Micas watched the news daily, so he would have known who you were."

"You didn't."

He grinned sheepishly. "I've been out of the loop, so to speak. I'd been on Earth for several months and hadn't kept track of what was happening on Meenus Prime. But I know Micas would have and he would have known who you were."

She shook her head, confusion creasing her brow. "I still don't understand."

Jerrod began to pace. "He kidnapped you at the university, right?"

"Yeah, how did you know that?"

"Your car is still there and Micas' fingerprints are all over it."

"Oh." Her eyes widened in surprise. "I'd forgotten all about my car."

"I think he left it there on purpose. Micas isn't . . . or wasn't, stupid. He knew a lot about my job and how I did things. What I looked for. Your car would have been something I'd have investigated and he would have known I would have dusted for prints. What do you remember about that night?"

"Not much. He hit me from behind, tied me up. Most of the two days are still a blur. I do remember that we passed a doorman on the way in. He actually stopped to talk with him."

Jerrod raised an eyebrow. "Don't you think that's a little strange? That was his second mistake. Once someone noticed you were missing, your picture would be all over the news. I think he was counting on the doorman remembering you and reporting it."

"I don't know, Jerrod." She shook her head with a frown. "How do you know he would have reported it?"

"I don't. But there are other slips he made. Your fingerprints were all over his house, his car. My assistant found your purse in the trash bin in the basement. You were also the only one he kept alive for more than a day."

Her face paled and she swallowed, raising her shaking fingers to her chest. "Oh, my God! There were more?"

"Yeah, five that we know of for sure. All died the same day he brought them home. My guess is he wanted to keep you alive so we would find you there."

"But I killed him before any of that could happen."

"Yes. When Micas didn't show up for his appointments that morning his assistant went to his apartment and found the body. I was the first one they called. The doorman had followed you and saw you board the transport for Klindor. That's how I tracked you, but I wasn't sure it was you until I saw the video."

She closed her eyes and covered her mouth. Her face paled and protectiveness swept through him. He hated to see her like this, all the spunk gone, defeated.

Jerrod grabbed her hand, pulling it away from her trembling lips. "I'm so sorry he did this to you, Kira. In some way I feel responsible."

She opened her watery eyes and stared at him. "Why? You didn't make him pick up the whip."

"No. But I didn't see this side of him. I should have. What kind of investigator am I that I can't even see the signs in my best friend?"

"Because he was your best friend," she whispered.

How had it gone from him comforting her, to the other way around? Leaning forward, he kissed her cheek and inhaled the scent of salty sea air on her flesh. She stiffened and pulled away, confusion and wariness darkening her gaze.

"What now?" she asked hesitantly.

A wry smile tugged at his lips as he brushed a stray curl behind her ear. "I'm going to do my best to keep your name out of this. I don't want your life ruined because of him."

"Why would you do that?"

He ran his thumb along her bottom lip, thinking about his next words and just how much he would tell her. "Because you did what you had to do and shouldn't be punished for it. There's something about you that touches me somewhere I haven't been touched in a long time. I can't stop thinking about you and I want us to have the opportunity to see where this goes."

She bit her lower lip and his cock tightened. This was the wrong time for sex. They had things they needed to talk about, but the lure of her full lips tugged at him, made his pulse quicken with the need to feel her mouth against his.

"I'm scared," she whispered. "What if they don't agree? Because of the bar, what if they think I went with him willingly?"

"It's all on the tape, sweetheart. It's obvious you were fighting him. I'll take care of this," he whispered as he took her face between his palms. "I promise."

A single tear slipped free and he kissed it away. The salty taste lingered in his mouth. When she didn't back away he placed another kiss on her cheek, her skin soft and warm beneath his lips. Slowly, he worked his way to the corner of her mouth. Her lips parted in response and the smell of mint and coffee floated across his cheek.

"I want to kiss you, Kira. This isn't the bar, and this is a hell of a lot more than just sex."

Her gaze met his. Her green eyes were filled with passion and just a hint of fear.

"I'm not Micas," he whispered. "I would never do what he did."

"I know."

She licked her lips and he closed his eyes, swallowing his groan. He'd spent his whole adult life jumping from one woman to another. Not one of them had made him feel the things Kira did. He wanted to protect her, take care of her.

He wanted more than just sex. He wanted to hold her and watch the surf play across the sand, talk about her ideas, her desires. He just wanted to be with her and he'd do whatever it took to keep her safe.

He waited, their gazes locked. The indecision slowly faded from her eyes and she leaned forward, gently touching her lips to his.

9

His lips were soft against hers, coaxing, and she shuddered, wanting so much more. For days she'd wondered what his kiss would be like. His tongue touched her lower lip, encouraging her to open for him, to allow him entrance into her mouth.

With a sigh, she parted her lips and welcomed the onslaught of his kiss. The soft texture of his tongue glided around hers, teasing, stroking, sending a stream of desire coursing through her veins. His mouth molded to hers, his taste all consuming. She sagged against his chest, her fingers fisting in the soft cotton of his shirt.

His groan rumbled in his chest, vibrating against her hands, and she answered with a moan of her own. One hand buried itself in her hair, holding her steady while his tongue plundered her mouth, exploring every crevice.

Pulling away, he laid his forehead against hers and brushed his fingers across her cheek.

"I want to do it right this time," he whispered. "Where's a bed?"

She let out a small laugh. "Down the hall on the other side of the center fountain."

He stood and grasped her hand, pulling her down the hall. She followed him into the massive suite and jumped as a flash of lightning lit up the room. She wasn't afraid of storms, but the ferocity of the ones here made her jittery.

Trying to take her mind off the weather, she glanced around the room. She had actually been staying in the smaller one. This room just seemed too big for one person.

A king-size bed took up the far wall opposite the massive

window, its deep blue satin sheets and comforter a stark contrast to the dark rock of the wall behind it. Other than a dresser, there wasn't much here.

Another flash of lightning flickered and she glanced outside. The sky was almost black, the clouds a menacing swirl of dark cotton. The ocean waves were angrily slapping the shore, the foam breaking against the rocks.

She hugged her arms around her chest while Jerrod lit the candles on the dresser, bathing the room in soft light. "Does the storm frighten you?" he asked softly as his arms encircled her waist from behind.

She leaned back, the warmth of his chest seeping into her. He rested his chin on her shoulder and she smiled.

"For the most part I like them, but sometimes the sudden crack of thunder can startle me."

"You're safe here." The back of his fingers brushed her neck and she wanted to purr like a contented kitten. "Right here in my arms."

For a moment they remained by the window, each lost in their own thoughts. Her fingertips trailed along his forearm. The scent of jasmine-scented candles filled the room, mixing with Jerrod's masculine, woodsy smell. Closing her eyes, she inhaled the erotic combination.

"You're so beautiful when you smile."

She opened her eyes and caught his reflection in the glass as he watched over her shoulder. His fingers tugged on the buttons at the hem of her shirt, slowly releasing one then working his way to the next. His hand skimmed across the flesh of her stomach, making her muscles twitch. Finally, the last button was free and he parted her shirt, revealing her bare breasts. His palms brushed over her nipples in small circles and they hardened beneath his touch.

With a soft moan, she rested her head against his shoulder. His teeth grazed the sensitive spot behind her ear, setting her body on fire.

"I want you, Kira." His hot breath brushed along her flesh and she sighed, arching her back, putting her breasts more fully into his hands.

He squeezed and she moaned softly. His hands moved to her shoulders to push her shirt down and she stiffened. "Jerrod."

"Shh," he whispered as he slid the shirt down her arms. She closed her eyes, waiting for the shocked gasp to escape his lips, but it never came. His fingers trailed along her scars, soothing her heated skin.

"Oh, baby. I'm so sorry he did this to you." He kissed one of the scars and she melted at his tenderness. "But in some ways, I'm not." His lips moved higher, skimming across her shoulder. "I would have never met you if he hadn't."

The backs of his fingers brushed the side of her neck, sending goose bumps along her flesh. "So gorgeous," he groaned before turning her chin with his fingers and capturing her lips in a kiss she felt clear to her toes.

She wanted him so much. Her pussy throbbed and juices flowed, coating her panties. She moaned and turned to face him, her arms wrapping around his neck, pulling him closer. His strong arms circled the small of her back, pressing her stomach against his thick cock. Every pore in her body hummed with need. She knew how good he would feel and she was desperate to get him inside her. She wanted him filling her, stretching her.

She shifted, rubbing herself along his length and he moaned deep in his chest. "Damn, Gorgeous, you're killing me."

She chuckled seductively and pulled him with her to the bed. With a light shove, he pushed her to the middle then fell on top of her, his warm weight pressing her into the cool comforter.

Spreading her legs, she moaned into his kiss when he ground his hips against her throbbing pussy, teasing her, making her hungry for more.

Moving his lips lower, he cupped her breast. His tongue slowly circled her nipple and she fisted her hands into the blanket, trying not to scream in frustration. "Jerrod."

"Patience, Gorgeous."

With deliberate slowness he covered the hard nipple and sucked it into his hot mouth. She squealed, the pleasure bordering on pain.

The fingers of his other hand worked lower, unbuttoning her slacks before slipping inside her panties to fondle her sensitive clit.

"You're wet, Kira," he whispered against the skin of her neck. "But I want you wetter."

She groaned, wondering how in the hell she could get any hornier than she already was.

Rising up, he pulled her slacks and underwear off, dropping them to the floor with a playful grin that set her heart racing wildly.

"You're still dressed," she pouted playfully.

He crooked a finger. "Then come undress me."

She sat up with a smile, anxious to finally see his naked flesh. Her fingers trembled in impatience as she pulled at the buttons of his shirt. In aggravation, she tugged, popping the buttons free in her haste. They pinged against the rock and floor tile, sounding loud in the silent room.

Biting her lower lip, she trailed her hands along his massive chest, tan from the sun, hard and bulging with muscle. His skin was smooth, hairless, and his chocolate brown nipples hardened beneath her touch. Moving lower, she grinned when his washboard abs jerked beneath her fingers.

Grabbing the button of his slacks, she worked it loose then slid the pants down his hips while he removed his shirt and tossed it across the room. His hard cock sprang free and she encircled him with her hand just below the purple head. He put his hand over hers, moving it up and down in a slow pumping motion. A drop of pre-cum escaped and she rubbed it around his head of his cock. She put her finger in her mouth and licked it off, meeting his heated gaze.

Jerrod dragged in a ragged breath. Her finger in her mouth, licking his cum, was almost his undoing. Damn, he wanted her.

"Lie back," he instructed, his voice rough with need.

She smiled seductively, stretching her body out along the bed. The woman had one hell of a body. All soft curves, smooth skin, and those breasts. He could play with those things all day. He dropped his gaze between her legs and smiled at the patch of hair just above her pussy. She was definitely a true blonde. The golden curls glistened with her juices. Juices he wanted to taste again.

Settling on his knees in the middle of her splayed thighs, he lifted her knees and bent to lick along her slit. She hissed and bucked her hips toward his face.

"Like that, Gorgeous?"

"Yes," she groaned as he pushed one finger deep into her dripping pussy. Removing it, he placed it in his mouth, licking her juices from his knuckle.

"You are such a tease," she admonished.

"Tease, huh?" He chuckled and once again lowered his head. "I'll show you a tease."

With infinite slowness, he separated the lips of her sex and gently licked, barely touching her swollen clit before retreating. Her hips undulated in silent invitation. Her whimpers spurred him on. She was so sweet, so fucking hot. It took every bit of willpower he had not to plunge into her and bury himself deep. He knew from experience it would be pure heaven. Her tight walls would squeeze him, milking his cock dry.

He rose up partially and watched her face as he pushed two fingers into her wet passage. Her lips parted as she gulped in air, her face flushed pink in her rising passion.

He switched to the tight bud of her anus and gently slid his fingers in while his tongue circled her clit.

"Jerrod, damn it," she groaned. "Please."

It was all he could take. Removing his fingers, he settled between her thighs. He toyed with the opening of her pussy with the head of his shaft, teasing her and himself. Her hips pushed forward, taking him part of the way inside her.

"Oh, fuck!" he shouted, then plunged balls deep.

She screamed and lifted her legs higher, dragging him deeper. Immediately, he began to move, grinding against her clit on the downward thrust. She moved with him, met every thrust with one of her own. They fit together so perfectly he never wanted it to end.

Pausing, he lifted her legs over his shoulders and drove deeper. She whimpered, her fingers fisting in the sheet by her head. He kept his movements slow, gentle, until he felt the beginning throbs of her climax. Her muscles rippled along his shaft and he couldn't hold it any longer. With a growl, he increased his rhythm, plunging harder, faster.

"Yes, oh yes," Kira yelled. Her whole body tensed beneath him.

With one final plunge, he came with her, emptying his seed deep within her. Every muscle in his body quaked with the intensity of his release. He'd never felt anything like it.

Her legs lowered to cradle his hips within the warm cocoon of her thighs, her hands feathered along his back. With a sigh, he rested his forehead against hers.

"I could stay like this forever." His eyes opened with a start. *Did I just say that out loud?* Meeting her gaze, he grinned sheepishly. "You're one hell of a woman, Miss Kira."

She smiled. "It's the afterglow talking."

He chuckled. "That's one hell of an afterglow."

Rolling to his side, he pulled her with him, wrapping his arms around her in a protective embrace. They had so much they needed to talk about, feelings they needed to explore. Or at least ones he needed to explore. She'd given no real indication she had any feelings for him at all, other than passion.

Tomorrow, he thought as his eyes closed and he drifted into sleep.

10

KIRA AWOKE WITH a start, her frightened gaze roaming around the still-dark room. Small, quick images from her dream floated through her mind, but never close enough to catch or see clearly. Someone else had been in the room with Micas. She'd thought it before but she was certain now. She didn't know who but she'd heard his voice. Clear, deep and evil.

She shivered and tried to push the sound from her mind. Jerrod lay beside her, still asleep. Deciding not to wake him, she headed to the kitchen to start coffee and breakfast. She'd had no idea if what she had dreamt had been what actually happened. She still remembered so little of those two days. Maybe someday it would all come back, but what if the other man was still out there, looking for her?

Stopping in the doorway, her heart leapt at the sudden thought that came to mind. Jerrod? She stared at him in the bed. He lay on his back, the sheet around his waist. She watched the slow rise and fall of his chest in sleep, one arm thrown over his forehead, the other across his waist.

No. It wasn't Jerrod. It couldn't be Jerrod. The voice wasn't the same. Trying to steady her racing heart, she continued to the kitchen.

Standing at the counter, cutting fruit and watching the sunrise over the ocean, she hit the knife blade against the cutting board a little harder than necessary. The bang echoed through the room and she froze, waiting to see if Jerrod had heard it. When it remained silent, she continued making breakfast, her heart heavy with confusion.

She couldn't stop thinking about last night, about the things he made her feel. Was she in love with him? She didn't know. She'd never been in love. She'd spent her whole adult life worrying about her career. Men were on the backburner, unless it was sex. Then it was get in, get some then get out. Which is what made the bar such an incredible idea. No one expected anything out of you beyond the moment.

But Jerrod had changed everything. For the first time in her life she wanted more than just the moment. She wanted what they'd shared last night. It had been sweet, tender and so hot.

Jerrod came up behind her and wrapped his arms around her waist. His body was warm and she sagged against him, melting into his embrace.

"Good morning, Gorgeous." He buried his face in her neck and inhaled. "Mmmm, you smell good. I missed you in my arms when I awoke."

A small smile curved her lips. "I couldn't sleep so I thought I would make us some breakfast. Are you hungry?"

"I'm starving," he drawled, sleep making his deep voice sexy. His palms slid up and cupped her breasts. A shot of desire went straight to the pit of her stomach. Taking a steadying breath, she brushed his hands away and turned to face him. "I meant for food, Romeo."

"Darn." His lips spread into a sexy grin, making her want to sink to the floor in a puddle. "And here I thought you were making a pass at me."

"Making a pass, huh?" She held up a piece of pineapple and placed it on his tongue. "What on Earth would give you the impression I would want to make a pass at you?"

He chewed, his eyes crinkling with mischief. "Maybe," he mumbled as his arms wrapped around the small of her back, pulling her close, "it was all the begging you did last night."

She stiffened with an indignant frown. "I did not beg."

He chuckled and kissed her forehead. "We'll call it a . . . soft pleading."

She halfheartedly swatted his chest, making him chuckle. "I have coffee made if you'd like some."

"I'd love coffee."

She pointed to the counter on the other side of the room. "There are cups by the pot."

While his back was to her, she took a moment to admire his tight butt in the slacks he wore. He'd left his chest bare and the muscles of his back rippled as he moved. The early morning sunlight landed across his shoulders, making them appear golden and absolutely perfect. Swallowing a wave of lust, she turned back to the fruit just in time for him to face her.

"So what's with the hidden house?" he asked.

She glanced at him over her shoulder. He stood with his hips leaning against the counter, one arm holding the coffee cup to his lips, the other tucked under his biceps. God, he looked good. His slacks hung just below his belly button, showing off one hell of a muscled stomach. Her gaze met his and he raised an eyebrow in amusement.

She quickly cleared her throat and kept cutting the fruit. "It's Mirage's. When she was a little girl her dad used to beat her and her mother. Everywhere they ran, he found them. As an adult, she tried a relationship one time and ended up with someone like her dad. Thank God, she got away from him. Once the bar was successful, she had this house built. It's her safety blanket. The one place she can run to when she feels trapped or afraid." Kira smiled slightly. "She hasn't used it in a while so I'm hoping she's getting over some of her fears."

"It's interesting she would open a place like Fantasy Bar, not to mention work in it."

Kira shrugged. "It's public, in the open. I think it's the only place she feels safe enough to have sex with someone."

"That's a shame. I hate that there are men out there that abuse women."

"Did you and Micas ever talk about stuff like that? Did he know your view?"

Jerrod frowned. "You know, now that I think about it, he always changed the subject or just remained silent. I don't think he ever expressed an opinion."

"I guess now you know why."

She set two plates on the table overlooking the beach. Between them, she placed a bowl of fruit and a platter of croissants.

"Breakfast looks great." Jerrod took a seat and immediately dug in.

"I hope it's okay. I'm not a big breakfast person, so I didn't have the usual 'hungry man' food in the house."

Jerrod grinned. "It's fine. After all, I'm certain you didn't expect me on your doorstep."

"True," she replied with a chuckle and took a bite of her croissant.

"Why did you run?"

The question startled her and for a second she just stared. "Which time?"

"This time."

She glanced down at her plate and pushed her fruit around with her fork. "Mirage remembered who you were. I knew you would eventually figure out who I was, if you hadn't already. I should have turned myself in, but I panicked."

She hated that about herself. Normally she was a strong person. She'd had to be to make it in the business industry. Despite strides women had taken, there were still planets where they were considered weak and inferior.

"Panicking is natural, Kira."

She shook her head. "Not for me." She sighed and waved her hand. "Let's change the subject."

"All right." Jerrod stabbed at a strawberry. "Let's talk about us."

Kira's startled gaze met his. She certainly hadn't expected that and her heart lodged in her throat. "I . . . umm . . . what about us?"

"First off. Do you agree that there is an us?" His intense gaze bored into hers and her mouth went dry.

Do I? "Yes, I agree we have . . . something."

"So do I. And it's something I want to explore."

She lifted one shoulder. "How?"

"Spending time together for one." He grinned. "What are you doing after all this is over?"

"I was thinking about that." She smiled and placed a strawberry in her mouth.

"Well, let's hear it."

"I want to open a resort."

He raised an eyebrow in interest. "A resort?"

"Yeah. Fantasy Resort, and at the center will be Fantasy Bar. Same principle just on a much bigger scale. We could even offer classes or a group setting for an orgy-type environment."

"Classes in what?"

She shrugged. "Masturbation, oral sex." For a moment she paused, unsure she even wanted to include this one, but also knew it would be popular. "Sensual spanking. It doesn't have to be classes, it could be a club setting, where people with similar interests come to experience things together."

"Sounds interesting." He wiggled his eyebrows, making her giggle. "Where would you put it?"

"Here."

He pointed to the beach. "Right here?"

"Well, in this general area. Mirage owns this. Ten acres on each of the three sides, but I own some beachfront property further to the south. It's more tropical than here and definitely more level."

"How much land do you own?"

She grinned. "Over fifteen thousand acres."

He choked on his coffee and grabbed a napkin to wipe his mouth. "How much?"

She leaned forward, enunciating her words. "Fifteen thousand acres. Not too shabby for a girl on her own, huh?"

He raised his cup in salute, his lips lifting in a smile.

"It's the perfect spot. It's right by the ocean and close enough to Vorkin City that getting guests there would be relatively easy."

"Sounds like you've really thought this out."

She nodded, her excitement building. "I probably have about fifty percent of what it would take to do this. The rest I can borrow." She bit her lip. "What do you think?"

"I think it's a great idea."

"You'll be on Meenus Prime though. I don't know how often we'll see each other."

He pushed his fruit around and remained silent, studying his plate. "The big question is . . ." He raised his gaze to meet hers. "Do you want to see each other?"

For the first time, she saw uncertainty in his eyes. It made him appear vulnerable and she wanted to relieve him, let him know she felt the same as he did. "Yes. Can we make it work?"

"We can make anything work if we want it bad enough." He pursed his lips and waved his fork in the air. "Maybe I'll retire from investigation and become a partner in this little venture."

"A partner?" Her heart warmed at the idea. The two of them running the resort, working side by side, together always.

"Yeah. Think you could handle me underfoot all the time?"

"Of course. I like having people to walk on."

He snorted. "Cute. What about the university?"

She drew in a deep breath then let it out slowly. She'd decided this morning that she wanted to close that part of her life. "I don't want to go back." She shrugged. "Too many bad memories, I guess. Of course all this is contingent on your idea working." She frowned. "What is your idea exactly?"

"Let's just say the high regent owes me one."

"Owes you one?"

Jerrod reached across the table and took her hand in his. "Trust me. I promise, a year from now we'll be overlooking the new Fantasy, hand in hand, jumping from one of your clubs to another."

She chuckled. "I would hope that some of those times we'll be alone."

He brought the back of her fingers to his lips, the warmth of the soft kiss sending electric shocks up her arm. Tingling warmth settled between her legs and she squirmed in her seat, fighting the rising passion that blazed hot and unrelenting.

"You can have me whenever or wherever you want, Gorgeous."

"Oh." She glanced out the window, toward the beach and the beautiful blue sky. "How about there?"

"Now?" he asked, his lips tilting upward into an adorable grin.

"Right now."

11

JERROD COULDN'T TAKE his eyes off Kira as she strolled along the beach, shedding her clothes as she went. Completely naked, she smiled seductively at him over her shoulder. His whole body heated beneath her emerald gaze. Her eyes sparkled with devilment. He was beginning to see a side of her she'd only hinted at before—playful, mischievous and absolutely delectable.

Her firm ass swayed as she sauntered toward the waves and he swallowed his lust, determined to not rush things. Unfortunately, his cock had other intentions.

"Are you coming?" she called over her shoulder before diving into the sparkling water.

She emerged on the other side of the wave and he stood mesmerized by the water glistening on skin. Damn. He put his hand over his bulging shaft and squeezed. Would she always affect him this way? He hoped so. He looked forward to a lifetime of being turned on by this woman.

He'd awakened that morning knowing exactly how he felt about her. He was in love. For the first time in his life he was actually in love with a woman.

At first, the idea shocked him, that he would have these feelings for someone. Especially this quickly. But no longer than he'd known her, he couldn't imagine his life without her.

"Jerrod?" He mentally shook himself and smiled at her as she waved to him from the water. "The water's great. Are you going to stand there all day or are you going to join me?"

He unbuttoned his pants, his chest tightening at the thought of being next to her. "Have a little patience, minx."

She grinned. "But I want you," she purred.

That was all he needed to hear. In a rush, he dropped his pants in the sand and took off toward the surf. Once in the water, he dove under and grabbed her legs, pulling her down. They both emerged laughing, and Kira splashed water in his face. "You brute."

"I may be a brute," he growled playfully, grabbing her around the waist. "But you want me."

"Who says?" she teased back.

"You just said."

"Well, okay." She slid her palms up his chest and around his neck. Her eyes narrowed seductively. "I guess I did say that."

"You guess?" He bent down and bit the side of her neck, relishing the tremor that skimmed through her.

"Okay, I did."

He bit harder, and she erupted in a peal of giggles. Palming the cheeks of her ass, he lifted her. Her warm pussy settled against his hard cock and he groaned deep in his chest. "Feel what you do to me, Gorgeous?"

She ground her hips along his length and his whole body shivered in anticipation of sinking inside her tight walls.

"Is all that for me?"

"Every last inch."

He covered her lips with his, the waves crashing around them, rocking their bodies against each other. She tasted of melon and coffee, rich and sweet. One hell of a heady combination and he couldn't get enough of her. Grabbing the back of her head, he anchored her and deepened the kiss. Their tongues battled for control, their bodies clamoring for fulfillment.

"Jeez, Kira," he murmured between kisses. "I want you. Now."

Lifting her hips, he set her at the tip of his cock and drove deep. She threw her head back, her yell scaring a flock of ocean birds searching for food on the shore. They flew over, their high-pitched squawks drowning out Kira's moans.

Her walls encased him like a glove, squeezing him, dragging him deeper. Never in his life had a woman made him this out of control, this hot. God help him, he never wanted it to end.

Her mouth descended on his, her tongue delved and teased. He met her demanding kiss and made a few demands of his own. Not only with his mouth but with his cock. She sighed as he relentlessly thrust deeper, hitting her womb.

"Jerrod," she whimpered, then screamed as her release gripped her. Every throb of her pussy pulled him closer to his own bliss and with a shout, he burst deep inside her.

A strong wave hit them and his legs wobbled, causing him to almost lose his balance. "Whoa," he laughed and held her tighter against him, spreading his feet wider to keep them balanced.

Kira slid down his body, her feet coming to rest unsteadily on the sand beneath them. She grabbed his forearms for support, her tiny hands gripping his muscles. She looked so adorable, her face still flushed from their passion. A breeze blew her hair into her eyes and he brushed it back, his heart in his throat. She had all the power. She could crush him if she wanted to and the very idea threw him for a loop.

"Nice show."

Jerrod turned and stared at Simas in surprise. "What the hell are you doing here?"

Simas stood on the beach, his hand behind his back. "Just checking. Making sure you found her."

"Of course I found her. I told you I knew where she was."

Something didn't feel right. Kira's whole body went rigid and her hands trembled. He glanced down at her pale face, concern racing through him. She didn't look well at all. "You all right? What's wrong?"

"It's his voice. I've heard it before."

He glanced at Simas, still on the beach, watching them with interest. Kira's lower lip began to tremble and his concern intensified. "Where, Kira?"

"At Micas' apartment. He was there. He was with him."

Kira's stomach rolled with nausea. Missing images and sounds from those two days came rushing back. She'd never seen his face but she'd heard him encouraging Micas, telling him to hit her harder. His teeth had bitten into the flesh of her back, drawing blood. She cringed at the remembered pain.

Jerrod touched the side of her face and leaned in close. "Are you sure?"

"Yes," she whispered.

He turned to face Simas and pushed her behind him. "Stay behind me, understand?"

She nodded. "Yes."

She glanced around his shoulder. Simas still stood on the beach, his leer making her shiver in dread.

"We're not dressed, Simas. At least turn your fucking back," Jerrod snapped.

Simas smirked but turned.

"What the hell are you really doing here?" Jerrod asked.

"I told you. I wanted to make sure you found her."

They slowly made their way out of the water and Jerrod handed her shirt to her. As quickly as possible, she put it on, covering herself as best she could.

"Why? So she wouldn't point her finger at you and let everyone know you were at Micas' apartment egging him on?"

Simas spun around and faced them. His face contorted into an evil scowl. "So you know."

"Not until just now."

Kira stood behind Jerrod, looking around the beach for anything she could use as a weapon. There was nothing and her heart sank. They were in real trouble.

"How long have the two of you been doing this?"

"Micas caught me years ago with a woman. He was fascinated with what I'd done, turned on by the blood and the screams." Simas shrugged. "We began to do it together. Until he developed a fascination with her."

"Why me? I'd never met him," Kira screamed in frustration.

"Yes you had. You just don't remember. He was at the university party, the one that introduced you as the new head of the department. I told him not to take you, but once he did, there was nothing I could do. It had to be played out."

"But why did he keep her alive when he killed the others so quickly?" Jerrod asked.

"He was playing a game. He wanted to prove he could do it and not get caught. He was flaunting it in your face, Jerrod. Granted, he wasn't supposed to show her to the fucking doorman!"

Jerrod shook his head. "Why? What kind of sick thrill do you get out of doing this?"

Simas' lips spread into a nasty grin. "It's all about control, friend."

"That's bullshit and you know it."

Simas shrugged and took a step closer. "It's all in your perception."

Jerrod reached behind himself and pushed Kira back, making sure to keep a safe distance between them and a man he'd considered a friend. A friend he'd apparently never known at all.

Damn, they'd hid it well. He hadn't had a clue either of them were crazy.

"How did you find me? I didn't tell you where I was going."

Simas held up a small device and smiled. "Tracking device. Ingenious invention. I put it on your ship before you left Meenus."

"Son of a bitch," Jerrod mumbled.

"You might as well move aside, Jerrod. I'm here for the woman and I won't leave without her."

"What do you want with her?" He knew, he just needed to keep Simas talking until he could figure a way out of this mess.

Simas rolled his eyes. "She can identify me, but then you know that. Stop trying to stall. Both of you have to die."

He pulled a gun from behind his back and Jerrod swore.

"How will you explain it, Simas?"

"She killed you in her attempt to escape and I had no choice but to shoot her. Sad really. She's such a beauty, so hot and delectable. Do you remember, Kira? Do you remember the feel of my mouth on you, the pain as my teeth sank into your tender flesh?"

Kira whimpered behind Jerrod, her hands balling into fists

against his back. He had no doubt she was remembering and it probably terrified her.

"Stop it!" Jerrod snapped. "I'm not going to let you do this, Simas."

"And how do you think you're going to stop me?"

Jerrod lunged forward, grabbing the gun. "Kira, move," he yelled, hoping like hell she followed his instructions.

They struggled, his heart in his throat. The gun was facing upward and Jerrod fought, trying to point it toward Simas. Time seemed to stand still then move in slow motion. Simas' face was red with his exertion, his determination to keep the upper hand. He was stronger than he looked, and Jerrod's arms began to shake with his efforts.

Suddenly, he became angry. Angry with himself for not seeing what they really were, angry that they'd pulled the wool over his eyes. Jerrod brought up his knee, slamming it into Simas' groin. Simas fell to the ground, his howl of pain echoing off the rock cliffs behind him.

"Damn you, Jerrod."

Jerrod stood over him, his chest heaving, his disgust for the man he considered a friend eating at him. "Damn *you*, Simas. You'll pay for what you did."

"How?" Simas sneered up at him, his expression triumphant. "How am I to pay and keep her out of it? Huh?"

"Oh, I assure you. I'll figure a way." He moved the gun to his other hand and glanced to his left, looking for Kira. She stood by the cliff, just below the path that led to the house. What the hell was she still doing there?

"Kira, go to the house."

She nodded then a shot rang out. Jerrod watched in anguish as she fell to the ground, motionless. "Kira!"

Spinning around, he caught Simas on his knees, gun in hand. He must have had another one hidden on him somewhere. Without thought, he aimed, shooting Simas between the eyes. He didn't even wait for his body to hit the ground before he took off toward Kira's lifeless body.

Kira groaned. Hot searing pain shot through her. She tried to open her eyes and see Jerrod, but the pain made even that small movement nearly impossible.

She'd heard the second shot but she had no idea who'd fired.

"Kira. Kira, baby, answer me."

Jerrod's hands touched her face and tugged at her shirt. Relief washed over her and she bit her lip to stop the sobs. "Simas?" she croaked.

"He's dead. He won't bother you again."

He applied pressure to her seeping shoulder wound, and she winced.

"You're going to be fine," he soothed.

"I don't feel like it at the moment."

She opened her eyes and caught him smiling at her. Love. It was the only word that came to mind. She loved him. She knew it now without a doubt.

"Let's get you some help."

She nodded and closed her eyes, falling into the relief of unconsciousness.

12

JERROD WATCHED ANGER crease the brow of High Regent Kimpak, then disgust. Kimpak's gray hair was pulled tight into a ponytail, making him look older than his one hundred and twenty years, but his green eyes still sparkled with intelligence. He was a good regent. A kind one. Hopefully that kindness would be present today.

"I've seen enough," Kimpak groaned then turned away.

Jerrod stepped forward and closed the computer screen. The click was loud in the silent room. Simas had been under the false impression he'd covered all the angles. Edit himself out of the films, make sure everyone knew it was Kira who had killed Micas, then frame Kira for Jerrod's death as well. The whole incident would have ended in her *supposed* suicide. He shuddered every time he thought of how close Simas came to succeeding. "It was self-defense, your Excellency."

"Is that why you hid her face?"

Jerrod nodded. He knew the regent would notice—he'd just hoped Kimpak would choose not to say anything. "Yes."

"You know her identity?"

"Yes."

"Well."

Jerrod met Kimpak's level stare with determination. He would not give up Kira. "With all due respect, your—"

Kimpak held up his hand and scowled. "You would give your career to keep this woman's identity a secret?"

"Yes. She's a highly educated, highly respected woman who was at the wrong place at the wrong time. To reveal her identity, even if it was self-defense, would ruin her. I refuse to allow that to happen." Taking a deep breath, he continued. "Micas was my best friend, but I had no idea what he was into or how sick he was. Simas being involved was another shock, and I feel responsible for the deaths of those women. I'm a better investigator than this. I should have seen it."

Kimpak shook his head. "You were too close, Jerrod. Sometimes it's most difficult to see what's directly in front of you."

"Regardless, I won't let you or anyone else take this woman to hell and back just because she was trying to save herself."

"I saw the video, Jerrod. I know what happened to her and why she did it."

"Then I see no need to reveal her to the public. We can say the woman died of her injuries."

Kimpak appeared surprised. "So you're going to reveal Micas and Simas' activities?"

"Yes. My only request is that you allow me to speak with their families first. I want their parents to hear it from me and not the press."

Kimpak sat silent for several minutes. Jerrod's nerves screamed with unease and he felt like a caged animal. He needed to pace, move, something. Finally, Kimpak spoke and Jerrod prepared himself for the worst.

"I never would have thought Micas, or Simas for that matter, could do those things. It makes me ill to think how many others there might have been."

Jerrod swallowed. He'd thought the same thing numerous times since seeing this video. "There are five others that we know of because of the hidden videos we found. They were unable to escape Micas and died of their injuries. Simas edited out his involvement, but his work was hurried and sloppy. It's obvious where the edits were made. Those videos are in there as well if you'd like to see them."

Kimpak help up his hand and actually paled. "No."

Jerrod nodded but said nothing more. He just waited.

"Tell the woman I commend her bravery and determination to

survive." Jerrod's heart soared. Was Kimpak going to let him keep her a secret? "I will go along with your plan."

"Thank you, your Excellency."

Kimpak eyed him speculatively. "This will be your last assignment, I take it."

It wasn't a question but an observation. And a very accurate one.

"Yes. I wish to retire and pursue . . . other interests."

A small smile lifted the corners of Kimpak's mouth. "You've been a good investigator. One of my best. You will be missed."

Jerrod inclined his head, relief that Kimpak hadn't fought him over the issue swimming through him. "Thank you, Regent Kimpak."

BOREDOM WEIGHED HEAVILY on Kira as she paced Mirage's bedroom. She'd been here for almost a week now, waiting for Jerrod to return. Hopefully with the news it was all over, that they could finally go on with their lives. Together.

With a sigh, she rolled her shoulder. It was still sore and the wound would leave a nasty scar, but that was no worse than the ones on her back. A forever reminder of just how nasty people could be. She loosened the sling and let her arm hang straight, stretching it out. Jaimee had told her it might be a while before she could lift it over her head.

"Kira," Mirage admonished as she came into the room carrying a tray laden with food. "You're supposed to be resting."

Kira scowled. "I've rested enough. If I don't get out of this room, I'm going to go stark raving mad."

Mirage laughed. "All right, I'll tell you what. Eat your lunch and I'll let you go downstairs and help me get ready for tonight."

Kira smirk at her motherly attitude. "What am I, eight?"

Mirage smiled. "Maybe ten."

"Very funny."

Kira sat on the bed and picked at the food. If she continued to eat everything Mirage brought her she'd gain fifty pounds within a month.

"I just want to make sure you're well before you overdo it just like you always do. You would do the same to me if the situation were reversed."

Kira grinned. "True."

Kira picked up her fork and studied the piece of meat dangling from the end. She just wasn't hungry. She dropped it back to her plate with a sigh.

"Lord, girl," Mirage admonished. "If all you're going to do is push the food around your plate, let's go ahead and go downstairs."

Kira jumped up and headed toward the door, ignoring Mirage's laugh.

"You're not in a hurry, are you?"

"Yes," Kira sighed, making her laugh even harder.

"Come on, mother hen," Kira shouted over her shoulder and practically skipped down the hidden back staircase that would take her to the main bar. Once through the door, she glanced around the nearly empty room. Just the bartenders and a few waitresses were around. The normally dim lighting was now bright, casting light into dark corners. The smell of vanilla and spice clung in the air. A man sitting at the end of the bar caught her eye and she sucked in a breath, her heart pounding in her chest.

"It's about time you came downstairs."

She smiled, letting her gaze travel down his dark blue shirt and slacks. The color deepened the sapphire of his eyes, making them sparkle.

"Jerrod," she yelled then slung herself into his open arms.

Jerrod laughed, holding her tighter. "Careful, Gorgeous. Don't hurt yourself."

"I don't care. I'm just glad you're back." She pulled away and stared at him, biting her lip in anxiety. She was dying to know what happened, but her heart raced with the fear it might be bad news. "How did it go?"

"Everything is fine. No one but us knows who the woman in the video was. It's over, sweetheart."

Relief gripped her, making her giddy. With a squeal, she hugged his neck. "I love you, Jerrod."

She froze. She hadn't meant to say that. What would he do? Would he ignore it? Or play it off as nothing?

"I love you too, Kira," he whispered and her heart soared. He smiled and cupped her face between his hands, his eyes shining with all the love he felt. "Let's go start that resort."

She wiped at the tears falling down her cheeks. "Yeah."

One year later

JERROD STOOD BESIDE Kira, his arm along her shoulder as they surveyed the new Fantasy Resort. Everything had gone as planned and they were now ready to open the doors. They'd been booked solid for almost two months now. As soon as word had spread of the new resort, people began to call. The opening party they had planned would be a huge success.

Kira smiled and snuggled closer to Jerrod. It had been a wonderful year. Days full of work designing costumes, decorating rooms and working out class schedules. The nights were full of snuggles, long talks and passionate lovemaking that never failed to leave her breathless. But nothing compared to the night before—when Jerrod had placed a diamond ring on her finger.

"Now that everything is in place, it's time we took care of this. Marry me, Kira."

She'd accepted, gladly and without reservation. He was and always would be the man of her dreams.

RIDE A COWBOY

DELILAH DEVLIN

1

THE HOUSE KATELYN Carter had bought sight unseen was kind of like her—weathered by storms and in need of a lot of TLC.

After a quick glance around the empty road, she set her truck into park and stared. She let her eyes blur and tried to imagine how the old house must have looked once upon a time before the harsh South Texas sun baked its exterior. She wasn't encouraged. Even from behind her dirty windshield, she could tell the one-story ranch needed a lot of work, and at the very least, a fresh coat of paint.

A lone tear streaked down her face, surprising her, and she sniffed. One last cry—she deserved that much. Then no more feeling sorry for herself. She had too much to do and a whole new life stretching in front of her.

A loud honk sounded and Katelyn swung her gaze to her rearview mirror to find that a dusty, older-model pickup truck had pulled up behind her. She swiped away the tears with the back of her hand, and then stuck her arm out the window to wave the driver past.

Instead, the driver-side door opened and a tall Texan in faded jeans and a cream-colored cowboy hat stepped onto the pavement.

Katelyn cursed under her breath and quickly tilted down the mirror to see whether her mascara had smeared. She didn't really care what a stranger thought—that was the old Katelyn. Still, some habits die hard.

When boot steps stopped beside her, she glanced up . . . and found herself trapped within a moss green gaze that raised the temperature within her cab a notch. The rest of him was just as captivating. Dark brown hair peeked from beneath his hat. His jaw was angular, his chin chiseled. Shallow crow's feet surrounded those amazing eyes and crinkled when he frowned—as he was doing now. But they were wrinkles cause by the sun, not the weathering of a few years, like hers.

Damn! Here stood the first man she'd met since her separation who made her think of all the steamy possibilities, and he was too young.

She didn't realize she'd cursed out loud until his soft chuckle washed over her like a silky caress. Her cheeks flamed instantly.

"Women don't generally cuss me 'til *after* they know me better," he said, his baritone voice thick as molasses.

The timbre and tone of his voice appealed too much. She lifted a single brow, trying for off-putting and hoping he didn't notice her lashes were still wet from tears. "Obviously, they're not too discerning."

His smile dimmed and his eyes narrowed, sweeping over her face and body hunched behind the steering wheel. "Not from around here, are you?" he asked, leaning closer.

She reminded herself she was alone, in the middle of a country road, with a large, predatory-looking man looming over her—and she'd just insulted him. She hit her automatic lock button.

"Whoa," he said, lifting his hands. "I didn't mean to scare you, ma'am."

Ma'am! Now she really did feel like the spinster librarian she was.

"Look . . . " He straightened away. "I just stopped to see if you were having car trouble."

"Funny, but I wasn't having any trouble at all 'til you stopped," she said, making sure he understood her unsubtle dig, and hoping he'd take the hint and leave.

The cowboy looked around and then down the gravel road toward her home, before returning to give her a questioning glance. "You lost then? The main highway's about three miles behind you."

"Nope, I know exactly where I am." She kept her response terse and lifted her chin. No way was she going to encourage the conversation to continue, no matter how handsome the man was—or more to the point, *because* he was so attractive. "Not that it's any of your business. I was just double-checking the address."

He pushed back his cowboy hat and leaned down again. "Well, I wouldn't want you to waste any more of your valuable time," he said, his gaze raking her face, "but you're at 118 Amman Road. The letters are worn off the mailbox."

The longer he stood there, the more certain she became she needed him gone. Something about him, his steady gaze and his large sturdy frame, made her . . . want . . . something more, something she was better off not having right now. "Then I'm in the right place," she said, keeping her expression challenging.

His hand rubbed the back of his neck and he shook his head. "Well, I'll be damned," he said softly. When his green gaze returned, his expression was hard to read, but intense, almost searching.

Katelyn shivered. All that attention from a handsome man unnerved her. She needed time alone to dam up her defenses against her unwanted reactions. Handsome she'd had and wasn't what she needed now.

"Seein' as how you don't need any help," he said, "I'll be on my way." One last glance with a naked promise she couldn't misinterpret, and he left . . . taking Katelyn's breath right along with him.

In the mirror, her gaze clung to his broad back and nicely rounded backside until he reached the door of his cab and glanced back. She whipped away her gaze and hoped like hell he hadn't caught her looking at his ass. Sinking in her seat, she burned with embarrassment while he passed by, giving her one last smoldering glance.

Katelyn's heart slowed and her hands released their tight grip on the steering wheel.

He was just a man—he had nothing she needed or wanted—*ever again*. Except maybe sex. She did miss that. But she'd never have sex with entanglement again. Complicating that fact, she'd come to a small town to start her life anew and couldn't afford the kind of scandal a fling with a younger man would cause.

Pushing thoughts of the tall cowboy aside, she pulled onto the long gravel drive and forced her mind back to what needed doing before she could rest that night. Hard work was what she needed—not anything the young cowboy had to offer.

And looking at her new home, she guessed she'd get plenty of cowboy antidote. A long day's work lay ahead of her—and that was before she could unpack the U-Haul trailer laden with all her worldly belongings. She squared her shoulders. She'd make it through the next couple of days like she had the last few years—one step at a time.

Her gaze lifted beyond the house to the field of ripening buffalo grass and broken rock behind the chain-link fence surrounding the two-acre property. The landscape was so different here.

Atlanta had just revealed the first hints of spring. Crocuses had pushed up through the lawn. Daffodils bloomed beside the porch where she'd planted them during the first year of her marriage to Chris, when she'd still had so much hope for their future together.

Here, the few live oaks that dotted the landscape looked like bushes in comparison to the tall pines of her former home.

And good Lord—the heat! Only April and already eighty degrees and climbing fast.

Katelyn opened her door, grateful for the stirring breeze. It was Monday; Thursday she started her new job and she wanted all her things in their proper place before she began her new life. She'd begin as she meant to continue—building order out of the chaos her world had been.

Besides its less than pristine appearance, she quickly discovered another problem with her new home—the ancient air conditioner didn't work. She raised every window she could and propped open the back door to let a breeze waft through the house. Warm though it was, the temperature outside was still better than the stale heat inside.

After wrestling with her bed frame, mattress, and small night-stand, she decided to get a good night's sleep and start again early the next morning. She lay down on top of cool crisp sheets and sighed her relief. But despite her fatigue, she tossed on her mattress, unable to fall asleep.

She would have liked to blame her restlessness on the warm

weather. But the temperature of the room had little to do with the heat pooling between her legs and everything to do with the cowboy in the faded jeans.

After pounding her pillow for the second time, she surrendered to her body's demands and did something she'd only recently developed the skill to accomplish, masturbating to orgasm being something her husband had considered a theft of his own pleasure.

Moonlight glared through the top of the window and obscured her view of the front yard, but she relaxed, knowing darkness, being a good hundred yards distance from the road and the spindly oaks in her front yard obscured the view inside her bedroom. She didn't live in the city anymore.

With one last guilty glance out the bare window, she slid her fingers beneath the edge of her panties. And if her mind drifted to the tall Texan in the cream-colored cowboy hat, well, she'd just put it down to a momentary weakness. He'd never know.

Feeling as low as a snake, the cowboy hid in the shadows just outside the woman's window and watched while her fingers disappeared beneath the edge of her pale panties.

Such a private thing to witness. A weakness betrayed. A deep passion exposed.

He'd walked the quarter mile from his house to hers, following an urge so strong he hadn't questioned it. While she'd worked steadily, well into the evening, brushing away a year's worth of dust from her wooden floors and wrestling with furniture, his gaze had followed her efficient movements, roaming the curves of her firm breasts and ass and the tempting length of her legs beneath the frayed edges of her cutoff jeans.

When at last she'd turned off the light, he'd been rewarded for his patient vigil as she'd drawn off her T-shirt and bra and slipped the shorts down her thighs. Although too dark to see the color of her nipples, he'd discerned their size and witnessed them drawing into beaded points when she'd rubbed them as though easing an ache. He'd licked his lips, anticipating their velvet texture on his tongue. Then she'd drawn a small top over her head that hugged her breasts like a second skin and did little to cool his ardor.

He'd grown hungrier by the moment, coveting each sweet curve of her body, determined to stake a claim, and soon. She might be a little older than he'd have liked, but the difference in their ages didn't mean a thing to his cock. The large, hard knot of his erection pressed uncomfortably against the front of his jeans.

But the physical attraction was only part of what drew him, what kept him skulking in the darkness outside her bedroom. The hint of sadness glinting wetly on her dark eyelashes when they'd met earlier on the road had done crazy things to the inside of his chest. The pain-filled defiance in her gaze hadn't deterred him one bit. If any man was going to chase the shadows from her past, it'd be him. The loneliness he'd sensed in her was echoed tenfold in his own heart.

Her low whimpered moan carried on the air between them, tightening his thighs and balls, building a painful urgency he had to relieve. He flicked open the button at the top of his jeans and eased out his rigid cock. He'd share this private act with her, giving the ache a face—*hers*. Blue eyes the color of a clear Texas sky. Hair as pale and soft as corn silk. Her face was etched on his mind, and now on his body.

With his hand closing around his shaft, he joined her, imagining sinking into the moisture her fingers drew from her pussy.

Her thighs parted, her knees rising high and splaying wide as her hips undulated on the mattress.

His hand glided up the rigid shaft, squeezing when he reached the end, then glided back down. His hips pulsed in time with hers, driving his cock within his circled fingers until the friction became nearly unbearable. He dropped spit onto his palm and resumed the rhythm, the moisture easing the movements. He imagined sinking to his knees between her thighs and pressing into her. How hot and tight she'd be, clenching around his cock like a wet fist, like his was doing now.

Her fingers pulled out partway and swirled faster. She must be getting close. Her little clit ached for direct stimulation. Someday soon, he'd purse his lips around it, flutter his tongue on the hard little knot, then suck on it until she came, screaming his name.

Her cry was wispy, restrained, but was enough to push him over the edge, and he spilled cum into the dirt at his feet, jerking his cock those last desperate strokes.

Tomorrow, he'd give her a proper introduction. And learn the name of the woman he planned to make his own.

THE NEXT MORNING sunlight streamed into her bedroom through the bare window. The air was stifling hot, and she lay drenched in sweat, her hair clinging to her face in sticky clumps. She flipped back the covers.

An ominous rattle sounded from the floor, and she froze.

She didn't need to be a native Texan to recognize that raspy rattle. Easing up to stand in the middle of her mattress, she peered cautiously over the edge. A rattlesnake lay on the floor next to her bed in a fat coil, its tail erect and quivering. Even if the snake hadn't paralyzed her with fear, he lay in a patch of sunlight between her and the bedroom door—she wasn't getting out of this predicament by herself.

She needed the cavalry, or at least the local sheriff's department. Moving slowly, she reached for her cell phone on the bedside table. Her heart nearly stopped when the dry rattle grew louder and the snake's head drew back with its mouth open and fangs exposed.

Her hands shook as she punched 911.

"Wendall County Police, how may I help you?" a female voice chimed.

Relief nearly made her weak. "Um . . . this is Katelyn Carter," she said, rushing to get the words out. "I'm at 118 Amman Road. I'm new here and I have a problem." Her voice trembled with fear as she explained her dilemma to the dispatcher. "Can rattlesnakes climb?"

"We'll send a unit right over, ma'am. You sit tight, now. I don't think that snake's gonna do any climbin'."

"Wait!" For the first time Katelyn realized she stood in the middle of her bed wearing only a tiny pair of bikini briefs and a thin white camisole that was transparent due to her own perspiration. Embarrassment warred with her fear.

"Yes, ma'am?" The dispatcher interrupted her thoughts.

"Uh . . . I'm not dressed. Can you send a female officer?"

The woman on the other end of the line chuckled. "Ma'am, we don't have any female officers, but I'll make sure only one fella comes in. You just stay right where you are."

As she powered off her cell phone, Katelyn could already hear sirens in the distance and wondered irritably whether the whole Wendall County police force was responding to the call. It wasn't long before booted footsteps made their way through her house.

One of the officers called out to her, "Miz Carter, you in there?"

Despite her fear, Katelyn cringed inside. The house was a mess—littered with cleaning supplies, wadded packing paper and half-emptied boxes. Worse, total strangers were about to see a whole lot more of her than anyone but her husband ever had. She inched her hand down to pull up the sheet to cover herself, but halted when the snake grew agitated by her slight movement and began to writhe in a tight circle around itself.

Wilting with embarrassment, she replied, "I'm in here."

A broad, amused face peered around the corner of her bedroom door. The officer's gaze widened slightly as it paused on her before seeking out her intruder on the floor. He whistled when he spotted the snake. "It's a big 'un all right. We won't come in just yet, ma'am. I can tell that rattler's gettin' annoyed. We've sent for a rattlesnake wrangler to come pick up this bad boy." He gave her a kind smile. "It'll only be a few minutes. You just hang tight—and don't move, ya hear?"

Long moments passed while Katelyn counted the drops of sweat that slid down her face and the brown and black diamonds that crisscrossed the snake's back. She had just begun to wonder what a "rattlesnake wrangler" was when she heard more voices from the living room and heavy footsteps just outside her bedroom door.

"Ma'am, it's Daniel Bodine."

That voice! Warm as whiskey, it poured over her. Katelyn nearly groaned.

"I'm coming in now. Don't you move a muscle."

A moment later, the cowboy who'd figured in her dreams—hot and sexy dreams—filled the doorway of her bedroom.

As nervous as she was, Katelyn couldn't help noting his broad shoulders nearly spanned the doorframe, and he had to duck to clear his hat beneath it. In one hand he held a long pole with a hook at the end of it; in the other, a white sack.

His gaze met hers briefly, and he nodded once in her direction. A flush of red tinted his cheeks as he moved slowly into her bedroom, then all of his concentration focused on the snake.

As he approached it, the whispery rattle grew louder and the snake's attention moved to him. When its head rose with fangs exposed, the man reacted in a blinding whir of movement, pinning the snake's head to the floor with the hook. Then the cowboy placed the toe of his boot just below its head and tossed aside the pole.

Her heart pounded with fear as the snake frantically whipped its body about.

Daniel grabbed the snake just below the head, then straightened and held it up for a moment, letting it relax its full length toward the floor. He whistled appreciatively. "Whoa, he's a big 'un all right." He dropped it into the white sack and pulled the drawstring closed over it. Finally, he turned to her, his gaze flickering over her before sliding politely away. "It's okay, ma'am. You can come down off the bed now," he said softly.

"Thanks," she said, her voice croaking like a bullfrog, "but I think I'll wait until my legs stop trembling before I attempt it." She hated admitting her weakness and flushed, feeling the heat color her cheeks and spread down her neck to her chest. She wanted to raise her hands to hide her breasts, but knew it was a little late to save her modesty.

"Let me help you down." He stepped toward the bed, his hand stretched out.

"N-No," she said, suddenly breathless. *Don't let him touch me.* After last night, she already felt as though he'd touched her—intimately. She'd come, pretending his fingers stroked her slick flesh.

"It's okay. I swear I don't bite," he said, his voice softer, huskier. His hand closed around hers, and he tugged gently.

Katelyn drew in a sharp breath at the heat of his touch and the calluses that roughened his palms, and let him help her to the floor. When she stood beside him in her underwear and bare feet, she ducked her head and pulled at the cotton camisole that stuck to her skin, aware he could see the dark outline of her nipples through the cloth.

Sure enough, his glance swept down her body and back up.

A warning flashed in the back of her mind, but she couldn't help the slight catch of her breath as his gaze paused on her breasts. But rather than the suggestive comment she expected from the sassy cowboy of yesterday, he tightened his jaw and he looked away.

The telltale sign of awareness and tension had a similar effect on her body and she felt her nipples bead beneath her damp camisole.

He cleared his throat and stepped away. "I'll just put him in the truck and be on my way," he said, his voice now brusque. "I wouldn't want him to scare you again." With a hot glance that said he hadn't really been talking about the snake, he turned on his heels and left the room.

She slumped against the bedpost and wondered what that had been all about and why her heart still pumped madly . . . and not from fear or embarrassment. She blew out a pent-up breath and moaned. Who the hell was she kidding? The look on his face had held a promise. One she was dying to know.

Katelyn, girl, you're in trouble now!

2

D ANIEL SWORE AND slung the sack into the bed of the pickup truck. For the second time in as many days he'd managed to act like a teenage boy in first lust in front of the prettiest girl he'd ever seen.

Dwight Emerson strode up beside him just as he reached for the door to the cab. "Mmm . . . mmm! Now, if that ain't the way to start off a morning. That there's one pretty filly."

Knowing Dwight had just gotten an eyeful of the woman he'd already decided would be his own, Daniel chose to ignore his friend. It was that or plant his fist in Dwight's grinning face. And he certainly didn't feel like discussing the sexy woman and her sweet assets with anyone. Especially a yahoo like the sheriff.

Daniel just wanted to get away and let the tension dissipate that had gripped his body the moment he'd laid his eyes on her wearing less than his heart could take—and a whole lot more than she'd worn last night when she'd stripped in the darkness. A deep shame still burned through him for his actions of the previous night.

He'd spied on her like a horny twelve-year-old boy.

"Yup, my eyes just about fell outta my head when I spotted Miz Carter standin' in the middle of her bed, all pink 'n' pretty. Didn't know sweat could look so hot." Dwight shook his head mournfully. "Too bad I'm a married man."

"Bet Maria wouldn't be too happy hearing you talk like that," Daniel said, sending him a warning glance. He glanced away and asked the question that was burning a hole in his gut. "What's her first name?"

"You talkin' about Katelyn Carter?" Dwight's eyebrows rose. "Now, she's a little long in the tooth, but it don't look like you even noticed that fact," he said, a wicked twinkle in his eyes.

Oh, Daniel had noticed all right—but he couldn't change the day she was born. Daniel resisted adjusting the crotch of his jeans and narrowed his eyes at his erstwhile buddy. Try as he might, he couldn't push from his mind the memory of her moist, sleep-tousled blonde hair and wide blue eyes. His body was as taut as a barbed wire fence and his groin ached. If she'd looked down the front of his body even once, he'd have frightened the tart-tongued woman even more than the snake.

Wanting to change the subject, Daniel asked, "How do you suppose that rattler got into her house?"

"Cain't be sure, but Miz Carter left her back door open all night. She don't have no screen door on it. That snake was probably just lookin' for a warm spot to spend the night. Cain't think of anyplace warmer, kin you?"

Daniel ignored his teasing and paused for a moment, his hand on the door as he digested that bit of information.

"So, you decided to stay in town for yer vacation?" Dwight's question intruded on his thoughts.

Daniel's gaze drifted back to Katelyn Carter's front door. "Yeah, I've got a lot to do around the place. I'm gonna catch up on chores," he lied. He wrenched open the door of the cab and climbed inside.

"Well, enjoy yerself, and stay away from the station. I want you rested—I'll need you this weekend." Dwight winked slyly at him and cocked his head toward the house. "Maybe you should check on her later. Make sure your new neighbor's doin' all right after her excitement this morning."

Daniel didn't respond as he inserted his key into the ignition. He was way ahead of Dwight.

"You know," Dwight continued, "she could probably use some help unloadin' the rest of the stuff she's got in that trailer. And Daniel . . . I didn't notice no ring on her finger." He winked again and grinned, then touched the brim of his white sheriff's hat before sauntering back toward the house.

Daniel cursed the fact that his interest in the woman was so apparent. He'd have liked to keep it to himself awhile—savor the heady emotions running riot inside him in private. Thank God he had a few days off. He needed time off to get himself under control. By the time he went back, he wanted the heat banked that burned through his body at just the thought of *Katelyn.*

Such a pretty damn name.

The long list of chores he'd hoped to accomplish during his vacation would just have to wait. They weren't nearly as urgent as his need to be around the woman. But first, he had to make a run to the hardware store.

Not that it was gonna be easy convincing her she needed his help.

Last night during the long walk home, he'd thought long and hard about how to get beyond the bone-deep wariness that made her expression defensive and almost brittle. He'd decided not to rush her, to take her slowly—one step at a time.

First he'd gain her trust, then he'd gentle her with his voice and hands. Kind of like breaking a nervous filly to bridle.

Last night he'd grinned at the thought. Today, he wasn't so certain she could be brought around to trust him. Someone had hurt her, made her skittish around men. The man who'd had her before was a damn fool.

Her body was tanned and toned like a model's, and she carried herself like a queen—even when she stood in the middle of her bed in her underwear. She had class stamped all over her face and body.

What the hell did he have to offer a woman like that?

AROUND NOON, KATELYN was busy putting away the last of her dishes into the cupboard when the dull thud of a vehicle door slamming shut echoed through the house. Sighing, she made her way around unpacked boxes to the front door to see who her visitor was just as Daniel Bodine stepped onto the porch.

Desire flushed her skin, unwanted and perverse in its choice of obsessions—which Daniel was quickly becoming. Inside, her body softened and moistened. Outwardly, she lifted her chin and waited.

He pulled off his cowboy hat, revealing chestnut brown hair cut short, but not short enough to hide a tendency to curl.

Her fingers itched to sift through his rich, curling pelt.

Daniel cleared his throat. "Howdy, ma'am."

Katelyn waited behind the screen of her front door, glad for the barrier between them. He was a sight to behold—muscles stretching the shoulders and arms of his pale T-shirt. Her heart pounded just looking into the green gaze that watched her steadily. Pleasure washed over despite her intentions, causing a tingling sensation in places she'd thought numb from years of neglect.

His face wasn't pretty-boy handsome. Instead, it was almost harshly defined and very masculine. Something about the way he stood so still and kept his unwavering gaze on her face told her he was an honest man—but he was still too good-looking for her peace of mind.

"What can I do for you, Mr. Bodine?" she finally managed to blurt out.

The corners of his mouth lifted just a fraction—just enough to warn her he knew she'd been checking him out. "I couldn't help noting earlier," he said, his voice dropping lower, "you don't have a screen on your back door. It isn't safe to keep it propped open like you did last night."

She frowned, not sure where the conversation was leading and not liking what his rumbling voice was doing to her body. She squeezed her thighs together to stop the instinctive yielding. "I kept it open because it was hot as a furnace in the house, but a repairman is coming out tomorrow. I won't have that problem again."

His gaze dropped and he cleared his throat again, twisting his hat in his hands.

She wondered cynically if this feigned shyness was an act he used to convince women to trust him.

When he raised his gaze to hers again, his expression was clear of any humor—and seared her with its intensity. "Ma'am, I know this house has a lot of problems. The previous owners were friends of mine. I take on jobs as a handyman from time to time, and I'd be glad for the work. I'd like to help you get this place to shine again."

Katelyn's breath caught. *How does he do that?* When he looked at her like that—like she was the prettiest woman he'd ever seen—she felt herself melting like a Popsicle in the sun. It was likely a practiced technique, but she was falling for it. Falling into those moss green eyes.

"Ma'am, what do you think?"

Me, think? This tower of a man—any woman's wet dream—could sap her resistance with just a look and that smoky, deep voice.

Katelyn sighed. The little sound that escaped broke the trance that had her leaning toward the screen door. She lifted a hand to her mussed hair, buying some time to get her reactions under control. But touching her hair was enough to remind her, she was a mess and he was probably only staring at a smudge on her face.

Her prejudice against handsome men might be coloring her impression of him. His eyes looked at her steadily without a hint of sexual innuendo. Her gaze turned to the ancient pickup parked in her driveway and she guessed he might need the money every bit as much as she needed help.

If she were truthful to herself, she'd admit the thought of having him underfoot made her feel more alive than she had in years.

Taking a deep breath and hoping she wasn't making a big mistake, she replied, "Mr. Bodine, it's not that I can't do this all by myself—and that would be my preference—but I want things in their proper place by Monday. That door's just one more thing I won't have to do."

"I understand, Miz Carter. You don't really need me."

She gave him a sharp nod. "That's right. If I'm satisfied with your work, we'll talk later about what else you might do for me." She blushed when she realized how that last statement might be interpreted, but a quick glance at his face eased her mind that he hadn't read anything into it.

He still wore the same steady expression. "I'll get started on it right away." He replaced his hat on his head and turned away.

Phew. She released the breath she'd been holding, and then her brain unclenched as she had another thought. "Wait!" she called out to him.

He hesitated on the porch step, and then turned. "Yes, ma'am?"

"I can't afford too much just yet. I start my new job on Thursday."

He appeared to relax.

He must have thought I changed my mind, Katelyn thought.

"That's okay," he said, nodding solemnly. "You can pay as you go. I also know which hardware stores have the best prices—and I get a discount." He smiled and continued to his truck.

That little smile nearly blew her away. A hint of a dimple in his left cheek had her thinking she was in trouble for sure. For a moment she melted, her toes curling against the hardwood floor.

Then she remembered the path those kinds of thoughts could lead, and she stiffened her spine. Glad she'd let him know up front where she stood, she turned from the sight of his strong shoulders and tightly muscled backside as he hefted a large toolbox from the bed of his truck and slammed the front door shut.

DANIEL STUBBED HIS toe against the top step of the back porch and cursed under his breath as he set down his toolbox. Deciding he'd better remove the solid door to get it out of the way while he worked, he reached for a hammer to tap the pins from the hinges. As he worked, he let his mind stray back to his beautiful employer.

Katelyn Carter had thrown him for a loop—again. No woman had a right to look that good with dirt smudging her cheeks and sweat dampening her hair. Looking into those baby blue eyes brimming with suspicion, he'd almost talked himself into believing that showing up on her doorstep so soon was a very bad idea. And letting her think he was a handyman didn't sit right.

Uncomfortable with subterfuge, he still couldn't think of a better way to spend time with the lady. He needed to get his foot in the door before the rest of the unattached males in Tierney, Texas discovered this exotic flower of womanhood. He knew he didn't possess a glib tongue or a pretty face, but usually he was satisfied with what he did have. This morning, however, Katelyn made him wish he was so much more.

Daniel sensed if she knew what kind of hammering and painting he really had on his mind, she'd probably run screaming. As he tapped at the pins, he imagined himself alone with her in the moonlight. He'd start with stripping that tiny excuse for a T-shirt from her body and lick the sweat from between her plump breasts—

"Mr. Bodine?"

Her voice startled him, causing him to jerk, and he nearly mashed his thumb with the hammer. "Yes, ma'am?"

She stood beside him, so close his ears began to burn. That T-shirt clung to her skin like he'd imagined doing. She licked her lips nervously, drawing his gaze upward to follow the pink tongue as it flicked once around her lips.

Daniel lost track of the conversation.

"Mr. Bodine?"

He blushed when he realized he hadn't heard a word she'd just said. "Pardon me, ma'am?"

"Um . . ." She blinked and her glance fell to his lips.

Was she thinking about kissing him too? He pushed back his cowboy hat and leaned toward her. "Ma'am?"

She shoved a glass into his hand and slipped back inside the house before he had a chance to say thanks. Grinning, he was heartened to realize she was just as disturbed by his presence as he was by hers. He chugged down the sweet tea and reached into the kitchen to set the glass back on the counter.

Slipping the hammer out of his belt loop once more, he tapped at the bottom of each hinge to unseat the pins and freed the door from its frame.

When he looked around, she was standing next to him again, a frown creasing the soft skin between her eyes. "I'm sorry. I forgot what I came to ask you in the first place." She blushed and twirled a curl of her blonde hair around her finger. *Definitely disturbed.*

"Shoot," he said, leaning the door against the side of the house.

"I was wondering if you'd help me bring in some of the heavier items from the U-Haul trailer."

"No problem." He wiped his hands on his jeans and walked toward her.

She backed away hastily. "Oh, I didn't mean right this minute."

"No time like now."

They met at the door that separated kitchen from living room, and she stood sideways to let him pass. He inhaled her scent, a heady mixture of lemon furniture polish and her, and tried not to notice when their chests met. The startled awareness that bloomed red in her cheeks had him hardening in an instant. Walking through the house, he was conscious of her shadowing his every step.

He stepped out onto the front porch, noting that she'd moved the trailer in front of the porch steps. "You'll have to tell me where you want me to put everything."

"Oh no, I didn't mean for you to unpack it all by yourself." She moved to unlock the trailer, but when she reached inside to grab the first box, he gently placed his hands on her waist, eliciting a gasp from her. Picking her up, he deposited her back on the porch.

His hands burning from that quick contact, Daniel hefted the box high. Her waist had felt taut, the muscles strong. "I'll let you know when I need your help," he said, his voice gruff. "You just point me in the right direction."

A frown knitted her eyebrows, and her chin rose. "They're all marked. That one says bedroom, so take it on back to my room. You know where it is."

He gave her a sideways glance, careful not to let his face show his amusement at her irritation from his taking charge. "Yep, I'm not likely to ever forget that."

Her face flamed red, and she stammered, "Well . . . well, I'll just leave you to it, then," before she escaped.

Chuckling, he continued on to her bedroom. Katelyn Carter was mighty cute when she blushed. Fact was, there wasn't much about her that he didn't find attractive. She was just the right size—she could rest her cheek right over his heart. She wasn't too fat or too thin—just soft and sexy. Daniel had every intention of finding out just how soft and cushiony those womanly curves, above and below, would feel pressed to his body.

He knew instinctively the real pleasure would be getting to know the parts of Katelyn not visible to the eye.

Whistling to himself, he returned to the trailer again and again.

Never a man to question the vagaries of fate, Daniel knew his life had forever changed the first moment he saw her. Tierney was a small town, and he knew most of the unattached women in a hundred-mile radius. None had ever made his heart skip a beat, or tempted him to wrap her in cotton wool and take every care off her slim but capable shoulders. There was something fragile and wounded in her expression that was at odds with the defiant tilt of her chin.

He wondered if she'd realized just how transparent her attire had been that morning . . .

Katelyn tried to ignore Daniel's presence in her kitchen as she continued to labor, unpacking boxes throughout the afternoon. It was getting late when she heard the creak of the floorboards behind her.

He once again had his hat in his hands. "Ma'am, I'm finished. I'd like you to take a look at that door."

She followed him back to the kitchen. The new door was in place, and he had painted the casing surrounding it to match the rest of the frame. He opened it and allowed the door to close again.

"It looks fine," she said quickly, wanting to put more space between them. Standing so close with darkness encroaching around them created an intimacy that undermined her discipline. "How much do I owe you?"

"How about you just run a tab?"

Katelyn nodded, at a loss for anything else to say. He was doing it again—staring at her with that look that made her tremble inside. She touched her hair. "I know I must look a mess," she said, and bit her lip. *God, did I sound like I was begging for a compliment?*

He raised his hand toward her face, slowly, as though letting her get used to the idea before his touch settled on her skin. His thumb smoothed over her chin, rubbing. "You've got a smudge here," he said, his voice a low, sexy rumble that produced a prickling deep inside her pussy.

Her mouth parted around a tiny moan and his thumb slid over her lower lip. Before she had a chance to think better of the idea, her tongue slipped out and lapped the callused pad, tasting salt, feeling the roughness that made her nipples tingle.

Daniel's chest rose and his jaw tightened. His thumb pressed inside her mouth and she sucked it. With a sharply drawn breath, he bored his gaze into hers. "Tell me you don't want me to kiss you, Katelyn."

He'd said the words—torn away the flimsy barrier between unspoken yearning and surrender. She shook her head. "I . . . can't."

His hands cupped her face, gentle and reverent, as he leaned closer. His breath was sweet and brushed her lips first, prompting her to open her mouth. When his lips slid over hers, he murmured and closed his eyes.

Now, Katelyn had shared many kisses in her life. But Daniel's tasted sweeter, made her feel cherished, even beautiful. His fingers threaded through her hair and he pulled her head closer for a deeper joining.

She stood still, letting the sensation of his mouth, pressing and molding hers, draw heat like a small, smoldering ember into a flame that licked over the places he hadn't yet touched—her breasts, her pussy . . . her heart.

He raised his head, dragging in a deep breath. "I should go."

"Yes, you should," she whispered, staring into his heated gaze. Katelyn stood at a crossroads, her destination hers alone to choose. Her body yearned for more of his soft caresses, but she wasn't sure she was strong enough not to want more.

Contrary to what her mind was thinking, she lifted her hand and placed it on his chest, molding her palm to fit the curve of hard muscle that flexed as she caressed.

His body went rigid beneath her touch. "Be sure," he rasped, his chest rising and falling faster.

Be sure? Kate wasn't sure of anything except she needed to be touched, filled—by Daniel. Katelyn stepped closer, aligning herself, chest to hip, with his body. In an instant, stinging delight drew her nipples into tighter, distended points. She swallowed and lifted her gaze to his. "This doesn't mean a thing," she said, her voice tight. "I don't want you to tell me sweet lies and this isn't about forever."

His nostrils flared and his head dipped, his lips hovering above hers. "Katelyn, darlin', who said anything about forever? What about just having fun?"

3

Torn between excitement and a dampening, perverse disappointment, Katelyn rose on her toes to close the distance between their mouths. *This is what I want—all I want.*

She believed the lie when his hands closed around her hips to hold her still while he pressed the ridge growing beneath his zipper into her belly. She rose higher, straining closer to his hardness.

He broke the kiss and pushed her away, his gaze burning. "Turn around and face the wall."

Katelyn's eyes widened and her body thrilled to the curtness of his tone. She thought she'd craved a softer, more romantic joining all these years, but the electric excitement, prickling every erogenous zone she possessed, said her body was delighted at his coarse command. With deliberate, breathless slowness, she turned away.

"Put your hands against the wall." His voice was closer, stirring her hair.

Katelyn shivered and braced her hands against the wall, and then waited, her heart pounding so hard she heard her own heartbeat in her ears. The tips of her breasts pressed achingly against her bra. Moisture dampened the crotch of her panties.

She jerked when his hands gripped the notches of her hips and a leg slipped between hers. He nudged her feet, one at a time, until they were shoulder-width apart.

Her breaths were shallow, her excitement rising. Although fully clothed, every part of her was accessible, open for him to explore. *Where will he start? Should I tell him where I need his touch next?* Instead, she bit her lip.

Daniel's hands slid around her belly and slipped beneath her T-shirt. The heat from his palms and the scrape of his calluses set her stomach quivering.

"Easy, now," he whispered, his body pressing closer to her back. His fingers found the clasp of her bra and opened it. The cups parted over her breasts, and in the next breath he held both mounds, squeezing her gently.

Katelyn moaned and pressed harder into his hands, gasping when he thumbed an aching nipple. Her head fell back against his shoulder and his lips slid along her cheek to her jaw and neck as he massaged her breasts, kneading until she whimpered, weak with delight.

"Easy," he whispered. One hand slid down her belly to the top of her shorts and his fingers crept under the waistband, flattening against her stomach until he reached her curls.

His hand rubbed in drugging circles, until she thought she'd scream if he didn't reach deeper. "Please, please, touch me," she whispered.

"Yes, ma'am." The snap opened and the zipper rasped, and then his fingers slid inside her shorts to cover her sex. His fingers swirled in the wetness seeping from within her, and one long, thick finger slipped between her lips to push just an inch inside her pussy.

Katelyn's whole body trembled and her knees gave way. If not for the arm clamped around her belly, she'd have melted to the floor.

"Tell me what you want," he said, his voice harsh now.

A question she'd never been asked and hadn't the capability to answer, she was so carried away with the feelings swamping her body and mind. A strangled "Inside me" was all she could manage.

"Put your foot up on the box."

"Box?" she parroted and looked down, surprised to see the wooden case with her silverware on the floor. She lifted a foot and the distance and angle of her stance opened her further.

His fingers reached deeper into her clothing.

Katelyn sucked in a breath and her belly, dying by inches for him to touch the part of her that wept and clenched.

Fingers combed through the short curls, tugging gently, easing, then tugging harder, until her abdomen trembled again.

"Like that, do you?" he rumbled.

"Uhnnn," she moaned, and she widened her legs again, inviting him deeper between her legs.

When at last his fingertips scraped her wet outer labia, she arched, her hands leaving the wall in front to reach behind her. She needed an anchor, his body to touch. She found his shoulders and neck and draped her body across his front, her bottom rubbing his erection.

One large, rough hand squeezed her breast harder, while the other delved deeper until he parted her and rubbed around her opening, rimming her vagina.

Katelyn's pussy tingled and quivered, and her hips moved forward and back as she silently begged him to enter her.

Then his whole hand cupped her, warming her cunt, two fingers sliding deep. Liquid gushed from inside her to coat the thick digits and seep beyond to soak his hand. "Katelyn," he said, the word sounding like he'd dragged it from deep inside his chest. "You're so damn wet. Do you know how much I want to taste you?"

Her heart pounded. Her throat closed against a sudden rush of emotion. In all the years of her marriage, her husband's voice had never held that note of anguished desire—*for her*. A sob escaped, and he murmured against her hair, the hand cuddling her breast released it, pulling out of her shirt. Gently, he turned her face upward.

Her cheeks flushed hot and her eyelids dipped. She felt drugged, surrounded, overwhelmed. Her heart beat in her ears to join the sound of her shallow breaths and the wet, succulent sounds below as he drew lush excitement from her body. Her channel convulsed as the moment built, pulsing, clenching around his fingers.

He twisted and stroked, deeper and deeper—three fingers filling her now.

Then a rising blackness overcame her. Her whole world exploded in sliding caresses and the pumping of her hips. She cried out, unable to hold the sound inside.

"That's it, baby. *God!* You're so beautiful."

When she opened her eyes, his were closed tight, his nostrils flaring. She felt the ridge of his cock grinding into her bottom, and she knew pleasuring her had caused him pain. "Daniel?"

He opened his eyes and shook his head, drawing his hand from her panties. He turned her in his arms and held her, pressing her face to his shoulder. "Give me a minute," he said, his voice gruff.

"Why?" She was ready. If he asked her to lie with him now, she would. She wanted more of his kisses. Wanted his cock to fill the empty space inside.

"Because this was for you—and I moved too damn fast."

She grew still in his arms, barely breathing. "I don't understand." Part of her was elated that a strong, younger man wanted her so badly. Another part, not so ready and just plain scared, cried inside, "No, no, no!" She didn't want him thinking this meant any more than it was—just sweaty, consensual sex.

He hugged her close one more time and then set her away, his gaze sliding from the shorts riding low on her hips. He drew in a deep breath. "I'd like to start next on the floorboards of the porch. Tomorrow," he said quickly, like he expected her to object and he wasn't going to give her the chance.

While deep inside she felt a wail of denial rising in her throat, Katelyn relaxed. He'd given them both a reprieve—and her time to think about where she was willing to let this lead, without pressure or desire clouding her mind.

He stepped toward the front door, keeping his back to her. "You have several boards loose. A few might have to be replaced." He glanced over his shoulder, a question in his gaze.

Katelyn nodded. She knew he was right—about the boards and about needing time. For such a young man, Daniel Bodine was pretty smart when it came to knowing how far he could push a woman.

She didn't think she could take having him underfoot for long without doing something that might embarrass them both. "I'm not sure when I can afford more work . . . "

"It won't cost much, and it shouldn't take me long. How about I come by tomorrow morning and get started?"

He was so insistent she thought he must really need the job—or maybe he really did want to come back just to see her. Her heart melted a little. She lifted her chin. "All right, I'll see you then."

He walked out onto the porch and quickly loaded his tools, and then headed to his truck.

She didn't relax until his long, powerful legs disappeared into the cab. He gave her a short wave, and she was startled to realize he knew she'd been watching him all along.

Katelyn uttered a curse word she'd only heard in R-rated movies, surprising herself into a giggle. "That man's a terrible influence," she murmured, pulling her shorts up. Her gaze clung to the trail of dust rising in his wake. "It's not like I want to give him the idea I'm interested in forever."

DANIEL GUNNED HIS engine and let gravel spray behind him as he peeled out of her driveway. The look on her face when he'd been talking about the porch repairs had nearly done him in.

Her lips and eyes were glossy and soft from his lovemaking. Disappointment had turned down the corners of her mouth when he'd turned to leave. Just the thought that he could be sinking into her wet, tight pussy right now had him hard as a post and groaning.

She'd come apart in his arms, shivering and moaning so sweetly, he'd wanted to lay her down on the gleaming wood floors and stretch his body over hers to absorb her ecstasy. He'd never felt more a man than with her sweet cunt squeezing around his fingers and her hips jerking at every rasp of his thumb across her swollen little clit.

He brought his fingers to his mouth and inhaled the scent of her as he licked the salty-sweet flavor of her desire. Katelyn Carter could say this wasn't about forever a hundred times, but her body sang a different tune entirely.

KATELYN FELT AS if she'd barely had time to blink and the morning arrived, and she couldn't help the excitement thrumming through her body. She was up before the sun and had a large pot of coffee brewing when she heard Daniel's pickup truck pull up to the house.

"Mornin', ma'am," he called out as his booted heels climbed the porch steps.

Katelyn found herself smiling and realized she was truly happy to see him. She opened the front screen door and called back, "I have coffee made, would you like a cup?"

His slow smile melted the hard knot of anticipation that had rested in her belly as she'd waited for his arrival.

"I could use a jolt of caffeine to get me started today," he said, his rich molasses voice wrapping her like a warm blanket. "Sure I'm not too early?"

"Not at all. I was anxious to get started myself." She drew in a sharp breath and blushed. *God, is every word out of my mouth going to sound like an innuendo?* She rushed on, "The AC's working now, so I'd like to be done with the outside work before the worst heat of the day hits." She opened the screen door to allow him to pass. She didn't realize she hadn't left much room for him to enter until his chest rubbed against hers. "Coffee's in the kitchen," she said to him, suddenly breathless. To herself she thought, *He's going to think I did that on purpose!*

He didn't appear to notice the intimate contact as he preceded her into the kitchen, and Katelyn wondered what law of physics applied when the cozy room suddenly seemed to grow smaller as his tall, broad frame strolled inside. She hadn't forgotten how handsome he was, but she had thought time and the stern talks she'd had with herself the past couple of days would dull the sharp edge of her interest.

She pulled her gaze away and sighed. Even from the back, or maybe especially from that perspective, she was achingly aware of every masculine muscle stretching his T-shirt and of the round, taut buttocks his jeans revealed. It just wasn't fair. Coming or going he was too delicious to ignore.

He cleared his throat, and she blushed again because she realized he'd tried to draw her attention to something he said.

"I beg your pardon?"

He glanced over his shoulder, the corners of his lips curving in a slight smile. "Cups?" he repeated.

"Oh yeah." She walked to the cupboard, took down two and handed them to him. He poured coffee and she busied herself looking for sugar, creamer and spoons. She needn't have bothered. It turned out they both liked theirs black.

They stood awkwardly, leaning against the counters, sipping from their cups. She looked anywhere but at him, certain she'd betray her thoughts if their gazes connected. Memories of how he'd held her while she orgasmed simmered at the surface of her thoughts. Never had she been so at a loss for words. She was aware of every move he made, of the smell of his aftershave and the way he too avoided looking directly at her.

Perhaps he regretted their intimacy.

Her stomach sinking, she realized she'd been hoping for more all along—more of his kisses, more of the sexy rumble of his voice as he'd coaxed her into opening to him. She wanted to know the sensation of his mouth on her breasts and his cock thrusting inside her.

She'd dressed especially for him this morning. The soft pink T-shirt a deliberately feminine choice. Tucked into the waist of an ancient pair of faded blue jeans, the T-shirt clung to the curves of her breasts.

When she'd dressed that morning, she'd called herself every kind of fool, worrying about what she wore and wondering if he'd approve of what he saw. She'd been too bold, dispensing with her bra for the day.

Earlier, she'd reasoned the heat would make wearing one unbearable. A glance in the mirror that morning had assured her the T-shirt didn't fit *too* snugly.

Unfortunately, she hadn't taken into consideration her reaction to this man. While she held her breath, trying to think of a way to break the uncomfortable silence, her nipples drew tight, the points visible beneath the fabric. Embarrassed, she hunched her shoulders and plucked at the fabric to ease the fit. Glancing up, she caught him before he could avert his gaze from her chest.

Fascinated by his reaction, she watched him cross and uncross his legs, and then take a long swallow of his coffee. His eyes teared up, and she guessed he'd burned his tongue.

She pressed her lips together to suppress a feline smile of triumph. He'd noticed the tips straining against her T-shirt and his gaze had clung—and he was bothered.

The blush on his cheeks as he grimaced through another sip of the scalding coffee somehow reassured her. His reticence pleased her.

He set down his cup on the counter. "I better get started outside, ma'am."

"*Mr. Bodine*?" she said, keeping her voice soft.

"Yes, ma'am?"

She raised her gaze to his. "Don't you think it's a little silly for us to be so formal? Please call me Katelyn."

He released a long breath and nodded solemnly. "And I'd be pleased if you'd call me Daniel." Without waiting for a response, he went out the back door.

His haste to get away had her grinning.

Katelyn went to work as well. The previous two days she'd managed to unpack the boxes, but there was still a lot of cleaning to do. The windows alone would likely take the whole weekend. They were so covered with dirt and grime and many wouldn't open.

Gathering her cleaning supplies, she headed outside to begin her self-assigned task. She didn't question why she needed to start on the exterior of the windows. She was resigned to the fact that she needed to be near her handsome handyman.

All morning long, she savored her awareness of his presence as they both labored. Midday, she saw him pause to wipe a hand across his forehead. His damp shirt stuck to his broad back. She put down her scrub brush and realized she was just as soaked with sweat. She went into the house, enjoying the blast of cool air, and hastily poured two tall glasses of iced tea.

Carrying one in each hand, she went out to the porch. "Daniel, would you like a glass of tea?" She held out a glass to him and he stood to accept it. Once again, she was intensely aware of the height and breadth of the man. Her breath caught.

"Thanks, I could use a break. The heat's a killer today."

She murmured her agreement and tilted back her head for a long sip. When she opened her eyes, he was watching her. His gaze slid away, but not before she noted the tightening of his jaw.

"It's very warm," she drawled.

He finished his drink and set the glass down, his eyes narrowing on her.

"Would you like another?" she asked.

His gaze swept down her body and he swallowed. "Not right now," he said, his voice gruff, "but thanks." He picked up his hammer and a couple of nails and went back to work.

A spring in her step, she went back to her chores as well.

CHIPPING AWAY AT paint that glued one window to its casing, her gaze returned to the porch for the hundredth time that day. Only now, Daniel was drawing his shirt over his head, baring his broad back and tapered waist. His skin was tanned, and the ridged muscles rippled as he shouldered several long planks.

Her mouth grew dry, and her belly tightened. God, how she wanted him! If the sideways glances he'd given her throughout the morning were any indication, he felt the same way. Their sly appraisals of each other felt like foreplay, building a slow heat that threatened to flicker into flame with the slightest encouragement.

Realizing the direction of her thoughts, she berated herself. She should be ashamed. She was in full-blown lust over a man she didn't even know. The last thing she needed was another man in her life, especially when she hadn't completely shed herself of the last one. She was a fool to stand here drooling over a cowboy.

Placing the tip of the screwdriver into the corner where the window met the casing, she pounded the end with a hammer, working her way along the corner to free the window. She continued to pound away her frustration, until she felt a hand at her shoulder. Startled, she whipped around. Daniel stood behind her.

"Let me see if I can get that open for you."

She moved away and he grabbed the window to push it up. His

jaw tightened and his forearms bulged. With a crack, the paint gave and he shoved it upward.

Grinning, he looked back at her. She knew she must have looked like a deer in the headlights, but she couldn't seem to take her eyes off the broad, bare chest that stretched endlessly in front of her eyes.

"Need help with anything else?" he drawled.

The gravelly texture of his voice drew her attention upward. Her heart pounded as she read the intent in is expression and his face drew near hers.

The kiss was light. His lips rubbed softly against hers, never opening. It wasn't a carnal kiss. It was sweetly innocent and exploring. Her hands rose to rest against his damp chest and she felt a ripple of response as the muscles tightened and flexed beneath her caress.

She rose onto her tiptoes to deepen the kiss, but his head lifted. The look he gave her held a solemn promise. She didn't know how to interpret it, and was more confused than ever when he released her and went back to the porch to pry another board loose.

Why had he stopped? Her husband had never kissed her with just his lips, and his kisses always led to sex. Was she confused because she didn't understand Daniel's intent or because she wanted more? *The last thing I should need is another man in my life, especially one who could have any woman he wants.*

At midday she stopped to make sandwiches for them both and delivered the meal on a tray with drinks. She sat opposite him on the porch steps and barely glanced his way while they ate. The strain of the hard physical work, as well as her efforts to ignore her clamoring hormones, had finally left her tired enough to relax next to him and just enjoy the sight of his naked, glistening chest.

He cleared his throat, drawing her gaze upward. "There's a dance Saturday night." He looked away and shrugged. "It's an annual thing to raise money for the volunteer fire department. I'd like to take you."

Startled, she didn't reply immediately.

She guessed he thought she was trying to find some way to turn him down gently, because he said next, "I know I'm doin' things a little backwards, and I 'm sorry I've made you uncomfortable. If I promise to keep my hands to myself, will you let me take you?"

She studied his face. He was handsome, yes. But his gaze met hers directly. He didn't push. He didn't try to seduce her with honeyed words. She realized he was nothing like her husband. And she liked that little bit of uncertainty he betrayed. She wanted to say yes, and see whether this gentle man was everything he seemed.

But would it be fair to Daniel? She should say no for more reasons than the obvious one. *I should tell him now*. But she demurred, not wanting to mention a name that would only make another's presence tangible—her husband wasn't a part of her life now. She wouldn't let him be, ever again.

"Can't we just go on the way we are?" she asked, feeling like a coward.

"And what way is that, Katelyn?" he asked softly.

"Just us." Her hand settled on his arm and glided to his shoulder. "Just this."

His jaw tightened and he ducked his head. "You mean," he said, his voice just as soft, but with a bite that raised the hairs on her arm, "I'm good enough to fuck, but not be seen with you in public?"

Shocked by the blunt words spoken so quietly, she shook her head and blurted, "We haven't fucked yet." *Jesus, I just said that!* She bolted to her feet.

His hand wrapped around her ankle, holding her in place. His expression was set, his eyes narrowing. "That's right. We haven't." His hand slid up the inside of her leg. "Why wait? It's what we both want."

4

Inside, Katelyn screamed, *That's not what I meant!*

But she didn't draw away when his fingers slipped beneath the edge of her cutoffs and stroked her pussy through her panties. Her mouth opened around a gasp as molten desire seeped to dampen the silky fabric.

"Want it here? In the sunlight?" he asked, rising to his knees on the top step. His fingers pushed aside the crotch of her underwear and traced the furrow between her labia.

Moisture pooled in her eyes and between her legs. She didn't want his anger, didn't want anything to mar the beauty of the feelings growing secretly inside her. Didn't he understand she was doing this for him? "I'm too old for you, Daniel," she said, surprised by the quaver and the breathless quality of her own voice.

He leaned forward and hooked one hand around the back of her thigh to pull her hips closer, and glided his lips up the tender inside of her legs. "Looks like you're old enough," he murmured and sank a finger inside her cunt.

Her legs trembled, and she gripped his shoulders. "What will people think? I'm old enough to be your m—"

"Aunt?" He gently bit her skin. "Don't stretch the truth."

Her hands gripped his hair to bring him closer to the ache. "For God's sake, I'm forty-one years old, Daniel."

He paused and his gaze seared hers. "I don't give a fuck, Katelyn. I'm not exactly a boy." Then he snaked his tongue beneath her shorts to lick at her sex.

Katelyn moaned and widened her legs. "This is wrong. You

know it," she said, swaying on her feet at the lazy strokes he plied her with. "I'm not what you need."

He lapped her, the broad surface of his tongue skimming her lips, the tip insinuating between to tease her with glancing caresses that drove her crazy and had her squirming against him.

When he dragged himself away, his breaths were ragged. "You are everything I want," he said, his voice fierce. His expression was set, his gaze unwavering.

She believed him. He meant it—*now*.

His hands gripped her upper thighs, his thumbs stroking beneath her clothing. He leaned into her crotch and mouthed her through the fabric, his steamy breath penetrating to heat her already molten core. "*Jesus, Katelyn.*" He groaned and pressed his face to her belly. "Take your pants off 'cause I'm gonna eat you right here."

The hoarseness of his command and the hard grip of his hand thrilled her like nothing she'd ever experienced in her life. She stared at him, knowing that once again the pause was for her sake. He'd given her control.

She could deny him now—end this before she sank any deeper toward a love that might leave scars on both their hearts. Or she could take a chance.

Katelyn drew in a deep breath and looked out over her dusty, rugged front yard. She saw beyond the scrubby live oaks standing still as she was in a breezeless, sun-scorched day, to the sky as blue and wide open as her possibilities, and reached for the button at the top of her cutoffs.

Daniel held his breath while Katelyn fought an internal battle that had her lips alternately tightening and trembling. Her gaze was on the horizon and he wished like hell she'd just look at him—*see him* and everything he could be for her—if only she'd trust him just a little.

When she reached for the top of her shorts, his body grew still. A blush stained her cheeks and neck, and her lips firmed with a determination that filled him with pride. She was so damn beautiful and brave, it hurt his heart to watch.

Daniel didn't know how he knew, but his gut told him this

was new for Katelyn. Standing in the sunshine with a man at her feet, baring herself slowly to the light and his gaze—he'd seen her hesitation, the flare of panic widening her eyes when he'd issued the command.

He'd heard her shocked gasp when he'd licked the feminine folds between her legs—and *knew* she'd never been pleasured like that before. Forty-one years old and never loved by man—not like he was gonna love her now.

Her shorts slithered to the floor and she hesitated, her fingers at the top of her panties. Her gaze met his, worry and modesty creasing her brow.

"Don't stop now, Katelyn," he urged her gently.

"Must it be here?" she asked, her voice thin and a little high.

His body urged him to say no—he'd take her on her bed, the floor, the cab of his pickup truck—just so he could taste her, fill her. But instinct told him he needed her broken down a bit, gentled to his command—if he was going to make her his forever. "Take 'em off now."

She swallowed hard and her gaze dropped, but she slid the panties down her long, slender thighs. When she stepped away from them, her hands fluttered by her sides, like she wanted to cover herself. He wasn't about to let her hide from his gaze.

He lifted his hand to the sparse dark blonde hair that covered her sex. She held herself still, her chest rising and falling with her shallow breaths. He combed his fingers through her curls, all the while watching her face. "That pretty pink T-shirt too, sweetheart."

Her eyebrows drew together in a look of pure irritation, but she yanked the T-shirt up.

Then, without waiting for her to finish, he gripped her buttocks and pulled her close.

She yelped and the T-shirt slapped his back, but he was already tongue-deep inside her, his thumbs spreading her lips wide while he swirled as deep as he could reach.

Her fingers clutched his hair hard and her whole body quivered like a nervous filly. She didn't move, didn't breathe, just clutched him close and seeped sweet honey onto his tongue.

He licked higher and rubbed the flat of his tongue on the hood covering the hard kernel of her clit.

Katelyn moaned, a thin sound that gusted with her gasps as he sucked and swirled.

She was close, her cunt tightening and relaxing, pulsing faster and faster. With his thumb and forefinger he lifted the hood, exposing the bright pink knot, and closed his lips around it, sucking hard.

Katelyn cried out and her knees buckled. He held her tight and pressed his face against her belly. "Easy, now."

A soft sob racked her body. "Please, Daniel—I can't stand it."

"Lie down here," he said, and helped her lie on the edge of the porch while he scooted down the steps. He placed her legs on his bare shoulders and stroked her glistening flesh, parting her to take a good look. "You've got the prettiest pussy I've ever seen."

"Don't talk—I might change my mind," she said, moaning the last words as he opened her wide with his fingers and lapped her with his tongue.

"First time a woman's ever asked me not to talk," he murmured. He decided to give her pretty pussy something to swallow and slipped two fingers inside.

Katelyn's hips rose off the porch. "I didn't think men had cunnilingus in their vocabulary," she said gasping.

"It sure ain't in mine either, but it's not gonna stop me from eating you out." He licked the pink petals of her tender inner lips, taking the cream her body offered while his fingers fucked in and out of her tight, hot cunt.

"I can't believe I'm doing this," she said, her hands reaching to grip his hair.

He gave her a quick, wicked glance. "Beg to differ. You're not the one doing."

Her face was red, her mouth open and gasping. "But out here? In the open? Anyone could pull into the drive—the postman, a neighbor—"

He slid a third finger inside her pussy and circled his thumb around the tight little hole below.

Her back arched off the porch, giving him an interesting view of the underside of her creamy breasts. "Don't!"

"Don't what?" he teased, pressing harder on her asshole.

"*That!* Damn you!" She settled down again and glared down at him.

More liquid seeped around his hand and he groaned, knowing how she'd feel clasping his cock. "You like it," he said, and bit her inner thigh.

Her thighs moved restlessly on his shoulders. "Daniel?"

"I know. You're comin'. Close your eyes."

Katelyn's teeth clasped her lower lip and she shook her head.

"Trust me, baby," he said, crooning now. "Close your eyes."

She drew a deep breath and turned her head away, her hands letting go of his hair and reaching out beside her, flattening on the plank flooring.

Her trust was a fragile thing and he vowed not to disappoint her. With her thighs clasping his neck, Daniel leaned closer and planted hot, sliding kisses on her pussy while his fingers ground inside her, twisting deeper.

Whimpers broke from her throat as he worked his hand in and out. His thumb resuming its pressure lower, working the cream dripping from her cunt into the tight orifice until it relaxed enough to slip the thick tip inside.

She groaned and her hips undulated, countering his rhythm to draw him deeper still.

Daniel fluttered his tongue on her clit, stroking harder as her cries grew louder, and when her voice broke, he drew hard on it with his lips until she came, shuddering and spasming around his fingers. He didn't relent until her legs eased their hold and her body grew slack beneath him.

Although it damn near killed him, he gently pulled away and gathered her into his arms until she straddled his thighs, her head tucked against his shoulder. "You'll go with me Saturday night," he said, kissing her shoulder. With his hand fisting in her hair, he tilted back her head. "And there won't be any more talk about what's right or wrong with us."

Her eyelids lifted and her clear blue gaze met his. "I s'pose if I tried to disagree, you'd just add another word to your vocabulary, wouldn't you?" she said, the corners of her lips lifting in a weak smile.

He smoothed a finger over her lower lip and smiled down at her. "Do you think I have that much to learn?"

The smile disappeared and she leaned in to slide her lips over his, giving him a searing kiss. When she drew back, she said, "I think there are some definite holes in *my* education." She looked down to where her hands smoothed over his chest. "But there's something in particular I want to learn."

"Tell me what it is. I'll add it to the curriculum."

Her mouth curved and her gaze rose to his. "I want to know what it feels like to be filled with you, Daniel."

He blew out a deep breath and tried to ignore the insistent ache beneath her bottom, sure his balls were blue at this point. "I'd like nothing better, sweetheart."

Her head came up. "But?"

"After the party."

A frown creased her brow. "You think you have to bribe me to go?" Her gaze narrowed and she ground her pussy against his erection.

"I think," he said, gritting his teeth, "that you're trying to distract me—but I'm going to get my way."

"Because I'm dying for you to fuck me?"

He gave her a slanted glance. "Aren't you?" His hands clasped her bottom and he butted up against her naked cunt.

Her eyes closed and her mouth opened around a moan. As he rubbed into her open, juicy cunt, she gripped his shoulders tight. "But . . . ah . . . what about you? Don't I get a chance to please you too?"

He inserted a hand between their bodies and palmed a plump breast. "You do. Christ, I need this in my mouth."

She rose and pressed her nipple against his lips, a little smile curving hers. "Seems kinda one-sided."

"I'll get to the other," he murmured, and then opened his mouth wide to take in as much of her tit as he could.

She laughed and clasped his head to her breast. "That's not what I meant." Her inner knees hugged either side his thighs and squeezed. "One thing I do know how to do is give a blow job," she whispered.

Daniel groaned and gently bit the velvet-soft tip scraping his tongue. "Saturday night."

SATURDAY MORNING, DANIEL entered the white sandstone building that had housed the county library for as long as he could remember. His nose wrinkled at the smell of books, a smell he hadn't encountered since his last year of high school.

It wasn't that he was averse to books, or to reading, he'd simply been too busy—at first with the police academy, and then on the job at the Wendall County sheriff's office.

Then he'd purchased the property which adjoined Katelyn's about three years ago when it came on the market for a good price—it being in nearly the same sad shape as Katelyn's house was now. From then on all his spare time had been spent renovating the thirty-year-old house that sat on twenty acres of land. He'd cleaned, repaired and painted in hopes of preparing it for a family, but the right woman had never come along. He thought now, just maybe, Katelyn Carter was what he'd been waiting for.

Daniel stuck a finger in the buttoned collar of his uniform shirt to loosen it enough to breathe comfortably. He was nervous and feeling more than a little foolish, paying a call on Katelyn at her job. He'd congratulated himself on refraining from checking in on her for three whole days. There was no sense in scaring the woman by rushing her off her feet. He knew he'd almost blown it when he'd turned down her generous offer. But sex wasn't the only thing he wanted from her, and he knew she might get cold feet if she got everything she yearned for too fast and easy.

Katelyn needed to want.

She needed to yearn for his touch the same way he was dying to hear three little words from her—with an ache that wouldn't relent.

Today, he just wanted to see her. Even if it was only to let her

level a distrustful gaze on him. She thought he was a handyman—
something he'd encouraged her to believe—because he'd wanted
the chance to get to know her. That their physical relationship had
progressed so far, so quickly, only added to his unease. He hoped
she wouldn't be too disappointed or angry at his little deception.
But the time for the truth was now.

"Why, Daniel Bodine, if this isn't a surprise. Now I know you're
not here to check out a book, so what can I do for you?" The dry
raspy voice of Mabel Comstock harkened back to high school and
he broke out in a sweat. Just a glance from the little white-haired
woman from over the top of her glasses had always been enough to
make him squirm.

Remembering his manners, he doffed his cowboy hat. "Howdy,
Miz Comstock. It's good to see you."

"Hrmph." Her mouth pursed, and her eyes narrowed, "I know
this isn't a social call . . . " One gray brow quirked upward. "Or
maybe not for me. You wouldn't be here to visit the newest member
of my staff now, would you?"

He felt the heat creep across his cheeks and cursed his lack of
composure. You'd think a twenty-nine-year-old man, and a deputy
sheriff to boot, wouldn't be intimidated by a tiny curmudgeon of a
woman. He cleared his throat. "As a matter of fact . . . Yes, ma'am.
I'd like to see Miz Carter . . . if it's not an inconvenience."

Mabel Comstock's eyebrows rose and the corners of her mouth
quirked into a semblance of a smile. "Katelyn's in the computer
room." When he continued to stare blankly at her, she motioned toward a room at the back of the building. "That room's been in this
building for five years—don't be such a stranger, Daniel."

"Yes, ma'am . . . thanks." With relief, he headed to the rear of
the library.

Katelyn's back was to the door as he opened it and closed it
quietly behind him. She was on her knees on the floor, her torso
beneath the table. The view of her backside, heart-shaped mounds
that jiggled a little beneath the fabric of her slacks as she tugged
at something out of sight, had him grinning. He leaned against
the door and crossed his arms over his chest to wait. No sense in

spoiling a good opportunity to take in the scenery by announcing his presence.

She muttered something unintelligible before backing out from beneath the table. As her head popped into view, she caught sight of him. "Oh!" She slammed her head against the table as she tried to rise. Tears filled her eyes.

He rushed to help her up. "Are you okay?" He pushed her toward a chair. "Take it easy here for a second. I'm sorry I startled you."

Rubbing her head, she frowned at him, then took in his uniform in one long glance, from head to toe. Her expression was one of dismay. "You're a policeman?"

"A deputy sheriff," he corrected her.

"No, no one said . . . *you* didn't say." She looked at him accusingly, a scowl wrinkling her forehead.

"I assumed you knew." Well, it wasn't exactly a lie. He hadn't mentioned it, but he couldn't have known how much Dwight might have blabbed to her after he'd removed the snake. He knelt beside her so their gazes were level. He didn't want her staring at his uniform. "I guess there are a lot of things we don't know about each other."

Her glance slid away from his. "You're right. We really haven't talked very much."

Daniel bit back a smile and picked up one of her hands, so dainty within his ham-fisted palms, and squeezed it gently before letting it drop to her lap. "How about we spend some time together. You're coming with me tonight, right?"

Her gaze went to the glass door and back. "Daniel . . . I don't know . . . "

He drew a breath and felt a slow burning anger heat his cheeks while tension filled his arms and chest. "We had a deal, Miss Librarian."

Her eyes widened. "I'll still do that," she hissed, "but don't you think you should give . . . the rest a little time? I mean, you're a deputy . . . you have a reputation—"

"Seems the only one worried about the difference in our ages is you, Katelyn. I'm beginning to think it's just an excuse to keep what's happening between us safe. Like our relationship is in a box for you to take out whenever you have needs."

"That's not fair. We hardly know each other. Do you think I'm afraid to commit?"

"I think someone's made you afraid to trust."

Tears filled her eyes and she blinked. "Daniel, we need to talk—"

He shook his head. "After the party."

A fierce frown drew her brows together. "We'll never get around to conversation then."

Daniel smiled. "After you make good on your promise . . . we'll talk."

Her head canted and she gave him an assessing look. "We just had our first argument."

"Not so bad, huh?"

"I survived."

He rose, and held out his hand to help her stand. "You sure you're feelin' all right?"

"Uh-huh," she answered, sounding a little breathless as she stared up.

His gaze dropped to her lips, and they parted. That was invitation enough.

Intending only a quick kiss to her lips, he pressed his closed lips to hers, but was pleasantly surprised when her head tilted to align their noses, and she deepened the kiss. His hands smoothed over her ribs, slid around her back, then spread to embrace her. He pulled her close to him, and she leaned into him with a soft moan. He let her take the lead, and while she never ventured beyond the seam of his lips, her own melted against his.

Suddenly, she broke off the kiss, shoving at his chest, and he released her immediately. Breathing heavily, he fought to calm his racing heart. Glancing around, he found his hat on the floor and brushed it off before placing it back on his head.

His eyes sought hers. Her lips still glistened from their kiss. Choking down an inward groan, he said, "Tonight."

5

KATELYN CHOSE A pink cotton dress with a skirt that swirled around her calves when she turned. She smiled at herself in the mirror, wondering if this was starting a trend. A brand-spanking-new *pink* life. Her blonde hair was pulled away from her face, fastened with small silver barrettes, leaving the rest to fall to her shoulders. She hoped she didn't look ridiculous and like she was trying to appear younger than she was, but the truth was, the anticipation of seeing him again left her feeling like she was standing on the edge of something wonderful.

And if they ended up in bed together tonight, she didn't believe her secret was a betrayal. He might have access to her body, but this time around she wasn't going to entrust her inner self to anyone else's care before she was sure. However, yesterday she'd called an attorney and begun the process to end her marriage.

This was a victory she wanted to savor alone—she'd proven her strength of will, proven Chris was wrong about her. She wasn't the insecure young woman he'd married. She no longer needed his approval to validate her choices. She didn't need him—she didn't need any man. It was a liberating feeling taking this final step of emancipation.

Every bit as freeing as the rich sensuality of Daniel's kisses. Today, standing in the middle of the library where anyone could see them, she'd given herself permission to love again. Compared to the wicked things he'd done to her before, the kiss had been rather innocent, but she'd initiated a deeper joining, let her hands roam over his body in a possessive way,

Until she'd realized the hard, unyielding surface beneath her palms wasn't his muscled chest, but the Kevlar jacket he wore beneath his uniform. That had been enough to jar her back to reality. She hadn't known he was an officer. He'd kept his own secret.

She wouldn't hold it against him. They had to learn to trust each other and give themselves time to know each other. If the physical side of their relationship was on the fast track, well, *hallelujah* anyway.

The age difference that had rankled and made her feel ashamed might actually be a blessing. Because he was younger, she felt more in control.

A knock sounded at the door, and her heart raced. She grabbed her purse and let herself out the front door. When she finally glanced at the tall man who waited patiently for her finish locking up, he stole her breath away.

Daniel in faded blue jeans had been a sinfully delicious treat. Tonight, he was the full-fledged cowboy in a starched denim shirt with pearl-covered buttons. His jeans were dark, his boots highly polished.

The oversize belt buckle drew her gaze so long she knew he grew embarrassed, because he cleared his throat before saying, "Do you have everything you need?"

Surprising herself, she giggled. She hadn't felt so lighthearted in ages. "I do now."

She grasped his arm and smiled warmly at him, and he responded by crooking his elbow and placing a hand over hers. They looked at each other for a long time.

Daniel cleared his throat again. "If I kiss you now, we won't make it off this porch."

"And that's a problem?"

He nodded, his expression solemn, but his eyes wrinkled at the corners like when he smiled. "Yes, ma'am. I want to dance with you tonight."

She tilted her head and raised a single eyebrow. "And you're telling me this, why?"

"Because I don't want you thinking I don't want to kiss you."

She lifted a finger to her mouth and licked the tip, then traced his lips slowly. "Consider yourself kissed." She lowered her hand and blushed when he continued to stare.

His chest rose sharply and he glanced away. "Shit."

"Problem?"

"Yeah, I have to get through the evening with a hard-on."

She grinned. "That belt buckle's big enough to hide behind."

His gaze narrowed on her. "No, it's not."

A grin stretched her lips wider. "No, it's not," she drawled.

His hands clasped her hips and glided lower. He rested his forehead against hers and squeezed her bottom.

It was an odd embrace, but one she didn't want to end. "Where's your hat?" she asked, wanting to extend the moment and not really caring about the answer.

"In the truck."

"Hmmm." This close she inhaled his spicy aftershave and the smell of soap on his skin. She wondered if he noticed the attention she'd given her scent as well.

"Did I tell you I love you in pink?" he said, his voice a low rumble.

She shook her head without breaking contact. "Nope."

"Well, I thought it. That very first day you wore a little pink undershirt."

She gave a breathless gasp. "You noticed the color of my camisole? Wait a second, I was wearing white."

"I was only seeing the pink of your nipples through that camisole. It about drove me crazy."

She sucked her lower lip between her teeth—it was that or mash her mouth against his.

His gaze dipped to her mouth and he groaned. "I'm holdin' on by a thread here."

"Not helping?"

"Nope."

She laughed softly. "Do you need a few moments alone to compose yourself?"

"I need more than a few moments."

"A cold shower?"

"Don't think it would relieve the problem a bit."

She dropped her own voice to a purr. "Would it help knowing I'm not wearing any underwear?"

He closed his eyes tight. "Fuck, no!"

"Well, then, you're in luck. I am. Granny panties."

"White?"

She nodded, sliding her forehead against his. "Mm-hmm."

His grip on her bottom turned rigid. "I want to see."

"After the party." She gave him a quick peck on the cheek and pulled away. "Payback's a mother."

DANIEL'S HANDS TIGHTENED so hard the steering wheel groaned. He'd been sweating bullets since he'd helped tuck her and that flimsy little dress into the cab and pointed the truck down the highway. Her sweet floral perfume and the faint underlying hint of arousal had him wishing he hadn't been so stubborn. He couldn't put his finger on it, but something was different about her tonight.

The quick little glances she gave him lingered on his body, burning him. The little wistful sounds that escaped from her pink mouth had him so hard the clasp on the back of his belt buckle poked his rock-hard dick.

Katelyn sighed again beside him, drawing his gaze from the road to the rise of her chest as she inhaled her next breath. "Is it far?"

"No. We'll be there in twenty minutes."

"Long enough," she murmured.

Her tone had him worried. When her hand settled on his knee, he nearly jerked the truck off the road. He gave her a quick glance and frowned when she undid her seat belt and scooted closer to him on the bench seat.

"Katelyn, get your belt back on."

She tugged the ends of the belt in the middle of the seat and buckled them together, snuggling her hips next to his. "Mmmm. That's better." Her palm slid up his thigh and down to his knee again. She smoothed it back up and then casually let it slip between his legs.

His thighs tensed from the pleasure. "Katelyn? I don't know what you're thinking—"

"You just drive and leave the rest to me."

She angled her body toward him and reached for his belt buckle. Her hand slid behind the buckle and Daniel sucked in his breath to give her room to work. A soft *snick* and it loosened, and as quick as he drew another breath she'd freed the button at the waist of his jeans and slid down the zipper.

"Thought we were waiting 'til after the dance," he said, enjoying the change in plans and the fact that she was taking the initiative.

"This is for you," she said. "*After* will be for both of us." She pushed down the top of his underwear, freeing his cock.

Daniel eased back as far as he could on his seat. When Katelyn leaned toward him, he lifted his right hand off the wheel to give her access, and then settled it on her hair.

As she drew close, her breath bathed his hot flesh.

"You know, there are laws against this kinda thing," he said, gasping when her tongue laved the swollen crown of his dick.

"I know this cop," she said, skimming her tongue along the sensitive ridge just below the crown. "Bet he can fix a ticket."

His hand stroked her soft hair and the truck slowed until he realized he'd eased off the gas. He punched the pedal again. "That cop's gonna be sittin' in the cell next to you."

"Sounds like fun." Her tongue glided down his shaft, curving to his shape.

"*Damn*, baby."

"Just keep your eyes on the road."

"Easier said than done." He bit back a groan when she made the return trip up his cock, swirling her tongue along his length until she reached the head.

She stuck the point of her tongue in the little slotted hole at the end and wiggled it.

Daniel bit back an oath and widened his legs, one foot still on the gas, the other leg pressing against the door. "You're gonna get us both killed."

"Not if you do what I say. Don't be such a pussy."

He snorted. "Didn't know you had such a nasty mouth."

"Don't know everything, do you?" With that, her mouth opened over the end of his cock and she took him inside.

He gasped and lifted his hips fractionally, frustrated he couldn't ram upward the way he needed. His hand gripped her hair harder, encouraging her to take him deeper inside her mouth.

Down she came, murmuring and sighing around his cock, her tongue and lips closing tightly, her mouth sucking—deeper still, until his cock touched the back of her throat and he eased off his grip.

But Katelyn had more to give, more amazing depths to plunder. Her throat relaxed and he sank inside as she moved her head up and down in his lap. With his breaths catching her rhythm, he raked her hair with his fingers, the end rushing up to meet him.

When one dainty hand clasped the base of his cock and the other dug between his legs to massage his balls, he felt the sweet tension begin to unwind. "Baby, back off, I'm gonna come."

She reared back. "Gotta swallow. Don't want to mess up your clothes." Then she sank down again, taking him into the moist, hot cavern of her mouth and beyond.

Air whistled between his teeth and he cried out, fighting to keep the truck between the dashed line and the shoulder of the road while she sucked him off, murmuring her delight and encouragement.

After he'd emptied his balls, she sat back and shook her hair around her shoulders, a feline smile on her lips. "Think you can make it through a dance or two now?"

He pulled the truck to the side of the road and got out, adjusted his clothing and took deep cleansing breaths of air. When he climbed back inside, he snaked his hand around the back of her head and kissed her hard. "Don't ever do that again."

Ten minutes later when Daniel helped her down from the cab of his truck, he barely resisted the urge to shove her back inside. Her nipples poked against the thin cotton of her dress and her hair was a little messy, her lips swollen and her lipstick nearly gone. He didn't want to share the sight of her with any other man. While he smiled down at her, he gritted his teeth. He'd just have to be satisfied with the fact that her pink lipstick ringed his cock.

• • •

THE OPEN BAY of the firehouse was strung with lights and the music could be heard well before they crossed the road to the parking lot. Food was laid on banquet tables to one side of the open bay. Sodas, punch and pitchers of tea were on a table to the rear. A band played country music to which people of all ages danced.

Katelyn passed the evening in a happy haze. With Daniel's arm curved around her back, she felt proud and protected. His glance never rested on another woman in the room. He introduced her to several people and she felt welcomed. If she caught a few curious stares, warm smiles quickly followed. It appeared she'd worried about her reception at his side for nothing.

The music slowed.

"Would you like to dance?" Daniel murmured in her ear, his arms enfolding her from behind.

She glanced around at the other couples already circling the dance floor. "I don't know how to dance like that," she said, leaning back against his body.

"It's a two-step. It's easy. Trust me, I'll show you how."

She turned and raised her hands to him, giving him her trust in the deepest sense of that word. He grasped one of her hands in his and placed the other on his shoulder before pulling her closer. He began the steps slowly, heedless of the beat of the music, then picked up the pace as she learned. They circled the dance floor, swaying together with the rhythm of the music.

To Katelyn, dancing within the circle of Daniel's arms was a hint of the heaven she'd know later—when their bodies blended and merged while they made love. Their movements now were pleasurable, their bodies perfectly aligned and in sync. When the dance ended, they both smiled.

"See, I told you you could do it."

They had come to a stop in a darkened corner of the room. His hands still rested on her waist, and she tried to forget the other people were beginning a new dance, so near to them.

Daniel watched her as she gathered her courage and lifted her hands behind his neck to pull his head closer to hers. This time her lips caressed his as she learned their shape and texture, first with her lips then her tongue. She followed the closed seam of his mouth, and he opened his lips on a soft moan.

Daring filled her, and she swept her tongue into his mouth, sliding it along his. She tasted the punch they'd drunk earlier and his own unique flavor. She gasped when his tongue began to slide sinuously against hers.

"Would you like to leave?" she asked breathlessly, when she could pull her mouth from his.

He didn't answer, but his flushed cheeks and the starkly drawn features of his face told her he was as desperate for privacy as she was. Taking her hand, he pulled her along out of the dance hall to his truck.

The drive back to her home seemed to take forever. Neither of them spoke, but she was glad for the silence. She didn't want to think; didn't want to change her mind about what she knew would happen.

DANIEL'S HEART POUNDED fast. He tried to temper his expectations, to keep his excitement in check, because at any moment she could change her mind. Despite her boldness during the drive to the firehouse, he couldn't let his hopes take flight. He'd felt off balance all evening, having surrendered the pace and the direction of this night to her care the moment she had opened her front door.

Everything after that had been a blur. All he could see were her flushed cheeks, softly curling hair and that bit of pink fabric that kept him a sane man. He'd been all too aware of the curious, covetous gazes that had followed her that evening. He knew he'd have some competition for her time soon, if he didn't make his move quickly to place his brand all over her.

When they pulled up the drive she fumbled for her keys and he took them from her shaking hands and unlocked the door. She didn't turn on the light. Moonlight poured through the living room window. Silver tipped her eyelashes and the curls that lay against her shoulders. Shadows settled in the curves between her breasts visible above the bodice of her dress.

"Are you sure about this?" he asked, praying she was.

She didn't reply. Instead her lips parted, and a small, shivery sigh escaped. She moved closer and touched his face with her open palm, and then leaned into him to press small kisses to his chin, along his jaw and finally on his mouth. He let her take the lead, and when she urged him to open her mouth against his, he obliged. Gently, he drew her body closer until he couldn't tell whether it was the beat of his heart or hers that hammered madly at his chest.

Abruptly, she broke the kiss and rested her face against the crook of his neck. "I'm sorry," she said, but instead of pushing away from him she wrapped her arms around him.

He sighed, this wasn't what he'd hoped for, but at least she wasn't showing him the door. "Katelyn, you don't have anything to be sorry for." She raised her head, and he gave her a crooked little smile despite the ache that pressed against the front of his jeans. "We can just talk," he suggested.

She stood in the circle of his arms, looking at him for the longest. Then she pressed her hands against his chest. He let her go and did his best not to reveal his disappointment.

She turned slightly from him and held out her hand. "Daniel, I'm not a sure this is the right thing for us to do . . . "

His heart began to beat faster. "Baby, I'm not asking for more than you want to give."

She led him to her bedroom. Blood sang in his veins, and he tightened against moving as quickly as he really wanted to. Instead, he let her set the pace, surprised when she turned on the lamp next to the bed and slowly drew her clothing off a piece at a time, until she stood naked in front of him.

The bright color on her cheeks, and the way she stood shyly, her hands held awkwardly at her sides, told him she wasn't accustomed to being so bold.

Lifting his gaze to hers, he said, "You're so beautiful you make me ache from wanting you."

Without taking his eyes from hers, he stripped off his shirt, shucked his jeans and underwear and then remembered to search his pockets for his wallet and the foil packet he had tucked inside it. That he lay on the table next to the bed.

A small smile lifted the corners of her mouth. "I hope you brought more than one of those."

He pulled several more from his back pocket and gave her a lopsided grin. "Didn't want you to think I was taking anything for granted."

Glancing up, he saw her wide-eyed gaze staring at his cock, and he let her look her fill. When she finally raised her eyes to his, his voice was tight. "You can still change your mind, Katelyn."

Her own voice was a little hoarse when she said, "Are you crazy?" She sank onto the bed, and he was right there, climbing over her, parting her legs with his knees.

Kneeling between her legs, he ripped open a packet with his teeth and smoothed the latex down his shaft. Then he curled his back to take an erect little nipple into his mouth and suckle as he rooted with his cock between her legs.

Her hands closed around him and guided him inside her pussy.

Even through the sheath, he could feel her moist heat and the muscles of her inner walls clasp his dick. He let go of her nipple and stretched out on top of her, resting on his elbows to look into her face. "Are you all right?"

She nodded, a smile trembling on her lips.

He kissed her mouth and lifted, just their breaths between them. "Think I'm staying here awhile."

A faint smile stretched her full lips. "Feeling warm and cozy?"

"I'm feeling a lot of things, but cozy isn't one of 'em."

Her hands caressed his chest, her fingers circling his flat nipples. "Feel like a ride, cowboy?"

A short bark of laughter caught him by surprise and he rolled, taking her with him, stopping when she rose above him. "Sweet-heart, wanna save a horse? Ride a cowboy!"

6

HE'D KNOWN SEX would be different with this woman—somehow more, but he wasn't prepared for the rush of emotions that washed over him at Katelyn's first tentative movements.

She was awkward and self-conscious, perched on top of him. He could tell by the frown that wrinkled her forehead and the way her hands wouldn't settle on any one place for longer than a moment.

He couldn't believe she'd never topped a man before—and bit back an oath at the thought of the selfish bastard who'd taken from her, probably humping her like a blow-up doll for all the joy he'd given her.

The fact she knew how to give a blow job, but had never had the favor returned, burned a hole in his gut too. Katelyn deserved so much more.

He reached for her hands and placed them on his chest, then guided her knees alongside his hips. "That better?"

Her nod was sharp, her breaths harsh. "I feel so full."

She felt wonderful—lush and wet as her cunt caressed his length. "Am I hurting you?"

"No." She shivered, her eyes closing momentarily. When they opened again, she whispered, "Show me?"

He reached and cupped the back of her head, pulling her close for a rough kiss. "Just move," he said, his voice harsh. "Whatever feels good is right."

She levered up and lifted her hips, pulling off his cock, then slid down to take him all the way inside again.

Daniel held her hips, helping her lift and fall, again and again, beginning the rocking ride to completion. Gradually, he moved with her, gently countering her moves, until they stroked each other faster and faster. Her sighs and the soft, moist sounds her pussy made as she rode him, filled the quiet room.

Every lesson he'd ever learned in any other woman's bed had only been a rehearsal for this. He held his own painful arousal in check, concentrating instead on her pleasure, gauging her breaths and the rising color in her cheeks to know when she needed more from him.

Keeping his eyes open, feeling every muscle of his body harden and strain, he watched the emotions revealed on her face as they made love. Anguish, urgency . . . painful need.

Feeling her draw tighter above him, and hearing her soft womanly moans, he knew she was drawing near. He deepened his upward thrusts, sharpening his strokes, earning gasps and jagged sobs from her as she clutched his shoulders and met his strokes, sliding up and down his cock until at last she hurtled toward the abyss.

At the final moment when her whole body tightened and strained, he fingered her clit, scraping his callused thumb over the engorged knot of flesh until she cried out, her head flung back.

Daniel's heart felt squeezed inside his chest. She was so damn beautiful, sitting there lost in her release, her body shuddering so hard her tits quivered. Her inner walls clasped and rippled around his cock and he gritted his teeth, wanting to make this moment last and wanting to watch her make the climb again—with him.

In his heart, he knew no man had ever been so determined to give her this joy, and he wanted her to acknowledge what they shared was unique and meant to be.

When at last she collapsed against his chest, he rolled her to the side and pushed back the hair clinging to the sweat on the side of her face.

"That was some ride, cowboy," she said, her eyes closing as she drew in deep breaths. "You took my breath away."

He kissed her, sucking on her open lips to let her breathe, and then smoothed a hand over her hips, gripping her to cuddle her closer and keep the connection. "Think you got this horse broke to saddle?" he whispered, his head tucked on the pillow beside hers.

Her eyes opened and her mouth slid into a grin. "God, I hope not. I'm looking forward to more bumpy rides." Her inner muscles squeezed around him. "What about you? Did I leave you behind?"

"Mm-hmm. Eating your dust." Then he gave her a little dig with his cock, a reminder there was still unfinished business and no one was getting any sleep just yet.

Katelyn laughed softly and groaned. "I don't think I can move. Something's got me nailed to this bed." But her hand reached over to rest on his chest and her palm rotated on his flat nipple.

He leaned closer and sucked on her chin, then gave it a gentle nip. "How about I do all the work? I'm younger—I've got stamina."

Laughter shook her shoulders. "Statistically, I'm just hitting my prime."

He hiked her thigh over his hip and his fingers slipped between her buttocks to graze her tight hole before sliding down to touch were they were still joined. "Think you're ready for another sort of ride?"

Her breath caught and her eyes widened. "Just what do you have in mind?"

"Nothing you won't love, I promise. Nothing you can't take. I want to taste you. Make you come with my mouth. Then fuck you hard to make you come again."

Her breaths coming faster again, she nodded. "All right, cowboy. You're on."

When she tried to slip her arm around his shoulder, he shook his head. "On your belly. I don't want you to watch. Just feel."

"Daniel . . . "

"Trust me." Pulling his cock slowly out of her tight cunt, he kissed her again and then helped her to her stomach, pushing two pillows beneath her hips to raise her bottom. "Remember, I get to do all the work."

She sighed and rested her head on her folded arms. "You have no idea how awkward I feel."

"Sure I do. That's what makes this so much fun."

Kneeling beside her, he started at her shoulders, kissing and massaging the muscle until she relaxed, purring with contentment. Then, slowly, he worked his way down her slender back, licking the notches of her spine, pressing kisses into the dimples at the top of her buttocks.

When at last he arrived at her plump ass, he stroked his cock, making sure the condom was still rolled to the base and nudged apart her legs with his knees.

She opened, groaning softly. "I don't suppose we could turn the light off now?"

"Not a chance." He placed his hands on the sweet curves of her ass, enjoying the feel of sleek silk beneath his work-roughened palms. The difference in their textures, rough to soft, and their skin tones, suntanned to pale cream, made him feel like an outlaw about to steal a sacred treasure.

With both hands, he parted her and lifted her higher until her hips tilted at just the right angle to give him a view of her pretty pink cunt and small rosy hole. "I've been dying for another peek. Wanna spoil my fun?" He almost growled, his throat felt so tight and thick—just like his cock.

She laughed, but the sound was smothered when she buried her face in the bedding.

Although his cock pulsed and ached for relief, he schooled himself to go slow, savor the journey—and bring her past her embarrassment and modesty. With every gentle initiation he provided, he hoped to tighten the cinch around her heart.

He leaned closer and buried his mouth and chin and in the moist heat between her legs. Knowing his beard stubble chafed, he circled slowly, rubbing himself in her juices while her hips jerked and she emitted excited little cries.

But she didn't try to pull away.

His thumbs parted the thicker outer lips and he tongued her from clit to cleft, again and again, until her hips followed the movement up and down, like she was trying to draw out each stroke.

He almost smiled, but his dick throbbed and his balls drew painfully high and hard against his body. Still, he speared into her, stroking her silken sheath until more salty cream greeted his tongue. He dug his fingers into her, rolling them to coat them all the way past his knuckles then pulled them out to rub the moisture around her pink asshole.

Katelyn bucked beneath him. "Daniel!" she cried out, desperation driving the pitch of her voice higher.

But he was merciless. He drew her pink inner lips between his teeth and sucked them hard while he pushed one finger into her ass.

Her body shivered and her back arched. Her ass, however, drove higher against his mouth and finger, forcing a deeper penetration. He twisted inside her, loosening the tight ring of muscle, then drove another finger inside and fluttered them, back and forth until she was groaning and gasping for breath.

His cock drew so tight he was afraid he'd spend himself if he didn't get inside her quick. Keeping his fingers in her ass, he rose behind her and guided his cock into her pussy, snuggling his thighs between her widespread legs.

He knelt behind her and with his free hand on her rump, he slammed forward, gliding freely into her heat, tunneling fingers and cock as deep as he could reach.

Katelyn's knees pressed into the mattress to find purchase, and then she raised her bottom to meet his strokes, grunting softly with each hard thrust.

He stroked faster, harder, until his balls banged her clit and she keened, her voice breaking as he pounded. Then he felt the rush of cum emptying from his balls in hot spurts to fill the tight latex sheath. He shouted and pumped faster, clenching his teeth as his whole body spent itself in a final violent thrust.

Afterward, he gathered her quivering body close to his chest and soothed her with his hands sliding up and down her back until her heartbeat slowed and she slumped beside him. When she sleepily nuzzled his neck, he pulled the sheet over them and slept.

MORNING DAWNED AND Katelyn woke and reached a hand across the bed to Daniel, but he wasn't there. She pulled on a robe, belting it snugly at the waist, before going in search of him. But he wasn't anywhere to be found inside the house.

His clothes were gone and his pickup wasn't sitting in the driveway. She felt the first tremor of panic begin to tremble in her stomach. Had she been wrong about him? Had he left her as soon as he had what he wanted? He'd left no note of explanation.

She wandered out onto the porch and watched the first rays of the dawn peek over the horizon—vivid, crisp orange and mauve against the harsh gold that rimmed the Earth.

Sitting on the steps, she drew the top of the wrapper closed, and began to berate herself silently. *How could I be such a fool?* She laid her head against her bent knees and gave herself a stern order not to cry.

Then she heard the sound of a vehicle as it roared down the driveway. She didn't look up when footsteps ran up the porch and paused beside her. She couldn't look up when she heard Daniel's worried voice speak to her. "Sweetheart, I meant to be back before you woke."

"I thought . . . " she whispered, her voice thick with tears. "I didn't know if you were coming back." A moment later she was in his arms. Ashamed of her distrust, she hid her face against his shoulder as he rocked her. Finally, she raised her face to meet his gaze. "I'm sorry. I'm acting like an idiot."

"It's okay, sweetheart. Trust takes time, and we're just getting to know each other."

She relaxed against him, enjoying the feel of his solid chest beneath her cheek. "So, why did you leave?"

"I went back to my place to pick up the tools I need to start work on the eaves today. You were sleeping so soundly I didn't want to wake you. I'm sorry now, I didn't tell you."

She hugged him hard and pressed her face against his neck. He was apologizing to her, and she was the one who should be ashamed. But she held on to her silence for just a moment longer, savoring the feelings that washed over her. Love enfolded her as he rocked her in his arms.

"Strange as it sounds, Katelyn, you hardly know me, and I don't know nearly enough about you. Why should you trust me? How 'bout we talk? I know there's something bothering you, but there can't be anything so terrible we can't face it together."

It hurt so much to look into his face and see the love shining in his eyes. *How do I tell him?* She shook her head, knowing what she was about to say would make a difference. "I'm married . . . "

It didn't take more than a moment for him to react. It was as if a shutter closed over his face. He drew away from her emotionally, even before his hands lifted her off his lap and left her body.

Panic flared and stilled her heart. "Daniel, please let me explain."

"I think you summed it up just fine, ma'am," he said. He rose to his feet, turned on his heels and marched toward his truck.

She ran after him on bare feet, heedless of the stones in the driveway, "Please, Daniel. Wait!"

He slammed the door to his truck and started it up. She stood beside his window, but he wouldn't look at her.

"Daniel, let me explain."

He began to drive away, but she ran beside him, desperate now for him to hear her. "I'm separated—I've already filed for divorce. Daniel, wait." The truck pulled away, and at the end of the drive, he gunned the engine.

Slowly, she became aware that she had been standing there a long time, staring at the empty road. She wiped her tears on the sleeves of her robe, and turned back to the house.

She had plenty of work to do. She would get through this pain the same way she always had. She just needed to keep busy. Never mind this time the agony cut so much deeper than her husband had ever managed to do.

Hours later, she paused to wipe the sweat from her forehead. She dropped her scrub brush into the dirty water and decided to get a fresh bucket before she tackled the last window.

She heard a footstep behind her and spun on her heels.

Daniel stood there. His face was pale, his mouth a tight line. His expression was harshly etched.

Afraid she would just break down and cry in front of him, she turned away and dumped the bucket of water.

"We need to talk," he said, his tone hard, the pitch deep and strained.

She added soap to the bucket and began to fill it with water, ignoring him. He wouldn't listen to her before, why should she listen now? She reached for the pail, but his hands stopped her. They settled on her arms and clasped her tight.

He stood so close she could feel him against her back. "Katelyn, stop."

"Let me go, Daniel. I have work to finish up here."

"We're gonna talk. I shouldn't have left the way I did earlier. I'm sorry for that."

As strong as the relief that sang in her heart, anger blasted hot and furious. "Sorry?" She shook off his hands and turned. "You didn't even give me a chance to explain. Where was your trust? You demand it from me, but the first time yours was tested—"

"I had to get away . . . to think. I was too mad to make sense of anything you wanted to tell me. I needed a little time."

"Well, now you have plenty of it," she snapped. "I'd like you to leave."

"I'm not goin' until you settle down and talk to me."

"I don't have to do what you tell me to. There's nothing left to say, and I have work to do." She turned her back on him, picked up the pail and stalked toward the window.

She heard a muttered "Damn it, Katelyn" just before she heard the sound of him walking away. That made her even madder. His affections could only be a pale thing compared to hers if he could give up so easily.

Well, it's better to know now, she told herself. Convincing herself it was better this way, she closed her mind to the pain and scrubbed the dirty window.

Weary and heartsick, she finished up and decided she'd had enough for the day. Too little sleep the night before, and too many emotions that morning, had left her exhausted.

She entered through the back door and headed straight for the shower. The water soothed her aching muscles, and she let her tears mingle with the spray jetting down on her. After she dried off, she went in search of fresh clothing. She had just pulled an age-softened T-shirt over her head when the sound of banging from the front of the house registered.

Every admonition she'd given herself earlier, trying to convince herself she was better off without a man—especially one who quit when the going got rough—disappeared. She'd been lying to herself.

Heart pounding, she walked through the house and looked out the front window. It was Daniel. He was there on her porch, prying a board free. He hadn't walked out on her after all.

But was he here to finish the job or because he wanted another chance? She suspected the answer was up to her.

He must have sensed her watching, because he looked up. She couldn't read his expression before he turned his attention back to the crowbar and the board he'd almost worked free.

Unsure how she'd be received, she hesitated. She prayed she hadn't been misreading him all along. If he returned even a small portion of the love she felt for him, it would be enough.

Pushing open the screen door, she took a deep breath and walked out onto the porch. He ignored her now, and kept working. She didn't mind, deciding it would be easier to get through the explanations without him looking right at her.

"I'm sorry I shouted at you earlier," she said softly. "It was childish of me. I wanted to hurt you like you hurt me when you left this morning."

A board creaked ominously before it split. Daniel tossed down the crowbar and began to pull at the board with his hands.

He wasn't going to make this easy for her. And she knew she deserved it. She had been the one to lie. Or at the very least, omit an important piece of information.

"Please just listen, Daniel." She eyed his back. His head was cocked to the side, and his motions slowed, so she knew he was listening. "I was wrong not to tell you about my marriage," she began. "I don't consider myself married anymore. My husband

and I have been apart for more than a year. Our marriage wasn't a good one."

Pausing, she realized it was easier to say what she had to without him looking at her, but she needed to read his expression. She didn't know if she was reaching him.

"My husband was very controlling. And while he didn't ever hurt me physically, he made me feel . . . small and stupid. He also made me feel very *unsexy*." She heard him snort and she rushed to continue. "And there were other women. A lot of other women. Chris said he needed them because I wasn't woman enough for him." She turned away and stared sightlessly at the expanse of rugged buffalo grass before her.

"I believed him for the longest time. I don't know what changed in me, or when it occurred that I didn't have to take it. I moved out. And at first I thought I was doing it to punish him, and make him see how much he had hurt me. But then I started to realize I liked my life better without him. That was when I decided to leave Atlanta. I couldn't really let go of my past if I stayed there."

He didn't stop working, and she started to feel anxious that maybe none of what she was saying mattered to him or excused her.

"When I came out here to Texas, it was to get as far away from my old life as I possibly could. The last thing I wanted was another man. And trust one? I didn't think I ever could again."

The board came free in his hands, and he tossed it on top of a growing pile next to the porch. He picked up the crowbar and inserted the end between two old splintered boards high in the eaves over the porch. The muscles in his arms and shoulders bunched and sweat dampened the back of his shirt.

Needing to be closer to him before she could say what she needed to say next, she stepped behind him and put her arms around his waist, pressing her cheek to the wet circle between his shoulder blades.

He stilled immediately.

"Daniel . . . " Squeezing him fiercely, she whispered, "I'm sorry I didn't tell you. I felt that if I shared this, somehow I wasn't being strong. And I didn't want you to know how stupid I'd been. You've shown me more about passion and what love is supposed to be in the past days than I ever experienced in years of marriage to him. Every time you pushed, it wasn't just because you wanted something for yourself. You were giving me the world, but I was too scared to accept or see that." Frightened because she didn't sense any change in his rigid stance, she went for broke. "But I want you to know . . . I *trust you*. And I love you with all my heart."

She felt his chest expand as he took a deep breath. He lowered his arms and set the crowbar on top of the rail. Then he placed both hands over hers and squeezed them gently. They stood there for long minutes, relaxing, savoring.

"You're not wearing a thing under that T-shirt are you?"

The question, and his deep smoky voice, made her smile. She bit him playfully on the back, and she felt his response in the ripple of his stomach muscles beneath her hands.

Pulling free of her grasp, he turned quickly, grabbing her around her waist. Before she had time to even gasp in surprise, he sat her down on the porch rail and stepped between her thighs. Their faces were level now, his gaze spearing into hers.

"No more secrets," he said firmly.

"No more secrets," she promised, and her heart began to expand with hope.

"We will be married, Katelyn."

It wasn't a question, but she nodded a moment before his mouth pressed against hers, and his hips pushed against the part of her that ached to be filled.

Pushing the T-shirt up her body, Daniel's lips left hers only long enough to pull it over her head and fling it the ground. "I need to be inside you."

She understood. He needed to stake his claim.

Her hands were just as busy, opening the snap of his jeans to free him. He lifted her from the rail, and her arms clung to his shoulders as her legs wrapped tightly around his waist and he lowered her onto his cock.

He took a deep breath, and rested his forehead against hers.

"Damn it, Katelyn. You're more than enough woman for me. I won't ever play around on you."

Her eyes grew damp again. "Daniel, I believe you. But right now no more talk, you have to move."

"You keep telling me that. Thought all you women liked to talk."

Katelyn wound her arms around his shoulders and leaned her forehead against his. "This one likes talking just fine, but right now, I can't think. Fuck me, cowboy."

His mouth twisted in a wicked grin and he tilted his hips to stroke his big cock all the way inside her. "One cowboy coming up, ma'am."